AMBER FISHER

NO SIN, NO FEE

LIGHTS, CAMERA, MYSTERY

4

intro reel (recap)

Welcome to *Sinful House*, a reality TV show where the 7 Deadly Sins live together in the sunny beach town of Odyssey, California, and compete to become America's Favorite Sin!

Previously on *Sinful House:*

1. At a séance, a disembodied voice told Pride to seek out a painting called *Sum of All Prophets*. The painting is owned by a collector in Santa Barbara, California.
2. For reasons no one can explain, everyone—including Pride—believes the voice belonged to Pride's mother.
3. Pride used a map found in Walt Romanowsky's computer to locate Chenoweth International in a twisted system of tunnels that run underneath the city.

4. Pride, Envy, Wrath, and Sloth rescued a supernatural from the Chenoweth dungeon right before Envy burned two blocks of Old Downtown to the ground with her fire elemental.
5. The rescued supernatural turned out to be Peyton Cameron, twin sister to real estate mogul and city council member Portia Cameron.
6. The person responsible for orchestrating the kidnapping and torture of Odyssey's supernatural community turned out to be Pamela Arquette—the Odyssey city manager.
7. Pamela also orchestrated the murder of an elderly mortician. In an act of revenge for his friend's death, mayor Julian Gillespie then murdered Pam. With the mayor in prison and the city manager six feet under, the city is left without a fully-functioning government.
8. Stephanie Jones, local pooch salon owner, runs a community "newsletter" where she airs the town's dirty laundry. She had a kerfuffle with Pride and Envy at the grocery store, and now the cast members and Stephanie butt heads. Not everyone likes Stephanie, but everyone reads her newsletter.

You're all caught up! Stay tuned for more rollicking adventures. And don't forget to vote for your favorite sin at the end of each challenge.

Happy watching!

one

. . .

I awoke to the sound of someone screaming.

I launched myself out of bed, throwing my blankets to the floor as I scrambled out the door. I paused a second in the hallway, listening. The scream came a second time, and I followed it to the source just a few doors down.

I threw Envy's door open to find her standing in the middle of her room, her phone clutched before her face. Her features were bathed in the pale electric light coming from her screen. When she saw me, she started screaming again.

"Envy?" I asked, my heart thumping in my throat. "Are you okay? What's going on?"

Shaking, Envy strode over to me and thrust her phone in my face. She had her Instagram page pulled up. I saw a wall of photos, mostly selfies of Envy in various swanky locales. There were also the obligatory photos of food, cute neighborhood pets, and the sunset over the Pacific Ocean.

It was true that I found social media largely horrific. I mean, any technology that encouraged people to share badly lit photographs of scrambled eggs had to be bad for humanity. But that still didn't explain why Envy was screaming at 8 o'clock in the morning.

"Do you see what I see?" she asked, her voice frantic. "I can't believe this is happening! It's finally really happening!"

I shook my head, staring at the photos in dismay. "What's happening? What are you talking about?"

Envy rolled her eyes and jabbed a finger at the screen. "Do you see this? Look at my follower count! It's nearly tripled overnight! Oh my God, I knew this show would change my life. But I had no idea it would be like this." She looked up at me, absolutely beaming with joy. "Pride, I'm *viral!*"

I blinked, then frowned and shoved the phone back at Envy. "That's what you woke me up for? Some random morons you don't know are following you on Instagram? Envy, I thought you were in trouble!"

"Well, I'm sorry about that," she said. She didn't look the least bit sorry. "But I couldn't contain my excitement. I've been dreaming about this for ages. And you know how it finally happened?"

To be honest, my interest in Envy's internet fame was extremely low. Still, I was already there, and it looked like she wasn't going to let me get back to sleep until she told me the whole sordid story. So I plopped down onto her bed and sighed. "Tell me," I said.

She flipped through the phone and then shoved it in my face one more time. "Look," she said. "It's all because of this account. It went viral. And now, every-one's following me."

I took the phone from her hand and looked down at the photos. At first, I didn't notice anything interesting about them. I don't exactly have face blindness, it's just that I don't really care that much about other people. But just as I was about to say so, I did a double-take, and my heart screeched to a stop.

"Envy, what is this? Is this what I think it is?"

My housemate folded her arms over her chest, a smug look on her face. "See? It pays to keep your body in tip-top shape."

"Envy," I drawled, "these are photos of you taken through your bedroom window. *Half-dressed* photos of you," I stressed. I glanced back down at the screen. The photos showed Envy changing out of at least a dozen different outfits—meaning the person had been photographing her for weeks. "This means you have a peeping Tom! Somebody's been watching you from the street, snapping these photos, and posting them online! You can't be okay with that!"

Envy sighed and snatched the phone from my hand. "Leave it to you to be old Prudy McPrudyPants. Yes, I know what it means. And you're right," she conceded coyly, "it's not *exactly* cool for someone to spy on me and then post my private moments to the public. But it would be one thing if this account went viral, and I got nothing out of it. But you saw my numbers. I'm an up-and-coming star! From here on out, it's going to be nothing but caviar and champagne!"

I had no idea how photos of Envy in her underwear

would land her a prime slot on *Lifestyles of the Rich and Famous*, but at the moment, that wasn't my primary concern. "Envy, you realize this person is stalking you, right? You have a *stalker*. Whoever did this is dangerous."

But Envy dismissed my concern with a wave of her hand. "Oh, you don't know that. It could just be an innocent fan. Someone who loves me on the show and was so excited to find out—"

"It doesn't matter whether it was a fan!" I said, incredulous. "This has to stop immediately before it escalates any further. You need to hang blinds and curtains as soon as possible. And stop getting changed with the light on at night in the meantime. Undress in the bathroom or something."

Envy sniffed and stuffed her phone in her pocket before leaning against her desk and glaring down her nose at me. "I will not live in fear. I'm not going to inconvenience myself by changing in our *shared, yucky* bathroom just because some creepazoid might be mildly obsessed with me. I'm just gonna keep doing me. And neither you nor some no-name with a camera is going to change that."

It was way too early to fight with Envy about something that ultimately didn't really affect me. If she wanted to entertain some crazy stalker person by prancing around half-dressed in her bedroom, I certainly wasn't the person to stop her. I dragged myself to my feet and ran a hand through my hair. "It's your funeral," I said. "I'm going back to bed."

"No, wait." Envy blocked my exit, her lip curled beneath her teeth. "I need a favor."

I yawned and stretched, hoping Envy would take the hint, but she just stood there with those giant puppy dog eyes. And because I'm a sucker, I knew she had me. I groaned in defeat. "Good grief, Envy, can't it wait? I still plan to get like three more hours of sleep."

"Really? Aren't you, Sloth, and Gluttony starting your task today?"

"Yes," I said, "but Sloth won't be awake for at least another two hours."

"Well, anyway, I need you to do me a favor. Your task is to find out the deal with the traveling mermaid statue, right?"

I nodded. "Yeah, that's right."

"And the statue is hanging out in front of a clothing boutique, right?"

I glowered at her. I had a bad feeling I knew where this was going. "If you think I'm going to *shop* for you so you can take off new designer clothes for your stalker friend, boy, have you completely lost your mind."

Again, I tried to leave, but Envy threw her body in front of me. "Julio Villarreal is a *totally* famous designer," she crooned. "And he's actually opened a store in Odyssey! I read on Hip-to-Trends Online that his new boutique, Nautical Articles, has the *cutest* stuff. And it's even reasonably priced—for designer, anyway. Look, I just need you to pick out a couple of cute blouses. I don't need pants. All the window photos only show me from the waist up."

I gave her my blankest stare. "No."

"But Pride, you're the only one who can do it!" she whined. "We're leaving for our task in 10 minutes. Who knows when we'll be home? And with all the crowds Julio is getting, he might sell out of all the cute stuff! And I can't let Gluttony do it. You've seen what he wears." She made a gross-out face. "And if I ask Sloth to do it, all my blouses will be covered in chocolate by the time I get home!"

"Envy, be reasonable," I said, placing my hands on her shoulders. "The whole reason Julio wants us to deal with the statue is because the crowds are messing up his business. So I think you'll be fine to shop for yourself later."

Just then, I heard the creak of Envy's door opening wider as Lust stepped into the room. She looked like a picture. Her hair was swept into a high ponytail away from her face, her ears dotted with tiny sparkling studs. She wore a faded red t-shirt and jeans so tight, it looked like she was poured into them. She was looking down into her phone as she entered. "Hey, Envy? You ready? I want to have enough time to get a latte from Starbucks." She stopped in the middle of the room and put her phone away. When she saw me, however, she balked and backed toward the door. "Sorry. I didn't mean to interrupt."

"You're not," Envy said. She reached into her pocket and dug out a credit card, which she pushed into my hands. "Just get like three shirts," she said. "And don't spend more than $1,000. Thank you so much, Pride! You're the best!" She planted a kiss on my cheek before she and Lust giggled their way out the door.

I stood there staring after them like an idiot, Envy's

American Express resting in my palm. A thousand dollars on three shirts?!

Boy, was I ever in the wrong business.

———

"Wow, Tricia really wasn't kidding. This is a complete circus."

It was a little after noon by the time Sloth, Gluttony, and I pulled up to the site of our new task. Our destination was a brand-new clothing boutique called Nautical Articles specializing in beach and sea-themed clothing for women. From what I could see of the shop, it fit the Odyssey aesthetic. It was a cute, pink stucco building with an adobe tiled roof, a black-and-white awning, and fancy lettering in the windows.

The problem was, I couldn't see very much of the building from the street thanks to the throngs of people milling around out front.

The street was absolutely clotted with tourists. I'd heard that people had come from as far away as Europe to see the statue with their own eyes. Under normal circumstances, the Star of the Sea was an impressive sight. Looming 20 feet tall, the bronze mermaid statue was supposed to stand in front of City Hall, carrying a lantern in one hand and a mirror in the other. But today, she was not at City Hall, nor was she carrying a lantern or mirror. And that was the problem.

Men and women snapped photos, oohing and ahhing as they pushed their way to the front, trying to get a decent selfie. Kids of all ages ran around, screaming and screeching, laughing with the joy of going unsupervised even for a moment. Dogs yipped. News vans lined the street, their reporters and cameramen vying for the hottest spots with the best view of the statue.

In the backseat, I heard Sloth breathing heavily. I turned around to find her forehead pressed to the window, her hands trembling in her lap. "Hey," I said. "Sloth? You all right?"

My housemate said nothing for a minute. I could barely make out her expression reflected in the window. "There's just so many people," she said, her voice hushed. "This is my nightmare, you know? Do you know how hard it is to keep out the thoughts of this many people?"

As a mind-reader, Sloth's talent was both blessing and curse. She'd proven helpful in more than one case, though we all tried not to ask for her help. She didn't exactly enjoy reading minds—she found it unethical. But as useful as her ability was, it didn't come for free. Watching her now, the way she curled into herself, her chin trembling, I knew she was preparing for the worst.

At my side, Gluttony reached down between his feet and extracted a picnic basket. "I know you didn't think I'd let you tackle this task unprotected," he said with a smile. He reached into the basket and withdrew a freshly baked croissant. "I put *Nanny nanny boo boo, I can't hear you* magic in those," he said, handing the pastry to Sloth. "I thought you could use the help."

Sloth accepted the croissant, her eyes round, her lips

fluttering into a disbelieving smile. "You did this just for me?"

"Not just for you," Gluttony admitted. "I love croissants and they're time consuming, so I hardly ever make them. But I decided today was a good day for flaky, buttery perfection."

He handed a second pastry to me, which I eyed with caution. Gluttony was a kitchen witch, and his magic was above reproach. But sometimes it worked a little too well. "This isn't gonna make me go deaf for three days or something, is it?"

Gluttony grunted and shoved a croissant in his mouth. "Nope, this is just for not hearing things you wasn't never supposed to hear to begin with. Words meant for you will find you. Words not, won't."

That was good enough for me. I took a huge bite and moaned. I had to hand it to Gluttony—the guy was a beast in the kitchen.

Climbing out of the car, Gluttony whistled and made a visor of his hand as he peered around, surveying the sea of people. "Somebody could make a killing selling street food to these folks," he mused aloud. "Man, if I cooked up a mess of char siu bao or maybe just some corn on the cob? And then if I added a little bit of magic? Yeah, I could make me a few coins. How much y'all think something like that could go for? Think I could get four, five bucks a pop?"

Sloth scratched her head, her nose scrunched up. "Five dollars for corn on the cob? Only if it was gold-plated," she said.

We crossed the street, slowly pushing through the

crowd to make our way to the giant mermaid, who was the entire point of our visit. Unfortunately, she was the point of everyone else's visit, too, and people weren't too excited to have us pushing past them. "Wait your turn," a woman snapped at us, pushing her sunglasses to the top of her head. "Get in line, would ya?"

"Just heading for the store," I murmured with a fake smile, slipping past the woman without so much as a backward glance. After all, unlike these people, we'd been invited here.

But although we were heading for the front door, our pace slowed as we wended nearer the statue. In her natural state, the Star of the Sea was regal—a symbol of Odyssey's steady progress. She was beautiful, wearing a beckoning smile, kindness beaming from her lovingly rendered eyes.

Today, however, she looked nothing like that.

When the statue had appeared in front of Sinful House, she'd traded her smile for a terrifying scream, hands pressed to her cheeks. Now, one hand was propped on her hip, the other pressed against her forehead. Her lips were round, and she was blowing out her cheeks as though whistling out a relieved, "Whew!"

Back when she was hanging out on our lawn, we tried everything to get rid of her. Wrath and Greed even tried to dig her out with shovels. But nothing had worked. The statue stayed for a while, cursing our front lawn with her presence, and then one day, she was gone. No one knew where she went.

That is, until a few days later when she appeared on the lawn here at Nautical Articles.

When we were as close to the statue as the other tourists would allow, we stopped, gazing up at her.

"What do you think she wants?" Sloth asked.

I rolled my eyes. "She's a statue," I replied tersely. "She doesn't want anything."

"I don't know," Sloth drawled. "I mean, sure, she's a statue. But she's a magical statue that disappears and reappears later with a different expression. It has to mean something."

"Number one," I said, holding up a finger, "it doesn't have to mean anything. Sometimes things just *are* and there's no further significance to it. But number two," I held up a second finger, "you didn't *say* you wondered what it meant. You *said* you wondered what she wanted. Those aren't the same things at all."

"We best get to steppin'," Gluttony said, ignoring our exchange. "Julio's waiting for us. Let's go."

Inside, the shop was exactly what you would expect from a boutique called Nautical Articles. The over-the-top beach and sailor themes were enough to make me seasick. The walls were painted with a mural of Odyssey's beach. Sunbathers, joggers, children, and dogs were painted in pastel colors against the blue-green background of the Pacific Ocean. Overall, the effect seemed low-brow—the opposite of what you'd expect of a swanky, high-fashion boutique. Though I have to say, I didn't mind the dogs so much. I mean, if you're going to paint a mural, you might as well throw a dog or two in there. Nobody doesn't like dogs.

As the door closed behind us, gently blotting out the sound from the street, a man appeared from a back room. He was on the short side, with a svelte figure and a stern face. Dark, unsmiling eyes peered out from under a narrow brow topped with the biggest pompadour I'd ever seen on a man. He was deeply tanned, with rings glittering on every finger. A scowl was etched deep in the crevices of his face.

He stormed over to us, nostrils flaring as he waved his hands dramatically. "There you are!" he snapped by way of greeting. "You were supposed to be here 15 minutes ago."

"That's my fault," Sloth said with an apologetic smile. "I had some trouble with the coffee maker. Are you Julio?"

The man blinked, long black lashes fluttering. "Were you expecting someone else?"

"Maybe someone better dressed," Sloth answered.

I bit down on my tongue to keep from laughing. It wasn't that Julio was dressed badly, it was just that he didn't look like a fashion designer. I'd expected something outrageous, like maybe purple silk pants or a fluorescent cravat or even a jaunty hat. But Julio wore only black jeans with a black turtleneck. In summer, in Odyssey. He looked like a Hispanic Steve Jobs—if Steve Jobs wore a pompadour that could double as a tidal wave in a Godzilla movie.

But instead of taking Sloth's remark as criticism, Julio broke out a smile and patted Sloth on the arm. "Oh, I like her," he said to no one in particular. "It's not every day someone dressed in sweatpants throws shade on me. Well, I guess you're the psychics the network sent over?"

Sloth offered her hand. "I'm Sloth. These are my friends, Gluttony and Pride."

With the introductions over, Julio gestured dramatically towards the windows overlooking the crowd amassed outside. "So what's your plan of attack for all this?" he asked. "My grand opening has already been ruined, but more people are coming every day. I don't like the general public on the best of days. But now they're here, all up in my business, ruining my Odyssey debut. It simply has to stop."

"Well, I guess we have a few options," I said. "If we figure out how the statue is moving around, we might be able to coax her back to City Hall. But that doesn't guarantee she won't move again. But if we can figure out *why* she's traveling, maybe we can end her adventures permanently."

"I like the sound of that," Julio said, nodding enthusiastically, his pompadour threatening to topple over. "Though I have to admit, I don't care how *or* why. I just want her and these tacky onlookers gone."

"We wanted the same thing when she was lurking on our lawn," Gluttony said. "We tried digging her out and everything. All that did was leave a big mess in the front yard."

Julio swiveled his head, now looking at Gluttony with a whole new level of admiration. "The statue was at your house? Well, how did you get rid of her?"

"We didn't," the big man said with a heave of his shoulders. "She stayed for as long as she liked, and then she hightailed it outta there. That's when she came here."

"Well, that just isn't helpful at all, is it?" Julio asked with a sigh.

"Can you think of any reason the statue might have chosen this for her new location?" Sloth asked. "Maybe if we can find some common thread to her destinations, we can figure out what her motivation is."

Julio sighed and pushed up the sleeves on his turtle-neck. "Well, I didn't choose this location myself. My new assistant Cary did that."

Sloth nodded. "All right. And do you know why she chose this location?"

"He," Julio corrected. "Cary is a boy. Well, a man technically, I suppose."

Sloth blinked. "What does that mean?"

"Mama's boy," Julio said, nose wrinkled. "I secured a loan from Pennington Bank for the new boutique, and when I mentioned at signing that I needed an assistant, the broker practically shoved Cary off onto me. His mother's family owns the bank, so it wasn't like I could demur. Though, to be fair, so far, he's working out all right. I had him scout out the most premium spot in Odyssey for the boutique. And this is prime real estate, to be sure. But if I had known this location would come with a side of unwashed masses, I would have settled for the *second* hottest location in Odyssey."

"Did you know much about Odyssey before you opened a boutique here?" Gluttony asked.

Julio gave a flippant shrug. "Just what everyone knows, which is that it's one of the most happening spots in the country. Everyone says Odyssey will become the next Beverly Hills. I don't know about that," he said, glancing disdainfully out the window. "There's a lot of gentrification that needs to happen before this place can hold a candle to the likes of Bel Air or Greenwich. Still, I like to keep my thumb on the pulse of America. I came to Odyssey because it seemed like a worthy investment in the future of my business."

Gluttony snorted. "So then, lemme guess. You didn't know about all the paranormal stuff that happens here on the regular?"

Julio blinked, mouth opening and closing like a fish before he said, "Paranormal activities? You mean *other* things have happened here besides this meandering statue?"

"This place is crawling with ghosts," I said. "And there's some kind of energy flowing beneath the city, too. At least, that's the rumor."

I was referring to the "Nexus of Power" I'd learned about recently, a river of energy that flowed beneath the city and attracted all kinds of weirdos to it. Dozens of ghosts had succumbed to its pull, ending up trapped in a coffee shop basement. And we even had our own illegal supernatural bounty hunter organization doing terrible things to shapeshifters in the city's underground tunnels.

Of course, Envy had burned all that to the ground, but still. I figured the energy that started all the ruckus was probably still there.

"You know who you should talk to?" Julio snapped his fingers, his face brightening. "Just a moment."

He excused himself and hurried to the back of the store, disappearing behind a door. A moment later, he returned carrying a hardcover book which he thrust into my hands.

"Brittany Miller," he said, thumping the cover with a forefinger. "She was one of the first to arrive after the statue did. Long before these other Johnny-Come-Latelys showed up. Super cute girl and whip smart. She asked a flurry of questions about the statue. When I asked why she wanted to know, she said she's an art journalist researching a new book. She was studying weeping Virgin Mary statues in South America when she heard about the Star of the Sea. She got on a plane immediately to fly up here. You should talk to her."

I looked down at the hardcover in my hands. The book was titled *The Genius of Mind and the Madness of Art*. I flipped casually through the pages. The book contained several black-and-white photographic plates depicting various artifacts—paintings, sculptures, jewelry, even stained-glass windows. I flipped to the back cover. A black and white headshot of a young woman smiled mysteriously back at me. There was no summary to accompany the photo.

I tucked the book under my arm. "Can I hold on to this? It might come in handy later."

"Yes, keep it," Julio said. "I'm not much of a reader. I prefer to binge-watch documentaries on Netflix."

"Oh, me, too!" Sloth bounced on her toes, hands folded under her chin. "What are you watching right now?"

"Something about a lion-tamer being swindled by his internet lover," he said. "I can't believe some people even *have* internet lovers. What is the world coming to?"

"You should watch the one about the cat that took down a multi-billion-dollar pyramid scheme," Sloth said. "It's unbelievable."

"Seen it," Julio said, waving a hand. "Have you seen the one about—"

"Do you know if Brittany's still in town?" I asked, interrupting their impromptu film club. I hadn't seen any of the shows they were discussing, so I was bored. "The sooner we can talk to her, the better."

Julio nodded. "She's staying at the Odyssey Grand Hotel. Make sure you tell her I sent you. Here, let me give you her phone number."

We all whipped out our phones and quickly exchanged information. Sloth dialed the number and paced away from us. While Sloth called Brittany, Julio looked nervously out the window. More tourists were arriving every minute.

"They're going to destroy my landscaping," he muttered under his breath. "The city had better reimburse me for this."

"Have you filed a formal complaint?" Gluttony asked.

Julio rolled his eyes so hard, I thought he might pull a muscle. "Of course I have. But every time, they tell me Odyssey doesn't have loitering laws. *It's a beach town after all*," he quoted in a mocking, singsong voice. "Well, this might be a beach town, but it still needs to follow certain rules of decorum. *Certainly* they have laws on the books that would stop this sort of thing from happening, right? But when I said that, I was told the only way to legally get these people off the property was for the mayor to issue an emergency ordinance making loitering illegal. But apparently, the mayor is in jail?"

Gluttony and I exchanged looks. "Yeah, he's in jail for murder," I explained. "He offed the city manager. And believe me, she was no sweetheart, but you can't just go around killing people, either, so. Anyway, we're kind of between leadership right now."

Julio opened his mouth to respond, but Sloth returned to us at that moment, nodding vigorously with her phone pressed against her ear. "Yeah, great. We'll see you then." She stuffed her phone in her pocket and turned a bright smile to Gluttony and me. "Good news! Brittany can see us now. She's having lunch at the Odyssey Grand and invited us to come by." She looked over at Julio. "I assume there's not much else we can do here?"

Julio thought for a moment, tapping his finger against his lips. But eventually, he heaved a sigh and shooed us away. "The sooner you get on with this Brittany interview, the sooner you might have answers for me. Go on, skedaddle. In the meantime, I guess I'll stay here and look pretty, hoping somebody with money and good taste comes through that door."

"Why don't the two of you go?" Gluttony said, gesturing between Sloth and me. "Let me stay behind and interview some of the tourists. Divide and conquer, right?"

My brows drew together sharply as I glanced out the window. "Interview them about what? They don't know anything."

Gluttony clucked his teeth. "You have no idea what

they do or don't know. And we won't know until I ask. Besides, we don't need three people to interview this lady. The two of you go, make nice, get whatever information you can. I'll do the same here. We'll meet up tonight over dinner and go over our notes. Sound good?"

We ambled out the front door, and Gluttony flashed us a peace sign as he began working the crowd. For a big guy, he was pretty agile, winding through the crowd with natural grace. As we headed for the car, Sloth slipped her arm through mine, giggling as she pressed herself to my side. "How much do you want to bet he's just trying to determine how much he can charge these people for magical hot cross buns with cream cheese frosting?"

I grinned. "I wouldn't take that bet. That sounds just like something Gluttony would do."

two

. . .

Brittany Miller looked exactly like her photo, which surprised me. I expected the headshot to be twenty years old, like the photos of most professional women I'd run across on social media. But Brittany Miller was no older than her late twenties, with a head full of shining blonde hair, a smattering of freckles across her nose, and a glint in her smiling blue eyes. She looked precisely like a high school cheerleader, maybe even college. She was pert and perky, with a voice and energy to match.

I disliked her immediately.

"Thank you so much for meeting us," Sloth said as we slipped into the empty seats at Brittany's table. "I know it's short notice, but Julio is really keen to get that statue out of his hair."

Brittany motioned over a server, who poured a fresh round of iced water. "No worries, I'm happy to do it. Besides, this is good for me, too. I guess Julio told you, but I'm writing a new book, and the mermaid will make a great addition. And if I'm not mistaken, you've had your own run-in with the statue, right?"

"That's right," Sloth said. "She appeared one day, stayed for a week or two, and then she was gone. It's absolutely mysterious. A lot of weird things go on in Odyssey, but I've never heard of a traveling statue."

Brittany nodded as she took a deep drink of her wine. "A statue that can change location and alter her physical appearance is unique indeed," she said. "Not that supernatural statues are a new controversy—they aren't. I assume you've heard of the weeping Virgin statues that have appeared around the world for decades?"

"I've heard of them," Sloth said. "But I thought those were hoaxes."

"Most were," Brittany agreed. "The so-called tears were often condensation or oil placed on the statue. But your sculpture?" Brittany tutted. "I'm not sure this one will be so cut-and-dried." She placed her wine glass on the table and sat back, folding her hands primly on her lap. "So! What would you like to know?"

Sloth leaned onto her elbows and plopped her chin in her hand. "I don't know," she said. "What do *you* know?"

"Well, let's see. The city commissioned the piece a little over 30 years ago," Brittany began. She sounded like she was reading from a script. "The artist is a Portuguese sculptor named Paola Barbosa. Her parents died when she was young, and she was raised by an eccentric aunt in Amadora, Portugal. She graduated high school at 18 and moved to America, where she attended the prestigious Rembrandt School of Design. She's most known for an underwater Poseidon sculpture that now resides in the Caribbean Sea. She completed the Star of the Sea in a little under nine months and was supposed to begin work on a new commission for the city of Copenhagen. Unfortunately, that never happened. Soon after the Star of the Sea was completed, Paola took ill. She disappeared from society and became a hermit. No one really heard from her after that."

"Became ill how?" Sloth asked. "What was wrong with her?"

Brittany paused, bouncing her head from side to side in a dithering fashion. "Some say she went mad," she said finally, her lips pinched. "But I think that's a gross, uneducated thing to say. She suffered some kind of mental illness, but the details are unclear."

"Is she still alive?" I asked.

Brittany nodded. "Yes. She lived here in Odyssey until recently. Now, she lives with a caretaker in San Diego. I've asked for an interview with her, but I've been routinely denied. So if you were hoping the artist might shed some light on your case, you're probably out of luck."

That definitely was my plan, and I felt a ripple of disappointment in my stomach. "What about her other sculptures? I don't suppose they've been traveling around, have they?"

Brittany smiled and dropped me a wink. "You have quite the investigative mind," she said. "I looked into that. And unfortunately, all Paola's previous works are exactly where she left them. They've never once moved."

I was still mulling this over when Sloth reached for a dinner roll and began slathering it with butter. "You don't mind if I eat this, do you?" she asked, the roll already halfway to her mouth.

Brittany chuckled. "They're all yours."

"Great. So, what's up with this book you're writing? What's the statue got to do with it?"

A server appeared then, placing a Cobb salad in front of Brittany. She took a small bite, chewing thoughtfully before answering. "My first book was about the interplay between art and madness. Not about artists who suffered mental illness, but about artwork that inspired obsession in others. People who went to extraordinary lengths to collect or even *see* a piece of art. One of my favorite cases involved a prominent household brand. Their logo was said to contain a secret message. If you could decode the message, you could apply to be a member of a highly selective, secret organization. People went nuts trying to decode the message. It became one of the most widespread popular hysterias of our time."

"But that's all nonsense," I said. "Nobody is really encoding secret messages in toothpaste logos."

Brittany grinned mysteriously as she stabbed a piece of lettuce with her fork. "*That* was nonsense, true. But not all reports of secret messages were. In the 1800s, a Spanish painting called *La mujer y el mar* or *The Woman and the Sea* was said to be a treasure map in disguise. Fortune-seekers from all over Europe came to look at the painting. It took decades, but finally, a man named Eduardo Arroniz deciphered the painting and found the treasure. Unfortunately for Eduardo, he wasn't allowed to keep it. The loot was seized by the Spanish government as a national treasure."

Sloth bit off a chunk of bread. "So you think the Star of the Sea has a secret message encoded? Or maybe she's trying to tell us something with where she appears?" Sloth glanced over to me and raised her eyebrows. "I said something similar, but Pride said I was being ridiculous."

I said, "I never said that."

"You implied it."

"Either way," Brittany interrupted, waving a fork, "no, that's not what I think. My first book was about art and madness. This book is about the relationship between art and cognitive awakening. Epiphanies. Spontaneous healing. Magic. Extrasensory perception."

I was still mad at the way Sloth had misrepresented our conversation, but I'd have to return to that topic another time because what Brittany just said actually piqued my interest. "Extrasensory perception? You mean ESP?"

"Exactly," she said. "I'm examining the way both the creation and the viewing of art change the mind's reality. There's an idea in Jungian psychology called the collective unconscious. All of us receive drips and drabs of information from a universal source. That collective unconscious is why certain synchronicities happen. For example, you've probably heard the story about how Gottfried Leibniz and Sir Isaac Newton both invented calculus at the same time in different parts of the world. At first glance, this looks like the most miraculous coincidence of all time! But in fact, both men were tapped into something larger than themselves. They accessed the knowledge that permeates the universe and infects us all."

Brittany looked proud of herself as she took another delicate bite of her salad, but she had no idea how low she'd just sunk in my estimation. It might seem weird since I'm a psychic ghost whisperer who has visions when I touch people, but I don't put a lot of stock in this New Age Jungian pop-psychology nonsense. If you ask me, this sort of thing is why you have otherwise sensible people walking around saying garbage like, "My partner's love language is words of affirmation, but I'm a Sagittarius Sun with Sagittarius rising, so it's not my fault if I say just any old thing that pops into my head!"

It's cockamamie malarkey, is what I'm saying.

"So…you think the statue is connected to ESP somehow?" Sloth asked.

"Don't you?" Brittany replied, eyes wide. "Although, to be fair, that's just my gut talking. As a journalist, I have to consider all the possibilities, of which there are several." She placed her elbows on the table and knit her fingers together, resting her chin on top. "The first possibility is that this is all an elaborate hoax, like the weeping Virgins. Someone with a lot of time on their hands could have created fake statues they've been placing around town."

Sloth frowned, reaching for a second dinner roll. "We considered that, of course. But it seems like an awful lot of work. Plus, someone would have seen them."

"Not necessarily," Brittany countered. "Have you heard of the monoliths that appeared overnight around the world? Or the Georgia Guidestones? No one saw those structures erected."

Sloth rolled her eyes. "Those were in the middle of nowhere, not standing on the side of the street in downtown Odyssey."

"Fine, but think about the greatest stage magicians of our time. It's a time-honored tradition to use smoke, mirrors, and misdirection to create elaborate illusions that make audiences think people are levitating, flying, or disappearing altogether. The brain is easily persuaded," Brittany said. "With the right knowledge and tools, a dedicated prankster could pull it off."

"Still seems far-fetched," Sloth muttered.

"There are no possibilities that aren't," Brittany agreed with a chuckle. "The second possibility is that someone with extrasensory abilities is manipulating the statue from afar. Although it's rare, telekinesis exists. Someone very gifted could be altering the statue with their mind. Option three is that the statue never left City Hall, and we're all suffering from mass hysterical delusion. And then we come to my favorite scenario."

I couldn't wait to hear this. "And what's that?"

Brittany lifted the linen napkin from her lap and dabbed delicately at her mouth, careful not to smudge her lipstick. "Creating art is its own form of magic. Artists are life-givers. We like to say metaphorically that artists put themselves in their art. But what if it's not a metaphor? What if some sensitive creators actually impart their own consciousness to the works they create?" She shrugged, her eyes glittering. "Some of my research into the mystical world of art has hinted it may be possible. And if so, maybe the statue isn't being manipulated from the outside at all. Maybe it's acting of its own free will."

I stared, for a moment too stunned to speak. Then I blurted out, "You're suggesting the Star of the Sea might be *conscious?*"

Brittany shook herself then and squared her shoulders, placing her napkin on the table. "I'm really not suggesting anything one way or the other," she pointed out diplomatically. "I'm merely enumerating and exploring all the possibilities. As a journalist and researcher, that's my job. Follow the evidence wherever it leads. But these are the options as I see them. Either we're all being pranked, someone is moving the statue with their mind, we are all imagining this, or the statue is, for lack of a better word, alive."

———

"I don't care what that harebrained cheerleader says," I said, stabbing my slice of cherry pie with a fork. "There is *no way* a statue can come to life."

We had just finished having dinner together as a house, and now, Sloth, Gluttony, and I were discussing the day's events over dessert. Gluttony's specialty was pastry, but I didn't usually care for cherry pie. However, the discussion with Brittany left a bad taste in my mouth, so I was trying to mask it with warm, tart, juicy cherries nestled in a buttery, flaky crust.

Sloth, on the other hand, was absolutely energized. "I don't know how *you*, of all people, could say something like that," she said. "Your family disappeared off the face of the earth without leaving even a trace. You can see and talk to ghosts. I'm a mind reader. Greed can see the future."

"That last part's up for debate," Gluttony put in.

"All I'm saying is, the world is much more complex than we know," Sloth continued. "After all the things you've seen in Odyssey, how can you really say *anything* is impossible?"

I huffed and set my fork down on my now-empty plate, pushing it away. "Ghosts are one thing," I said. "They are well-documented throughout human history. Everyone dies. Every culture has some tale about life after death. What cultures do you know where statues come to life? And don't say *Ghostbusters*," I said, holding up a hand. "I said *cultures*, not movies."

Sloth stuck her finger in the red filling of her cherry pie before jamming it into her mouth. "I just think you're being myopic. And anyway, Brittany was the first to admit there were several possibilities. The statue coming to life was just one of them."

I turned to Gluttony, my hands spread before me, supplicant. "You're on my side, right? No way statues can come to life."

Gluttony wiped his mouth with a napkin, balled it up, and tossed it into the trash. "Three points!"

"No way was that worth three," Sloth objected.

"The trash is *right there*, Gluttony. That was two points, and you know it."

"Who died and made you the kitchen referee? You wanna be in charge so bad, how about you do the dishes tonight?"

"You're right," Sloth said with a smile. "That was totally a three-pointer. My bad."

Gluttony chuckled and returned his attention to me. "If you'd asked me a month ago, I would agree with you. Statues don't come to life. But we saw old girl right here on our own turf. We touched her. Tried to dig her out. She was solid as anything. She wasn't some sleight-of-hand magician's smoke and mirrors. She was here, screaming, and then she was gone. So if you ask me…" Gluttony shoved a final bite of pie into his mouth. "I guess I don't know if she's alive. But she's definitely not a hoax. Either someone is telekinetically moving her around like a chess piece, or she's alive. Ain't no other way about it."

Sloth nodded her agreement. "That's right. And I feel confident we can rule out the chess piece idea. Moving a statue around is one thing. Making her change form is something else altogether."

I sat back from the table and crossed my arms to think. Whether I liked it or not, they both made good points. But Sloth was wrong about one thing—we couldn't rule out any scenarios yet. We didn't have enough evidence. Still, there were only so many leads we could pursue at a time. Starting with how to bring a statue to life was as good a place to begin our investigation as any.

"So how about you, Gluttony?" I asked. "What did you find out from your interviews today?"

Gluttony whipped out his phone and peered down into the screen. "A lot, actually. I surveyed over 100 people, and here's what I found: About 25% of respondents would prefer a fruity, refreshing snack while they camped out at the statue site. Around 30% said a savory snack would be best. But 45% of statue tourists agreed they would gobble up anything sweet and decadent. Nobody talked about the mechanism for eating said treats," Gluttony mused aloud, "but I don't want to create any opportunity for litter or excess trash, so anything requiring utensils is out. I'm thinking some kind of hand-held pie. What do y'all think?"

I glanced over at Sloth. "You were right."

"I knew it," she said, smiling. "Gluttony, you *really* are as predictable as the weather at the North Pole. Did you do *any* real investigation while you were out there?"

"Finding out people's food choices *is* real investigation," he countered.

"How's that?" I asked.

Gluttony held up a finger. "For one, you can tell a lot about people by what they choose to put in their bodies. Take Greed, for example. You don't never see him eating chocolate cake or drinking pop. He thinks he's gonna get rich and live forever, so he gotta take care of his temple, right? But me, I know I'm gonna die young. So, I'm not trying to live off broccoli and boiled chicken, you know what I'm saying? I don't need to keep this hunk of junk healthy for the next 50 years. If you offer me some bananas foster and some fillet mignon,

I'm eating that. No question. *And* the chocolate cake, *and* the fois gras, and whatever else tasty you got."

Sloth tilted her head, frowning. "What makes you think you're gonna die young?"

"An old psychic woman told me when I was a kid," he said with a shrug. "Normally, I wouldn't put much stock in that, but what if she's right? None of us is guaranteed tomorrow. So I'm gonna stock up on the good life while I can. Which brings me to my second point." He held up two fingers. "Finding out what these folks like to eat matters so I can charge as much money as I can. Each dollar I earn here is another dollar I can invest in date night with my wife when this show is done. Twenty bucks here is a bottle of wine there. And you *know* I like nothing more than making my wife happy. It's like I always say, if you got em, better love em."

Sloth and I sat and stared at him for a little while, neither of us responding. It was sound logic to me—if you knew you were gonna die, that is. But I guess I was thinking about that the wrong way, because if you thought about it the *right* way, we were all gonna die. Some of us were just a little closer to the finish line than others.

Eventually, Gluttony shrugged and put away his phone. "Well, I'm gonna do the dishes while I still have the energy. You want to hand me them plates?"

I gathered all our dishes and passed them to Gluttony. "Are you sure? You cooked. You shouldn't have to clean."

Gluttony ambled into the kitchen where he dumped the dishes into the sink, squirted in some detergent, and turned on the faucet. "I don't really mind." He dipped a sponge into the soapy water and squeezed it out with a smile. "The kitchen is where I'm happiest. Thanks for offering, though."

I hung around for a second to make sure he didn't change his mind, and then I left Gluttony to it.

I wasn't ready to retire to my room, and there was no one hanging out in the recreation room, so I decided to go for a late jog on the beach. I went outside, breathed in the fresh, salty air, and stopped short just as I was about to skip down the steps to the sidewalk.

Standing on our porch, hands dug in his pockets, was a man. He was dressed casually in jeans and a t-shirt that said, "Vote for Pedro." When he saw me, he lifted a hand in greeting.

"Uh, hey, excuse me." His cheeks were ruddy, and a twisted, embarrassed smile gave him a friendly appearance. "I'm super sorry to bother you, but are you Pride from *Sinful House?*"

I gulped. This wasn't my first celebrity sighting, but it wasn't my thousandth, either. I was never sure how to handle these things, especially since you never knew if you were dealing with a fan or someone who hate-watched the show out of spite. Though, to be honest, both groups gave me the willies. "That's me," I said.

The man glanced around and took a tentative step toward me. "You're the one that sees ghosts, right?"

I nodded, the corners of my mouth tugging into a frown. "Sometimes," I hedged.

He hesitated. "Sometimes? Like, what, sometimes it doesn't work?"

"No. I mean, I only see them when they're there. Which is only sometimes."

The man chuckled, more color seeping into his face as tension leaked from his shoulders. "Oh, yeah, cool. That makes sense. Listen, um—yeah, I know this is super weird, but can I speak to you a moment?"

"You are speaking to me," I said.

The man smirked. "Right. Well, I don't know how to say this, so I'll just… I think my apartment might be haunted. I need someone to check it out, but I don't trust any locals. It's hard to know who's faking it and who's not."

I grunted. I'd run across more than my fair share of charlatans, and nobody hated them more than me. They were the reason most people didn't take me seriously. Well, them plus the fact that a lot of people just didn't believe in anything they couldn't see. "I can't say I blame you," I said.

"Right. Well, the haunting…it's getting worse. It's starting to mess with my mind. Like, I feel like I'm going crazy, you know?"

"You should see a therapist about that," I said. "Sometimes just talking about your problems can—"

"I've seen a shrink already, believe me," the man interrupted. "It's not exactly helping. I don't need a therapist, I need *proof*. I need someone to come to my apartment and tell me I'm not imagining things. I need a ghost whisperer."

Under different circumstances, I might think this guy was putting me on. Who approaches a perfect stranger and says, "Hey, I think my apartment's haunted. Can you come check it out?" I mean, it's not a good line for anything—picking up girls *or* luring a potential murder victim to your house, which are the only two reasons I could think of for why you'd need a line in the first place.

But this guy *looked* haunted. His skin was pallid, and purple half-circles beneath his eyes suggested he hadn't been sleeping well. He desperately needed a shave, and his dark hair was too long in an unkempt sort of way, like it hadn't been cut in a while. He was fidgety, too—not like crack-addict-in-withdrawal twitchy, but more like someone at a horror movie who was expecting a jump scare any minute. He was wound as tight as a coil.

Still, investigating private hauntings wasn't in my wheelhouse. And if anybody found out I did this, the crazies would explode out of the woodwork. I'd be up to my eyebrows in nutters begging me to come exorcise their dear aunt Matilda from their spider-infested garden shed. Even thinking about it sent a shiver down my spine.

"It's awful about your trouble," I said. "But that's not really…I mean, I'm not comfortable…"

"If it's about money, I can pay," he said. "I'm not trying to get anything for free. It's just—I'm at my wit's end."

"It's not about money. I just—"

"Tell him we'll do it."

I startled and looked over my shoulder to see the ghost girl standing beside me, legs akimbo, arms on her hips, staring up at me with a deep frown scribbled over her features. She was glowering at me, her brows drawn into a sharp V. For a child, she looked terribly menacing. "Tell him we'll do it, or I'll never speak to you again."

"Don't I wish!" I barked and immediately wished I hadn't.

The man in front of me blinked, taken aback at my outburst. "Sorry?"

Embarrassed, I looked away, rubbing the nape of my neck as color rose hot in my cheeks. "No, it's nothing, it's just—"

"Tell him you're having a conversation with your ghost friend," she said, the challenge unmistakable in her voice. "What, are you too embarrassed? Think he won't believe you? Think he'll think you're *nuts?*"

"Of course not," I hissed. I glanced quickly at the stranger before me, who was staring like I'd sprouted a second head. "Please, go away." I glanced up quickly. "No, not you. I'm talking to…it's just this…uh..."

"You're talking to a ghost, aren't you?" His voice was soft and devoid of ridicule. "Is there a ghost with us now?"

I shot a dark look at the ghost girl, who only returned my glare with equal venom. "Well, actually…yes."

He stepped nearer to me and closed his eyes. He breathed in deep through his nose and then went still. When he opened his eyes again, he looked disappointed. "I can't sense anything," he breathed. "I don't know which is scarier—to know there's a ghost you can't feel, or to feel something's there you can't know."

The ghost girl cleared her throat loudly, and when I looked at her, she gave me her best angry schoolmarm scowl. "He needs our help," she said. "You know what it's like, Pride. You know what it's like to think you might be losing your marbles because no one believes you about the ghosts."

I said nothing. She'd hit on a sore spot, and she knew it. It still burned whenever someone called me a whackjob or a nutcase or a lunatic. But while these days it just ticked me off, in the beginning, it made me doubt myself. It led to my doctor putting me on medication. Nothing makes you feel lonelier than questioning your own sanity.

Still, I had a lot going on, and I didn't need to add anything else to my growing to-do list. I started to say as much to the ghost, but she held up a hand, turning her face away from me. "I don't want to hear your excuses. If you don't help him, I'll start singing John Jacob Jingleheimer Schmidt, and I won't stop until—"

"Just a minute ago, you said you'd never talk to me again!" I interrupted.

"Well, I was lying. Don't make me do it, Pride." When I said nothing, she clenched her fists at her side, took a deep breath, and opened her mouth wide. "*John Jacob Jingleheimer Schmidt! His name is my name too! Whenever we go out, the people always shout JOHN JACOB JINGLE- HEIMER SCHMIDT la la la la la! John Jacob—*"

"All right, all right! I'll do it, just don't sing that awful song!" I sighed, my shoulders slumping in defeat. To the man, I said, "At least tell me your name first."

"Aaron," he said, fumbling his hand from his pocket and offering it for a shake. "Aaron Burton. I really can't thank you enough."

"Don't mention it," I mumbled, reaching for my phone. "Here. Put your information in my contacts. So, did you have a specific day, or—"

"As soon as you can fit me in," he answered, punching his info into my phone. "The sooner I can get this all sorted, the better. But it might be better late in the evening. That's when I usually notice something is…off."

"I just want to be clear about one thing," I said, taking back my phone and slipping it away. "I can't necessarily make the ghost leave. Assuming there is one, I mean. In that way, they're like humans. Except at least you can drag humans around. If you're strong enough."

"Oh, I understand," Aaron said. His voice was different now—rounder and lower-pitched. He definitely sounded less anxious. "But this is a good first step, right?"

He flashed me one last bashful smile before turning on his heel and wandering off into the night.

three

. . .

Gluttony and I went to see the statue first thing the next morning. Gluttony and Sloth had stayed up late baking peach and rhubarb hand pies to take to Julio's, and my sleepyhead teammate had promised to join us later after a few more hours of shut-eye. Gluttony, however, was in fine spirits. He was sitting in the passenger seat, bopping his head to the radio and musing aloud about his impending profits. "Five dollars apiece might be too high," he said on the drive over, "but I'm gonna start there and see how many takers I have. These folks won't know what hit them. These are some of the best pies I've ever made."

As I parked the car, I threw Gluttony a side-eye glance. "You didn't put any weird magic in there, did you? We're supposed to be investigating, after all. This whole thing might go smoother if everyone is in their right mind. So to speak."

Gluttony hauled the boxes from the back seat with a huff. "Ain't nothing in here but fruit and sugar," he said, dropping me a wink. "Come on now. Enough talk about magic. Let's go make some money."

Apparently, Gluttony and I had different priorities for the day. While he found a place to set up shop, I headed straight for the statue. Just like yesterday, getting through the crowd was difficult. It seemed impossible, but even more people had arrived. Everywhere you looked, there were parents, toddlers, dogs, teenagers— you name it. The only thing I *didn't* see were cops asking people to leave. I guess Julio hadn't made the right phone call just yet. Poor guy. Dealing with Odyssey's bureaucracy was a nightmare I wouldn't wish on anyone.

Finally, after stepping on too many toes and pushing aside at least a dozen strollers, I made it to the statue. Unfortunately, someone else was already there, and my heart sank when I saw her. I wasn't exactly sure what I had against Brittany Miller, except that she reminded me of the girls in high school who wouldn't let me sit at their table. But there was something else, too, I hadn't yet put my finger on.

Brittany hadn't noticed me yet. She was scribbling furiously on a tablet, her lips pressed into a hard line. When she looked up, she yelped in surprise. "You startled me," she said, her free hand pressed to her chest.

"You were concentrating pretty hard, I guess."

Brittany mumbled her agreement before hiding the tablet behind her back and gazing up at the mermaid. "Every time I see her, I forget how beautiful she is," she cooed. "I mean, I love paintings and illustrations as much as the next art lover. But sculpture is something else, don't you think? Can you imagine looking at a block of clay and seeing the human form beneath it? It's such a unique talent to see beyond the excess and carve away what isn't necessary to reveal an object's true nature. Especially in the case of bronze monuments. Do you know how they're made?"

"No," I said. "And I don't—"

"It's a very complex process of clay carving, mold making, wax pouring, and metal melting," she went on. "There are usually several people involved in the process, not just the sculptor herself. But my understanding is that Paola allowed very few people to intervene in her process. She didn't want anyone polluting her vision of the mermaid's true nature."

I grunted noncommittally at that. "You think that's what Paola Barbosa did? Just kept carving until the mermaid's true nature revealed itself?"

"Maybe," Brittany said with a smile. "But it's more likely she always knew what was there. Like she saw it with her third eye. That's what I find so fascinating. Artists are such *givers*. She didn't need to carve the mermaid for her own sake. She always saw what lay beneath. She carved it to make the beauty and glory visible to the rest of us."

And there it was. What I instinctively disliked about Brittany Miller. You could tell she was smart. Really smart. Yet she succumbed to some pretty cockamamie ideas, and that bothered me. Because if you're a natural-born idiot, it's okay if you believe in superstitions, conspiracy theories, or commercials. But if you're an intelligent person with a good head on your shoulders, talking about mortifying topics like third eyes was just a travesty. Brittany Miller's mother was probably ashamed of her.

None of this seemed polite to say, however, so instead, I just said, "Yeah, that's pretty cool."

Brittany clucked her tongue against the roof of her mouth and giggled. "I can see you're not interested in all my psychobabble about artists. That's okay. Why don't we just skip to the good part then? Did you notice this before?"

She placed her hand on my elbow and guided me around to the back of the statue. She got down on her haunches and beckoned for me to do the same.

I lowered myself so I was level with Brittany, though my knees protested like a vegan at an Arby's grand opening. Then she tapped a finger at the base of the statue. "Here."

Brittany's finger rested on a scribble of black ink that looked like a signature or autograph. Maybe some wayward gangbanger had tagged the monument, though Odyssey didn't seem to have much of a street gang problem.

"Yeah, it's graffiti. Probably some kid's way of saying they were here. Happened all the time in San Diego," I said.

Brittany nodded, her eyes never leaving the scribble. "I assumed that, too. But I haven't really seen any other graffiti in the city. And here's another weird thing." Brittany glanced around before pulling a handkerchief and a bottle of what looked like nail polish remover from her purse. She wet the handkerchief and went to work scrubbing the black ink, but it wouldn't come up.

She flashed me a smile. "That's pure acetone. It removes basically anything. If that were marker or paint or something, the acetone would remove it. But it doesn't. So what do you make of that?"

To be honest, I didn't make much of that at all. For all I knew, the writing was an integrated part of the statue itself. But then I realized that might have been Brittany's point—it wasn't left there by some hoodlum. It was an intentional mark.

I examined the scribble more closely. "Does that say Luis?" I asked.

Brittany brought a finger to her lips, smiling mischievously. "That's what it looks like to me, too. Does it ring a bell? Is that someone significant from Odyssey's history?"

I shrugged, stumped. "I'm the wrong person to ask about Odyssey's history. But it's not an uncommon name, especially for a city founded as a Spanish mission. There are probably a dozen Luises to sort through."

Brittany sighed. "Well, it could mean something, so I thought I'd point it out to you. Maybe it'll help with your case. Unfortunately, today is my last day in Odyssey. I'm on deadline, and I have some last-minute details to wrap up back home, so the investigation is now firmly in your hands. But you've done this kind of work before. You probably don't need me anymore, anyway."

I definitely didn't, and was about to say so when a shadow passed over me. Looking up, I expected to see

Gluttony, and I was readying a wisecrack about his hand pie side hustle.

But it wasn't Gluttony.

It was a woman. She had an oval face and peaches and cream skin with eyes the color of the Pacific Ocean after a storm. Her long, wheat blonde hair was parted in the middle forming curtains around her face. She looked familiar, though I couldn't quite put my finger on where I'd seen her before.

"She's absolutely breathtaking, isn't she?" the woman said.

"She's really something," I replied, rising to my feet. "Have you ever seen anything like her?"

Confusion washed over the woman's face as she blinked and did a double-take as though only just noticing I existed. And then I saw her eyes dart past me, and I realized with poker-hot chagrin that she hadn't been talking to me at all.

"Yes, she's stunning," Brittany said, her cheeks coloring. She actually reached for her hair and smoothed it down, an unconscious attempt to make herself more attractive. "Up close, she's the most amazing work I've seen in a long time."

"I sort of have a thing for mermaids," the woman said, her smile growing broader, eyes never leaving Brittany. "I think it's the whole 'enchant men with their voice and then drag them to the bottom of the sea to die' thing."

I cringed. It was possibly the worst pick-up line I'd ever heard, but Brittany seemed unfazed. "Those were sirens, not necessarily mermaids, but I take your point," she said.

I cleared my throat. "We have a siren at the house. Her name's Lust. She uses a form of psychic persuasion to get men to do what she wants. Or anyone who's into women, actually."

Both women ignored me. "This city gets its name from Homer's *Odyssey*," Brittany continued, "where sirens famously tried to lure Odysseus to his death with their song. I think that's why the city chose the mermaid as its mascot, though if you ask me, it's a strange choice, all things considered."

"Weren't the sirens of Greek mythology actually half-woman, half-bird?" I asked.

Brittany opened her mouth to respond when someone behind us croaked in a pitchy, breathless voice, "Hadley?"

We all turned around. Sloth was standing there, her brow wrinkled. But when her eyes landed on the woman's face, she stepped backward, hands flying to her mouth. "Oh my gosh!" she yelped. "You're not Hadley! You're Tabitha Antoinette!"

The woman—Tabitha—grinned and tossed her hair over a shoulder. "I am." She cocked her head to the side, her smile widening. "Who's Hadley?"

Sloth waved her hand frantically in front of her face, her cheeks blushing crimson. "Oh, no one. Just my sister. I can't believe I mistook *Tabitha Antoinette* for my sister!" She paused. "You really do look alike from behind, though."

I didn't know much about Sloth and her family, but I

knew Sloth had an older sister named Hadley, and the two did not get along. It was a source of real heartbreak for Sloth, who worshiped her older sibling like many little sisters. Apparently, the feeling was not mutual.

"Well, if your sister looks anything like you, then I take that as a compliment," Tabitha said.

I inched closer to Brittany and leaned in to whisper, "Who the heck is Tabitha Antoinette?"

But apparently, my whisper wasn't as whispery as I thought because Sloth gasped and punched me in the arm. "Who is Tabitha Antoinette? Oh my gosh, Pride, have you been living under a rock? She's only Hollywood royalty! She's been in like…a *million* TV shows! She was on that show *Filmore Sisters* where she played, what was it, a floozy secretary? And she was the assistant paramedic on that show *Nurse Kimmie*. And—oh, how could I forget the waitress on that one episode of *Housewife Confessions*?"

I felt my mouth twist into a frown. "So she's played bit parts on second-rate TV shows?"

For a second, I seriously thought Sloth might slap my face. The look she threw me was giving me big how-could-you-cheat-on-me-when-I-supported-you-through-law-school vibes. But while Sloth stood there fuming with what I think was embarrassment, Brittany cleared her throat and said, "It's really nice to meet you, Ms. Antoinette. I'm a big fan."

"Tabitha, please," the woman said, smiling. Then she turned to me, still beaming that 1,000-watt grin. "I was also an extra on *Burning Bridges*."

I couldn't tell if she was good-naturedly sharing a

laugh with me or if she was too self-absorbed to realize she just made my case. You never can tell with actresses. But I didn't have long to wonder about this because somewhere behind us, someone began shouting into a bullhorn.

"From the waters of life we came, and to the waters of life we shall return. Be renewed and born again with the gifts of the mermaids, children of the starless sea! Come with an open heart and a willingness to transform, and let the Star of the Sea guide you to salvation! See my website for details!"

I turned around and searched the crowd for the idiot causing the spectacle. He wasn't hard to find. A short man with a shining, bald head fringed with sparse curls was standing on a stepladder, mouth pressed into a huge bullhorn with the words "America's Goddess" painted on the side. He wore pink prescription glasses and was dabbing his face furtively with a handkerchief. Huge sweat stains marred the pits of his yellow Hawaiian print shirt.

"Citizens of Odyssey! The time to pay homage to the goddess of the deep is now! As the prophet for the goddess of the sea, I'm taking donations. Cash preferred. Come speak to me for details!"

Sloth sucked her teeth and narrowed her eyes as she peered at the mermaid preacher. "Who's that?"

Brittany sighed and rolled her eyes, shaking her head as she propped a hand on her hip. "That's Dewey Delaney, self-proclaimed prophet of the Children of Poseidon church. He's been doing this schtick every day. He's trying to recruit members for his congregation or something. You should see his website. It looks like he made it on Geocities back in the 1800s. Honestly, the mayor needs to come do something about him. He's an eyesore, a nuisance, and an embarrassment."

"So is the mayor," I sighed. "And anyway, he's in jail."

"Well, you can't blame the guy for trying to live his dream," Tabitha said. All eyes turned to her, and she stood up straighter, shrugging a slender, suntanned shoulder. "I haven't seen his website, obviously, but if he's talking about renewal and rebirth, it can't be *all* bad."

"Yes, it can," I said.

"What do you mean?" Sloth asked, directing the question at Tabitha, ignoring me utterly.

"Well, everyone could use a do-over. Take me, for instance. Before I dedicated myself to living my most authentic life, I was working in sales at a big corporation. It was draining the *life* out of me! Thankfully, I was on a vacation with girlfriends in Tokyo when I got picked up by a talent scout. I took a chance, redesigned my life, and here I am."

"Yes," I agreed. "Working as an assistant paramedic in a single episode of…what was it, again?"

"Anyway," she continued, "I'm about to make another change. Acting has been a godsend, but it's time to take my talents to another level. I'm starting a foundation to help women find their authentic selves and achieve their dreams."

"Are you really?" Sloth breathed. "Oh wow, that's so *noble*. What a wonderful way to use your celebrity!"

I thought calling this C-list actress a celebrity was a bit much, but what did I know? Sloth watched a lot more television than I did, so maybe to her, someone with a dozen unimportant roles on bad cable shows really was the bee's knees. Still, I didn't like the way Sloth was looking at her. It made me feel twisty inside.

"Well, you know, *we're* celebrities, too," I heard myself saying before I could stop it. "Have you seen the show, Tabitha? *Sinful House?*"

Tabitha blinked and turned a cold stare to me. "Sinful what?"

"It's a reality show," I explained. "We're the 7 Deadly Sins, and we solve mysteries." When no look of recognition crossed her face, I added, "I guess you haven't seen it."

"I haven't." She looked pointedly at my housemate. "Which sin are you?"

"Sloth," she answered.

"Well, you don't look like a Sloth to me," Tabitha replied. "And anyway, what a weird concept for a show! Like people don't have enough emotional baggage to deal with! Now they have to go around pretending to be a cardinal sin? Honestly, how does that affect your self-esteem? You know, we are what we tell ourselves. Having everyone refer to you as 'Sloth' can't be good for you. How do you cope?"

My housemate paused to digest that little tirade, then lifted her chin. Something hot and furious flashed behind her big gray eyes, but I wasn't clued in enough to know what she was thinking. "Well, I hadn't thought much about it," she admitted. "But now that you mention it, I guess it *is* a little dehumanizing."

Tabitha clucked her tongue in sympathy. "Hmm. If you ask me, you should be more upset than you are. Maybe you need to take back your power, you know? Find your powerful goddess."

I gestured to the Star of the Sea. "According to Dewey, the goddess is right here."

Brittany had the decency to chuckle at my joke, but both Tabitha and Sloth ignored me. Tabitha touched Sloth lightly on the arm and made her voice velvety soft. "Listen, I know we just met, but would you like to take a walk with me on the beach? I'm curious about this whole 7 Deadly Sins business. Maybe we can discuss the psycho-spiritual underpinnings of it all. Would you mind?"

Sloth squealed, clapping her hands together as she bounced on the balls of her feet. "Oh my gosh, are you kidding? Go for a walk with Tabitha Antoinette? Yes! Yes, let's go!"

Tabitha hooked her arm in Sloth's, and the two of them wended their way through the ever-growing crowd. I watched their backs as they sauntered off toward the water. I couldn't help but notice that from behind, with their long, blonde hair and the way they casually bumped into each other as they walked, they really did look like sisters.

"Repent and save yourselves!" Dewey was shouting, sweat pouring from his nonexistent hairline. "Let the living waters of her eternal sea wash you clean! Follow me on social media for more!"

four

. . .

L ater that night, long after the rest of the house had gone to bed, I lay awake in the dark, staring at the ceiling. Something was niggling at the back of my mind, but I couldn't place my finger on it. I rolled over onto my side and squeezed my eyes shut. *Come on, brain*, I thought. *If you can't be useful, just turn off for the night and let me sleep.*

But apparently, I was not the boss of my brain, and sleep refused to come.

Eventually, I sighed and threw my blankets off, swinging my legs over the bed and climbing to my feet. I rarely had insomnia, but it was usually nothing a hot mug of chamomile tea couldn't fix when I did. I went downstairs to the kitchen, heated myself up a cup, and was halfway to my bedroom when I saw light underneath Sloth's door.

Her door opened soundlessly, and I stepped inside. I found her sitting on the floor in the middle of the room, surrounded by a half-dozen boxes. She looked up at me, and her face immediately brightened. "Oh, Pride! I'm glad it's you. I actually wanted to talk to you, but I worried it might be too late."

I frowned. "Too late for what? Oh. You mean the time." I held my steaming cup of chamomile tea aloft. "I couldn't sleep. Looks like you couldn't either."

I closed the door behind me and sat at the foot of Sloth's bed while she continued to rummage through the various accouterments she'd assembled around her— books, stationery, electronics, clothing. She appeared to be sorting her belongings into various piles, though her categorization method made little sense to me. "You can sleep when you're dead," Sloth said, moving a rumpled t-shirt from one clothing pile to another. "Did you bring me any tea?"

"I would have if I'd known you were awake," I said.

She grinned. "I bet you really would have, too. That's what I like about you. You're so thoughtful."

I'd been called many things, but I couldn't recall *thoughtful* ever having been on that list. The compliment made me blush like a politician in church. "So, what are you doing?" I asked.

Sloth waved the question away. "Nothing, really. Just thinking. I called Paola Barbosa today."

I blinked. That was news. "You did? On your own?"

Sloth chuckled. "What, I'm not allowed to take the lead on this investigation or something?"

"It's not that," I said. "I just figured…she's the only real lead we have, so I figured we'd all call her together."

"Well, it doesn't matter. I couldn't get a hold of her. I spoke to her caregiver, a woman named Claudia, who was not especially happy to talk to me. She told me the artist wasn't taking interviews and made it clear she didn't want me to call back."

"Made it clear how?"

Sloth grunted with a shallow lift of her shoulder. "She told me I should be ashamed of myself, and I should get a life."

I grimaced. "I can see how that would upset you. Try not to let it get to you, though," I said. "Back when I was an investigator, people blew me off a lot. You learn to find other ways around obstacles. Claudia is just an obstacle."

"Well, that's what I wanted to talk to you about."

"Oh? You wanted to talk about Claudia?"

Sloth smoothed her hair behind her ears and rested her hands in her lap. "No. After you and Gluttony left Julio's, I spent most of the afternoon with Tabby," she began. I physically restrained myself from wincing. *Tabby?!* "She told me all about the foundation she's starting—what she's trying to accomplish and everything. And you know, I realized something. The things she told me resonated. She talked about being true to herself and not locking pieces of herself away to make other people happy."

"Well, you don't do that," I pointed out. "You're always completely yourself."

A shadow passed over Sloth's face, and she dropped her gaze. "Well, no one is ever completely themselves, least of all me. But anyway, eventually, we started talking about my wants and desires. And I told her that ever since Eleanor died…well, I haven't been as sure about my priorities as I used to be. I've felt…well, aimless, really. Confused. Her death left a hole in my heart."

I took another long sip of tea. This was the first I heard that Eleanor's death affected Sloth so profoundly. What did that say about me that I hadn't noticed before now? And what did it say about me that this was what I was worried about as Sloth was pouring her heart out? Why was I always so selfish and self-centered? What was wrong with me?

Panic began rising in my chest, and my heart skipped several beats as my blood pressure rose. I hadn't had a panic attack in a long time—I'd almost thought I'd outgrown them. Realizing I was on the verge of an episode made my anxiety even worse, but now was not the time to completely lose it, not when Sloth was trying to tell me something. So I closed my eyes and practiced a technique Dr. Xena taught me. "Find four things you can hear, four things you can smell, four things you can see, and four things you can touch."

So I listened. Sloth was still talking, and I let her words fall into me like puzzle pieces. Sloth's voice—that was one. Beyond her voice, I heard the whir of the air conditioner. That was two. I took another sip of tea. The comforting slurp was three. And finally, I heard the creak of the floorboards as Sloth shifted around.

I was already calmer, but I continued the ritual, finding smells, sights, things to touch. Before long, I felt like I might be okay.

That is, until I focused on what Sloth was saying.

"…and that's when Tabitha made her proposal. I mean, by that point, I was half in love with her, you know? She's got this *amazing* energy, and she's just so charismatic. So, when she suggested I work with her on building the foundation, it seemed like a good fit. Like it might fill my empty spaces."

I sat in silence, trying to make sense of what Sloth was telling me. I was having a weird déjà vu moment. Something about finding Sloth in the middle of all these half-packed boxes was prickling a memory. I couldn't place it at first. But then it came to me, and I sat up straight, my jaw falling open.

It was bringing back memories of Shayda.

Specifically, the day Shayda had moved out.

"Sloth?" I looked around the room, really taking in my surroundings for the first time. "Why are you packing your things? Are you…trading rooms with someone?" I asked hopefully.

My housemate's gaze softened, and she gave a slow, tender shake of her head. "No, Pride. I'm not switching rooms with anyone. I've decided to leave the show. I'm moving to Los Angeles with Tabby. I'm going to be her business partner."

A thousand different thoughts ran through my head, making me feel very overwhelmed. So instead of saying what I actually felt—which was that I was scared—I blurted out, "That's the craziest, most cockamamie thing I've ever heard!"

Sloth sat still as stone, her expression unreadable. Was she unfazed by my outburst? Upset? I couldn't tell. And the fact that I couldn't tell redoubled my anxiety. I took a deep breath and said, "I didn't mean to call you crazy. I don't like it when people call me that."

Still, Sloth said nothing. She didn't even blink. I plowed on. "But quitting the show? Come on, you can't quit! You have a contract!"

My housemate said nothing for a while. She merely looked down and began picking at a stain on her flannel horse pajamas. I don't mean she was dressed like a horse. But her pajamas had horses printed on them. "I'm sure I can get out of that. Tabby said there are ways. What are they gonna do, anyway? Arrest me? Take me to jail?"

"I don't know! Maybe? But that's not even…Sloth, we need you." I heard the whine in my voice, and I didn't like it, but I was about ten seconds away from a full-blown panic attack. I was long past counting sights and smells. I needed Sloth to *listen.* "Think about it. Without you, there's just six of us. And there's no such thing as the *Six* Deadly Sins!"

"I thought about that," she said. "And I'm sure the network will find someone to replace me. After all, I'm not the only lazy slob with a motivation problem in the United States of America."

This conversation wasn't going the way I wanted. For one thing, I didn't care at all about the show's fate. And that was the truth. Sure, living at Sinful House gave me a place to sleep and put food in my stomach. But that wasn't why I was subconsciously looking around Sloth's room for a paper bag I could hyperventilate into.

It was the possibility of losing Sloth.

I took a deep breath and decided to change tacks. "Sloth, be logical for a second," I said. "You *just* met this woman. What did she say to you to make you think this was a remotely good idea? Do you even know the first thing about starting a business?"

A wave of uncertainty washed across Sloth's face. "Well, no, not exactly. But I can learn."

I threw my hands up in exasperation. "If you want to start a business, you can learn while you're on the show! I'm sure there's videos about it on YouTube. Isn't this kind of sudden?" I gulped, grasping for an argument—any argument—that might keep her here. "Don't you think maybe you're just star struck? This is, like, a temporary brain fart. You're not thinking clearly."

My housemate drew herself to her knees and crawled over to where I was sitting. She placed her hand on my thighs and squeezed. "That's where you're wrong. I'm thinking *very* clearly. I need something like this. Something I helped build. Something to keep me grounded. Think of all the new skills this will teach me."

"A lot of people can teach you a lot of things for a lot less than the cost of breaking your contract and moving to Los Angeles," I countered. "Think about that, Sloth. What if it doesn't work out? Then what?"

Sloth sighed and sank back down to the carpet. "I'm not sure. But I'll cross that bridge when I come to it."

"No, we're gonna cross that bridge right now," I said, folding my arms across my chest. Slowly, anger replaced fear and anxiety as my primary emotion, which I welcomed. Anger wouldn't leave me curled up in the fetal position in the corner of the room, crying into my knees. "Sloth, I know you think you made a connection today, but that woman's an actress. An actress I've never heard of, sure, but still. How do you know she has your best interest at heart? Maybe she picked you because you're vulnerable and hopeful and, and, *vulnerable*—"

"Pride, did it ever occur to you that I already thought of all this? Did it ever cross your mind that maybe I used my gifts to see for myself what Tabby's intentions were?"

I blinked, and time stopped. My heart leaped into my throat, and my mouth went dry. "You read Tabitha's mind?"

Sloth nodded. "Of *course* I did. I had to know that she was the real deal, didn't I? You didn't think I'd agree to run off to L.A. without doing my due diligence, did you? What do you take me for?"

I set my now-cooled tea on the nightstand and dropped my chin into my hands. "I don't—I mean…I don't know. I should have known better. You're not an idiot."

"That's right. But don't beat yourself up over it. It's easy to underestimate me. Everyone does." Sloth smiled again, but this time, the expression came more slowly, with more reservation. "I really appreciate your concern," she said. "But if I worry about what might happen in the future, I'd never do anything worthwhile. What is it Envy always says? No pain, no gain? No risk, no reward?"

"Envy is an idiot," I spat, not really meaning it, but also kind of meaning it.

"That's not fair, but even if it were, she's *right*. I've been playing it safe for such a long time. You have, too, so you should know what that's like. I'm ready to do something new with my life. And I believe in Tabitha's foundation and what she's trying to do for women of all stripes. And I have faith that if Los Angeles doesn't turn out, then the universe will provide me a way to get back to safety. But don't worry," she said. "I'm not leaving until our task is finished. I'm not a quitter."

"I know you're not," I said, getting up and heading for the door. "But believe me, right now, our task is the last thing I'm worried about. Listen, it's getting late. I'm gonna head back. We're not done discussing this, though, right? You'll give me a chance to change your mind?"

Sloth grinned and returned to sorting her possessions. "No promises. Good night, Pride."

I let the door click quietly shut behind me. I returned to my room and climbed into bed, but I didn't fall asleep for a long time.

five

. . .

The next day, my teammates and I sat in an ice cream shop across the street from where the Star of the Sea stood gleaming in the sunlight. Sloth and I shared one side of the table, and Gluttony took up the other. Craig set up the camera on the other end of the shop where he could capture our conversation in the same shot as the Star of the Sea in the distance. My housemates and I were enjoying giant banana splits and going over everything we had learned so far—which was precious little.

Gluttony pulled a map from his backpack and spread it on the table, pushing our desserts aside. "We know the statue has appeared at JB's Grocery, Sinful House, and the boutique," Gluttony said. He circled these three locations with a red magic marker. "Where else?"

"Tigh's Dry Cleaning on the corner of Dolphin Cove and Breaker," I said, leaning over the map. I found what I was looking for and tapped the paper. "Here."

Gluttony circled it. "Great. Where else?"

Sloth dug out her phone and peered down into the screen. "Lots of places, actually. The Hightide apartments, Parsimonious Art Supply, Sailor's Drink and Sink Pub, Surfside Grille, and Flix on the Rocks, which I guess is the local movie theater."

It took a little while to find each location on the map, but Gluttony studiously sought each and circled them. When he finished, he circled City Hall twice and sat back to examine his handiwork. "That's every place?"

Sloth nodded. "Every place we know of."

"And did the statue appear more than once at any location?"

"Yes," Sloth said. "The apartments and the restaurant. She appeared in both places several times over a few weeks."

"Okay, that's good," I said, still poring over the map. "Maybe we can start with finding the overlap between the apartments and the restaurant? Something they have in common?"

Gluttony looked up at me, one eyebrow cocked. "Are you serious? You want to find an overlap between a place people live and a place people eat? Come on, now. Rudimentary logic should tell you that overlap is gonna be huge. This town doesn't have *that* many eateries. My guess is everybody at that apartment has eaten at that restaurant."

"Not necessarily," Sloth said, her cheeks propped against her fists. "The Surfside Grille is one of the more expensive restaurants in Odyssey. I'd guess plenty of the people who live at Hightide haven't eaten there. And anyway, we're not looking for a casual link, but something more significant."

Gluttony wasn't convinced. "Significant how?"

Sloth sighed. "I don't know…like, maybe someone died in each place. Or both were struck by lightning. Or both are haunted."

I mulled that over. "That's not a bad thought," I said.

Gluttony reached for the remains of his banana split, plucked the cherry from the whipped cream, and popped it into his mouth. "Okie doke. I'll see what I can dig up on any connections between the restaurant and the apartment complex. Anything else? Y'all see a pattern here I'm missing?"

I stared down at the map. Odyssey wasn't very big, and the circles were mostly concentrated near downtown. But then, most commercial properties were downtown. With the exceptions of the apartment and Sinful House, the statue only appeared in commercial areas.

"Is it significant she doesn't like to appear at people's houses? No single-dwelling homes?" Sloth asked.

"No way to know at this point," Gluttony grunted. "Honestly, we're tilting at windmills here. We need to start at the source. It's time to call Paola Barbosa."

"I don't disagree," I said, "but Sloth already called her. The caregiver declined our interview."

Gluttony leaned back, stroking his chin thoughtfully. "If we can't speak to the artist, we're flying blind on this task. I could probably whip her up a batch of cookies or brownies or something. Y'all know I have ways of getting people to talk." He chuckled to himself, but then stopped, eyes flitting to me. "But actually, Pride…I bet *you* could get her to talk."

"Me?" I pressed a hand to my chest, eyes flying wide. "I don't have that kind of magic. I can only—"

"There's not an artist alive who isn't curious about what happened at that Sam Lovelace commune," he said, a twinkle forming in his eye that I didn't like at all. "So maybe she won't speak to some no-account reality show contestant, but she might talk to the sole survivor of one of the greatest mysteries of our time."

I looked away, letting my gaze wander to the statue still surrounded by throngs of people. It was true that people loved unexplained mysteries—even more when it had to do with their own industry or niche. So Gluttony was right about that—if she'd talk to anyone, it would likely be me. The trouble was, I didn't want to talk about the commune. I had nothing to say about it. And I didn't want to use my personal history as a bargaining chip.

But I didn't see any other option. We had nothing else to go on, and I wanted to keep Sloth interested in our case. The more she thought about traveling statues, the less she'd think about traveling to L.A. At least, that was what I'd pinned my hopes on.

"All right," I said with a sigh. "You want to do this right now?"

Gluttony shrugged. "No time like the present."

The ice cream shop was mostly empty, so I didn't need to worry about disturbing the other diners. I got the phone number from Sloth, put my phone on speaker, and dialed.

On the third ring, a woman answered. "What is it?"

I gulped. "Uh, hello. I'm looking for Ms. Paola Barbosa?"

"Who is this?"

I glanced at Sloth, who gave me an encouraging thumbs-up. "This is Pride from the show *Sinful House*. I was wondering—"

"Ms. Barbosa isn't taking any interviews," the woman on the other end spat. "And I thought I already made that clear to your co-star."

I half-expected her to hang up, but the line didn't go dead. At my side, Sloth grabbed my knee and squeezed. "Tell her who you *really* are, Pride."

I cleared my throat. "Would it make any difference if I told you my real name is Sid Sheridan?"

Silence. After a long stretch, the ragged voice said, "*The* Sid Sheridan? The baby from the Sam Lovelace commune?"

I nodded. "That's right. Except, I'm an adult now. I was a baby then, but you know. I got older."

A pause. Then, "Just one moment."

A minute later, a new voice came on the line. It was even more ragged, with a hint of an accent. "Video chat me," the voice said.

I blinked. "Excuse me?"

"Anyone can claim to be Sid Sheridan, yes? If you are who you say, video chat with me. Show me who you are."

The line went dead.

Pressing my lips together, I dialed again, this time with video chat turned on.

She answered on the second ring. The woman staring back at me was older, maybe in her 60s. She was fair-skinned, with thinning silver hair at the temples that gave way to a dull onyx. I wondered vaguely how long ago she'd stopped dyeing it. Her eyes were small and black but bright as a raven's. Her mouth was a slash of pink, her chin pointed. It was the face of someone unused to smiling, someone for whom life was serious business.

I liked her immediately.

"Sidney Sheridan," the woman said, the barest of smiles gracing my screen. "It really is you."

"Yes, ma'am," I answered, a tremor in my voice. "Am I speaking with Ms. Paola Barbosa?"

"It is I," she answered. "Do you not recognize me?"

"I don't know what you look like," I admitted.

The woman scoffed, shaking her head in what appeared to be grave disappointment. "You young people. And here I thought you were a great investigator. Yet you haven't researched me at all? Have you not read my autobiography?"

I stammered, my cheeks coloring red. Now that she'd said it aloud, I realized I hadn't done everything I could to learn about the artist behind the wandering statue. It was a rookie mistake—but I'd been so preoccupied worrying over Sloth that I had shirked my basic responsibilities. I didn't want to admit that, though, so I said, "I was getting around to it."

"That's a lie," Paola said, "because I haven't written one. A poor investigator *and* a liar to boot. I'm unsure why I should bother giving you my time." Before I could answer, however, Paola pressed on. "I've seen the show, you know. *Sinful House.* You have the talent to be great. Truly great—and I know potential when I see it. I am, after all, a sculptor."

I recalled Brittany Miller saying the same thing—that sculptors were special because they could look at a block of clay and see the potential that lay beneath. Still, I didn't know how to respond to this. Was it a compliment or admonishment? It felt like both.

"Am I to understand my art is the subject of a current investigation?"

"Yes," I breathed, glad to be on a subject that had nothing to do with my so-called potential. "Your statue, the Star of the Sea, has been traveling around Odyssey. My teammates and I intend to learn why. We thought talking to you might shed some light on the statue's secret."

"So you want to pick at my bones, is that it?" She laughed, a dry, crackling sound, like a campfire in the thick of night. "I'll make you a bargain. You tell me something no one else knows about the Sam Lovelace commune, and I'll answer any question you throw to me."

I balked, my lips working, but no sound coming out. I looked to Gluttony and Sloth for help, but they both looked as clueless as I felt. "But…I don't know anything about the commune," I said. "Everything I know is what everyone else knows."

"Well, that's a pity," Paola said with a sniff. "Because I may or may not know some things that could help you with your investigation. But I suppose it doesn't matter. Perhaps you don't care to win as badly as you pretend."

"I *want* to win," I snapped back.

"And there it is!" She squealed in delight, turning to someone off-camera and smiling as she pointed into the screen. "There it is, Claudia, just as I thought. The *fire*. Any child that came from that commune *had* to have the fire." Returning her attention to me, she said, "You know more than you let on. I know you do. Bring me something unique and secret, *Pride.*" She said my name in a tone that sounded at once like mocking and reverence. "And I'll tell you my story in exchange."

And then she hung up.

"Well, that was worthless." I tucked my phone away with a sigh. "She really doesn't like to talk, does she?"

Sloth narrowed her eyes, her head leaning to the side as a yawn escaped her lips. "Is that what you heard? Because it's not what I heard at all."

Gluttony leaned forward onto his elbows. "So what did you hear, Sloth?"

"That's a woman who doesn't do milquetoast," she said. "She doesn't want to waste her time with boring or ordinary. She liked your *fire*, Pride. You have to find a way to show her more of that. More of *you.*"

"But there isn't any more," I said, frowning. "What you see is what you get."

Sloth pressed a napkin to her lips, completely missing the smear of chocolate fudge on both sides of her mouth. "I hope you don't take this the wrong way, but you might be the least self-aware person I've ever met. You really know nothing about who you truly are."

I had nothing to say to that, so I made myself busy collecting our plates and carrying our trash to the bin. I had no idea what the right way to take Sloth's comment was, or if there even *was* a right way. But I did know my ego was bruised, and worst of all—a small, shameful part of me suspected she might be right.

———

Back at Sinful House, I found Lust and Greed canoodling in the living room. Lust was stretched out on the couch, eyes closed, her head in Greed's lap. He was reading aloud from a book of poetry. When he saw me, he looked up, a sly smile flitting over his lips. "Well, hello there, Pride. How's your task coming?"

I sighed. It was no secret that my team and I had made little progress on our task, and I thought it was crude of Greed to call us out like that. I wasn't going to let him get the best of me, though, so I said, "Made some good progress today. Thanks for asking."

I knew the polite thing to do would be to ask Greed how his task was going, but I didn't for several reasons, the primary being that I didn't care. Plus, I wanted to get out of there. If there was anything I hated more than seeing Lust curled up on the couch with her head in Greed's lap, I couldn't tell you what it was.

As I was turning to head upstairs, however, Lust sat up and called to me. "Hey, Pride. Wait. Can I talk to you for a minute?"

I clenched my jaw and gestured up the stairs. "You

already are talking to me. But I can't stop right now. I'm busy."

Lust got to her feet, batting her lashes and twirling a lock of dark hair around a slender finger. "Busy doing what? Maybe I can help."

I tried not to glare at her, but I wasn't sure I succeeded. Every normal person knew "I'm busy" was code for "Leave me alone." Even I knew that. I had expected the lie to work, so I hadn't bothered thinking up an excuse. Caught off guard and really wanting to make an escape, I said the first thing that popped into my head. "I'm working on my taxes," I said, cringing inwardly at the absurdity. It was summer. Nobody did taxes in the summer. "But I'll be back down for dinner. I'll see you then."

I took the stairs two at a time. I could almost feel Greed laughing at me behind my back. Doing my taxes? That was the best I could come up with? I banged the heel of my hand against my forehead as I silently berated myself. *Stupid, stupid, stupid.* But it was no use beating myself up. I wasn't the first person to turn into a blathering idiot in the presence of a beautiful woman. But it was one thing to be reduced to a pile of goo in front of Lust. It was another thing to do it in front of Greed.

I stepped into my bedroom and closed the door, leaning against it as I squeezed my eyes shut, trying to blot the embarrassing scene from my memory. *At least I can binge-watch Netflix and drown my sorrows,* I told myself.

But when I opened my eyes, I saw I wasn't alone.

Wrath was slouching at my desk, one leg thrown

casually across the other, his hands dug in his pockets of his parachute pants. His lemon-blonde hair stuck out all over his head. He looked like he'd just woken up from a nap. But then, Wrath always looked like that.

"*There* you are," he grumbled. "I've been waiting for you for like half an hour."

"What are you doing in my bedroom?" I asked. "Did I give you permission to be in here?"

But Wrath sucked his teeth and waved his hand dismissively. "Come off it, man. You don't have anything worth stealing or whatever. I bet you don't even have any dirty magazines. There's no reason to keep me out. And anyway, private property is a tool of oppression. You should know that." He sighed and crossed his arms, thumbs hooked under his armpits. "Plus, I need your help."

With a sigh, I sat on the edge of my bed, untying my shoelaces and prodding my sneakers off with my toes. "What do you need? Is this about your task?"

Wrath shook his head. "No. I need a healer."

I put my shoes away and selected a pair of hedgehog slippers from the closet, sliding my feet inside. They were warm and fuzzy. "I can't help you with that," I said. "I don't know the first thing about healing. In fact, I don't think anybody at the house has that skill."

"Not healing in real life," Wrath said. "For my MMO. We have a raid tonight, but our healer called out sick. I've been waiting for this raid for like two weeks. You gotta help me, man. I'm gonna be in such a bad mood if I don't get this loot tonight. I've been trying for a god roll on this gun for *weeks*. It's the meta."

I chuckled good-naturedly at Wrath's joke. "Hilarious. You almost had me going there for a sec. Okay, but no, really. Why are you…"

Wrath was looking at me with a blank expression. I didn't know what he was thinking, but even I could tell he wasn't messing around. "Wrath? Are you kidding me? You know I don't play video games. I wouldn't even know where to begin."

Wrath leaned forward onto his elbows, smiling maniacally. "Check it out. You'll be perfect! Healing is dead easy. It's designed that way, so even girls can do it. Guys don't wanna heal—they get their girlfriends to do that. Guys wanna do DPS."

I frowned. "DPS?"

"Damage per second. I'm talking about dealing damage," he said. "Anyway, don't worry about the mechanics. I'll show you what to do. I made macros and everything."

"I just don't see the point," I said. "Of video games, I mean. You spend hours on those things, and for what?"

"Because it feels good, man." He said this like it was the most obvious thing in the world. "In real life, can you leap 100 yards at a time? Can you blast lasers at bad guys while invisible? Can you freeze your enemies in place and then one-shot them with a hand cannon? These games make you feel powerful. And when you're a scrawny little guy like me who can't even do a round-house kick in real life, well, video games just make sense. Who doesn't want to feel like a god?"

"You're supposed to love the skin you're in," I

pointed out. "Isn't that the kind of stuff you always say? Self-hatred is the tool of the patriarchy or whatever?"

Wrath gaped at me, the gears of his mind whirring before he said, "What are you even talking about? That's got nothing to do with this. So, anyway, will you come heal? Seriously, you can't screw this up, and it would be a huge favor to me. I'd owe you." He paused for a breath, and his face fell. "Please?"

The last thing I wanted to do was help Wrath play video games, and I was about to say so when my phone rang.

I clicked 'Accept' on the call. "Tricia? Why are you calling me?"

"Well, hello to you too, Pride. So we're just dispensing with life's little pleasantries, hmm?"

I glanced over at Wrath, who was still watching me. "I'm in the middle of something. So, why are you calling me?"

Tricia sighed on the other end. "All right. Straight to business. I realize this is highly unusual, but I need to talk to you about your case. Am I right in understanding that the three of you have made almost no progress discovering the Star of the Sea's secret?"

"Who told you that?"

"Craig."

I blinked. "Craig? My cameraman Craig? He ratted us out?"

Tricia sucked her teeth and snorted into the phone. "He didn't rat you out, Pride. It's literally his job to report what's going on at the house. Did you really think we relied on footage alone to keep our finger on the pulse of our cast?"

To be honest, I hadn't thought about it one way or another. I mostly tried not to think about the reality behind this "reality" TV show. "We haven't made much progress, no," I admitted. There was no sense in lying. Even if Craig hadn't turncoated on us, she was bound to find out eventually. "We tried talking to the artist, Paola Barbosa. But she'll only talk if I tell her something about that vanished commune no one else knows. And you know as well as anyone that I have nothing to offer."

"For once, your interests and ours align," Tricia said with laughter in her voice. "Why you've been so hesitant to go to Santa Barbara, I'll never know. But it's fine—I took matters into my own hands. I've called Arjun Singh and made an appointment for you to visit the painting."

"Arjun Singh? The painting?" I repeated.

"Arjun is the current owner of *Sum of all Prophets*," she said. "You know—the painting that psychic medium told you to find. The painting that might hold the key to your past. And—coincidentally—the missing commune."

I hesitated, clenching my fists at my side. "You made an appointment for me? Tricia, who do you think you are? You don't get to dictate the terms of my life. You're a producer on a TV show. Stay in your lane!"

"What's done is done. I can't make you keep the appointment, of course. But I recommend you do. Look, I'll be frank with you. The show needs this story-line to keep viewers coming back. The heyday of the episodic TV show is long over. Viewers expect a season-long arc. Or even a series-long arc! And you are the perfect person to deliver it." She paused, presumably waiting for a response. When I said nothing, she said, "I'll text you the details of the appointment."

Then she hung up.

I stared at my phone for a solid twenty seconds, feeling angry and sorry for myself and just generally annoyed. First, I had Sloth threatening to leave the show, and now I had Tricia bossing me around, forcing me to do things I didn't want. I felt helpless.

But I didn't have to feel that way. I could, to use Wrath's phrase, 'feel like a god.' Suddenly, playing video games with a technopath didn't sound like the worst thing in the universe.

"All right," I said. "I'll do it. Take me to your lair."

Wrath wrinkled his nose. "Don't call it that. Ever. Seriously, never say that again. Now c'mon. Let's go kill some cyborgs."

six

. . .

As it turned out, playing video games with Wrath was a blast. We stayed up until the wee hours of the morning eating cold pizza, drinking Mountain Dew, and killing bad guys. And he was right—it was exciting and did make me feel powerful. It was a much better adrenaline rush than having someone pull a gun on you, I can tell you that.

The downside, however, was that when I woke up the following day, I was exhausted. Even after I'd gone to bed, I hadn't slept well. My brain went into overdrive, replaying key moments of the game—mostly my screwups, like the time I accidentally healed an enemy player and the time I'd let myself run out of magic power and couldn't heal anyone. As a result, the whole raid got wiped out during the final battle. Everyone shouted at me about that—everyone but Wrath, who explained that everybody makes mistakes, especially newbies. He didn't even raise his voice.

If you're shocked, imagine how I felt.

I pulled on a hoodie and stuffed my feet into my slippers before shuffling down the hall to find Gluttony or Sloth. Neither were in their rooms—even Sloth had beaten me awake. I glanced at Sloth's alarm clock to find it wasn't technically morning anymore. I yawned and closed her door. Then I went to find something to eat that wasn't cold pizza or electric green sugar water.

I lurched downstairs to find Gluttony had made a mountain of blueberry cinnamon pancakes and cheesy scrambled eggs. He'd even covered everything with aluminum foil, so the food was still moderately warm. I made myself a heaping plate, warmed up some coffee, and was sitting down to eat when Lust joined me at the table.

She looked great. I mean, really great. An oversized t-shirt slipped down over one shoulder, revealing smooth brown skin and a lacy bra strap. She wasn't wearing any makeup, and a pair of My Little Pony pajama bottoms completed her outfit. Still, she looked like a million bucks. Or maybe like something you could eat with a spoon.

I blushed for even thinking that and turned away.

I pretended to be very interested in the texture of my eggs. Lust tried to wait me out, sitting quietly across from me and sipping a can of sparkling water. But after a while, she cleared her throat and said, "Pride, I was hoping we could talk."

I leaned back in my seat and waved my fork vaguely toward my breakfast plate. "I don't really like to eat and talk," I lied. "Can this wait?"

Lust leaned forward and folded her hands atop the

table. "All this tension between us isn't necessary. Everybody in the house feels it. Even Tricia said she thinks it's affecting our ratings."

I slumped in my chair, the delicious eggs turning to glue in my mouth. "I don't care what Tricia thinks," I said. "My personal life has nothing to do with her. She doesn't get to dictate what I do or don't do."

"Of course she doesn't," Lust agreed. "I'm just saying…this is about more than you and me."

I swallowed the eggs. "Lust, I just woke up. And I didn't sleep great last night."

But Lust acted like she didn't get the hint. "I know you're thinking about me and Greed," she said. "And I know you think you walked in on some intimate moment between us the other day. I don't even *like* poetry, okay? He was just trying to—"

Suddenly, I found myself without an appetite. I stood so abruptly, I knocked over my chair. "Yeah, I can't do this right now," I muttered, righting my chair and pushing it under the table. I grabbed my half-eaten plate and was almost to the kitchen when I said over my shoulder, "Another time, maybe. After I've had a nap or something."

She didn't follow me or try to force a conversation, which I appreciated. Still, I felt like a complete jerk for leaving her there like that. My therapist, Dr. Xena, always said it's important to let people you care about say what's on their heart because frankness is healing. And I did care about Lust—that was the problem. So the right thing to do was to face my problems like an adult, even if that meant I ended up a puddle of snot and tears.

But I didn't feel like being an adult. I only felt like guarding my heart. After all, it had already been broken once. Who knew if it could survive a second time?

Upstairs, I took a shower and then had no idea how to spend the rest of my day. I messaged Gluttony and Sloth to see what they were up to, but neither texted me back. My brain was too foggy to think about my case, and I was too tired for a jog on the beach. But I needed something to keep my mind busy and my thoughts off Lust. With no other ideas, I made a phone call.

A man answered on the first ring. "Hello?"

"Hey, Aaron. It's me. Pride. Uh, the ghost whisperer from the TV show."

Aaron chuckled. "Yeah, I know who you are."

"Great," I said. "Are you busy?"

"Not at all!" I heard muffled speaking on the other end and imagined Aaron covering up the receiver, talking to someone else. "What's up?"

"I was thinking about your request. I guess I could come to your apartment and check it out. I've got today free, but I have to take a trip out of town in the morning." I frowned, annoyed at Tricia for the millionth time for making an appointment on my behalf. "So, if now is good for you, I could be there in, say, 15 minutes?"

Again, I heard that muffled talking. Then, more clearly, Aaron said, "It would be better if you came later this evening. Say around 8 o'clock? I know it might sound crazy, but that's when I sense the presence most strongly."

That was interesting information. Most of the time, if a place was really haunted, it was haunted 24/7. Ghosts didn't typically keep to a schedule. "8 o'clock is fine. Sure. I'll—"

"Hey, hang on one second." I heard another male voice in the background saying something I couldn't decipher. Then Aaron said to him, "Seriously? Are you sure that's a good idea?" The voice answered, but again, I couldn't hear the reply.

Into the phone, Aaron said, "So, I have a weird request. My brother wants to know if you can bring your teammates and your camera guy tonight. Would that be okay?"

I balked, taken aback at the request. "Of course I *can*. But what for?"

"Well, if the apartment *is* haunted, that fits in with the theme of your show, right?"

"The show is about solving mysteries," I said, knowing that was only partially true.

"Yeah, well…my brother thinks maybe the network could use the footage as B-roll. Or maybe in a montage of what the Sins do when you're not out solving myster-ies. Uh…" Aaron paused, and I realized he was taking cues from the other person in the room. I guessed it was his brother. "…It could be good for votes—you know, showing yourself doing something altruistic. You never know. Anyway, maybe something interesting for the show will come of it."

It wasn't the worst idea I'd ever heard—I could use the votes. But there was a niggling feeling at the back of my mind, like maybe these guys didn't have a ghost problem at all and were setting us up. Maybe they were going to lure us someplace private, knock us out, hold us hostage, and demand ransom money from the network.

But of course, if that happened, Craig would probably rescue me like he'd done in the past. So, where was the harm?

On the other hand, maybe they didn't want to kidnap us for ransom at all. Maybe they wanted to discredit us as psychics and make us look like idiots on national television. What if they forced Sloth to play "Guess what I'm thinking" until she was exhausted and incapable, and they used her ensuing meltdown to prove we were all charlatans? It could happen—she was too nice to refuse, and then we'd be trapped with a couple degenerates until either Craig or Gluttony got fed up and used their girth to intimidate the brothers into letting us go.

But there I was, over-dramatizing things again. Probably they just wanted a cool celebrity story to impress half-drunk girls down at Sailors Drink and Sink.

Or, you know, maybe they had ghosts.

"I'll see if they're available," I said finally. "That's the best I can do."

"Yeah, that's cool. Of course. I really appreciate it. I'll see you tonight at eight."

———

I didn't need to convince my housemates to come with me to Aaron's. Neither had any ideas about how to proceed with our challenge, and they were grateful for the distraction. Even Craig agreed we needed a break from our dud of a case. "Filming you guys doing nothing is a colossal waste of my talent," was how he put it.

We rang the doorbell a little after 8 p.m., and Aaron answered immediately. He looked disheveled and disoriented. Half-moons like bruises adorned the soft hollows beneath his eyes. His skin was pallid, and it looked like he hadn't eaten a healthy meal in a while. Still, when he saw us, he smiled, the corners of his eyes crinkling as he extended his hand and greeted each of us.

When my hand closed around his, I felt a jolt of emotions—confusion, fear, apprehension. I saw Aaron standing in a bathroom with a collection of various pills in his palm. He deliberated, glancing up at his own reflection to find a face that was stricken and careworn, bloodshot eyes that needed sleep. Then I saw him flush the pills down the toilet.

I blinked and wiped my palm on my pants.

"I'm so glad you could make it," Aaron said, bringing me back to the present. "Please, come in."

I wasn't sure what I expected, but this apartment wasn't it. Aaron was a mess, but his apartment definitely wasn't. The place was as immaculate as it was tasteful. It was also entirely composed of white and beige, almost like he was scared of color. His sofa was beige leather and chrome, sleek, and looked brand new. He had a large, wall-mounted plasma TV, several comfy leather chairs (beige), a pristine area rug (white), a few lamps (beige and white) and hardwood floors (not white, but I guess they only came in standard brown.)

The place was so perfect, it didn't quite look lived in. The only giveaway that this was an actual abode and not a staged apartment was the easel set up in the corner of the room. It held a large canvas, maybe 24 inches across by 48 inches tall. I knew little about art, but the painting seemed professional—like it was painted by someone who knew what they were doing. It depicted a small gathering of people in a dark location—perhaps a cocktail party or a lounge. The whole thing was diffuse and dreamlike, colored primarily in hues of ochre, gold, and soft purples. When I gazed at it, I felt like I wanted to fall into it. It drew me in, is what I'm saying.

But maybe that's because it was the only thing in the room that didn't look like it had been soaked in Pottery Barn until all its personality drained away.

Beside the easel stood a side table containing a palette of oil paints lay beside a jar of brushes. The faint scent of turpentine hung in the air.

"Can I get anyone anything to drink? Beer, wine? Maybe a glass of water?"

I moved away from the painting and went to sit with Sloth and Gluttony on the beautiful but moderately uncomfortable couch. Aaron hovered over us, waiting to take our orders. However, we each declined, and eventually, he sat down across from us in a chair shaped like a hand (white).

"So this is my place," he said. "I hope you didn't have any trouble finding me."

"Odyssey is only so big," Gluttony said matter-of-factly. "Plus, we have a GPS. It was no big deal."

"Of course. Sorry. This is, um…well, let's just say I

rarely have guests. I used to, before my girlfriend and I split up. But she got all our friends in the divorce, so." He chuckled, but there was no mirth in it. It was more like a vocal fidget to offset his nerves.

I knew how he felt. None of our mutual friends had reached out to me after Shayda and I broke up, either. Which is how I found out they weren't actually so mutual.

"So, you think your place is haunted?" Sloth asked.

Aaron opened his mouth to reply but was interrupted by a second man breezing in, bringing with him the smell of aftershave and breath mints. He walked right into the center of the room, hands on his hips as he surveyed our little troupe. "Aaron? Why didn't you tell me your friends were here? And nobody has drinks or anything? Come on. Surely, we raised you better than this!" He swept over to the couch, taking Sloth's hand and kissing it on the back. "You must be Sloth," he said, his smile growing impossibly wider. "It's my absolute pleasure to meet you. I'm Aaron's brother, Cary."

Sloth blushed and stammered, quickly drawing her hand away and pressing it against her chest. "Nice to meet you."

"I offered drinks, but no one wanted anything," Aaron explained. He looked chagrined, his cheeks coloring, the tips of his ears growing red. "We were actually about to get down to business."

"Business," Cary repeated, a slight frown peeking over his lips. "We can't get down to business without wine. If there's one thing I've learned from working multiple side hustles at once, it's that it's always a good time for wine." He clapped his hands together and then disappeared the way he'd come. A moment later, he returned with a tray of glasses and a bottle of merlot.

"It's great that you took my advice and brought the whole crew," he said to no one in particular. He uncorked the wine bottle and started pouring. "Though you're probably wondering why we wanted you here."

Cary offered me a glass of wine, but I shook my head. He placed it on the table before me, anyway. "I didn't ask you here as Aaron's brother but as his agent. My dear brother is a very talented thespian who just hasn't found the right role yet."

"You're an actor?" Sloth asked.

"Well, one of us has to be," Cary answered. "I mean, by the odds. Every family in Odyssey has to have at least one actor. And unfortunately, I don't have the looks for it."

I couldn't argue with that. Cary had the kind of face that looked put together wrong. He certainly wasn't leading man material. Not that you have to be a beauty queen for a career in Hollywood. I mean, that guy from *Fargo* isn't exactly a lady killer, and he does all right.

Ignoring Cary, Sloth asked Aaron, "Theater or screen?"

Aaron blushed as he plucked a wineglass from the table and took a healthy sip. "Neither at the moment. I've been an extra on a few shows here and there, but nothing has really panned out. I tried ORCA for a little while, but...I don't know, it skews toward more hoity-toity productions than I'm interested in." He sighed, finished his merlot, and beckoned for Cary to pour him another. "I'd love to break into the movies, but at this point, I'd take any work I could get. Even work on a reality TV show."

"And that's why you're here." Cary pointed at us, still smiling. "Aaron has an actor's heart, but not an actor's head. He can't network. Anyway, I promised I'd do what I could to help him get an in. And now that we're all friends here, I'm sure you'll pass his information on to your producers, won't you? Oh, that reminds me." Cary snapped his fingers and disappeared once more. This time, he returned carrying white manila envelopes that he handed to each of us. "Aaron's headshot and resume," he explained. "I assume you know what to do with those."

Unless the correct answer was "Dump them in the bin on the way to the parking lot," I had no idea what I was supposed to do with Aaron's paperwork, so I placed the envelope on the table and said, "So…about the ghosts. Was that all just a ruse to get us here?"

"No." Aaron held up a hand to silence his brother. "It was probably bad form to listen to Cary on this. He means well, and it's true I need all the help I can get. I can't exactly afford this place on a server's salary."

Sloth looked around and whistled. "You must be a seriously good server. This place looks high end to me."

Aaron blushed and ran a hand through his already-bushy hair. "Oh. Yeah, well. This is all my mother's doing. But no, I definitely asked you here on the up and up. I really do need your help."

Gluttony folded his arms across his chest and asked, "So, what have you been experiencing?"

Aaron inhaled long and slow before turning to me, his eyes pleading. "I know you're the expert in this stuff. But…would you mind terribly taking a walk around the house before I answer questions? I don't want to bias you one way or another. Can you look around and just…I don't know, see what you see?"

If Aaron was having us on, he was doing a good job. I saw how his hands trembled and his eyes flit nervously around the room. He appeared both shy and reluctant. I'd investigated enough cases to know that people who aren't used to dealing with ghosts often behaved the same way Aaron was acting now. It didn't mean anything, but I trusted my gut.

Aaron thought his house was haunted. If so, there was only one way to find out.

"Of course," I said, climbing to my feet. "I'll look around."

"Take your time," Cary said in a lilting, singsong voice. "Wouldn't want you to miss anything hiding in a closet or whatever."

I heard the telltale note of disbelief in Cary's voice as I ducked out of the room. That had to be hard—to have a brother who thought you were making things up or had a few screws loose. And to be fair, either could be true. Still, I thought the point of family was to have your back. Otherwise, I wasn't sure they were worth the trouble of fraught Thanksgiving gatherings and daily group texts comparing the scores from online crossword puzzles.

I wandered down the hallway to the back of the apartment, where an open door on the right led to the master bedroom. Like the rest of the house, it was pristine. His queen-size bed was made, his floors vacuumed, and his dressers aesthetically styled. A paper bag from an art supply store sat next to the dresser, still filled with paints, brushes, and a tin of turpentine.

The walls were sparsely decorated, but I did note one thing of interest. Hanging in a black frame over his side table was a newspaper article about the Star of the Sea. It was dated a few months earlier and sported a large photograph of the original monument. I stepped closer to read it. Here's what the article said:

Police call for information after Odyssey's 20-ft tall bronze statue, The Star of the Sea, vanishes into thin air

A 20-ft tall, 1,100-pound bronze mermaid monument has disappeared from City Hall in Odyssey, California, causing borderline hysteria from art aficionados, true crime fans, and history buffs alike.

"It's not every day a statue just vanishes into thin air," says Veronica Bloom, spokesperson for the Odyssey Beautification Commission. "Especially not one of this size. But then again, unusual occurrences are no strangers to Odyssey. I just hope this works itself out and the statue is returned to her rightful spot. City Hall looks naked without it."

The statue disappeared between 8 p.m. March 13th and 6 a.m. March 14th. "She was there when I left work that evening," says Pamela Arquette, City Manager. "But she was gone when I returned the following morning."

The Star of the Sea, valued at over $100,000, was sculpted by Portuguese-born artist Paola Barbosa. The mermaid statue is an effigy of the fabled medicine woman Magdalena and carries a mirror in one hand and a lantern in the other. "The mirror reflects on the past while the lantern lights the way for the future," says Arquette. "She's an important bridge between what Odyssey used to be and what we still are to become."

Detective Kelly Doyle with the Odyssey police department says the statue's removal remains an unprecedented mystery. "Erecting a statue that size takes significant manpower and coordination. Its removal would require a similarly concerted effort. Yet we have no indication of any trucks or cranes moving through this area. We're all scratching our heads on this one."

Cate Burton, philanthropist and civil rights attorney, told *The Odyssey Trident* that at first, she was "heartbroken" about the mermaid's disappearance. But after careful consideration, sorrow has given way to anger. "The Star of the Sea is a vital piece of Odyssey's cultural heritage. Not only is she a stand-in for a beloved woman of color who gave Odyssey its vibrance and eccentricities, she's also a touchstone for a community that has already lost so much to the greed and moral turpitude running rampant through our fair city." When asked if she was satisfied with how the city was handling the search for the sculpture, she responded, "It's outrageous that we aren't doing more. It's disrespectful to the artist, to the

Native people who once roamed this land, and to every citizen of Odyssey who found comfort in the statue's warm, maternal presence."

Meanwhile, the police are hoping a witness will emerge and provide much-needed insight into this case. "Somebody had to see something," says Detective Doyle. "The Star of the Sea didn't just vanish into the night. We're hopeful that someone will find the courage to come forward and do the right thing."

I made a mental note to ask Aaron about the article. If he had a special interest in the statue's disappearance, maybe he could shed some light on my case. Because as it stood, I was really no better off than the day I'd been assigned the task in the first place.

I opened the door to his walk-in closet. The clothes were arranged by color, and his shoes were placed neatly along the wall. Several shirts hung in dry cleaner bags. On the shelf, I found a collection of belts, a hat, a pair of rainboots...

...And a sawed-off shotgun.

Working in the San Diego police department, I'd seen my fair share of weapons. Knives, mostly, but a few handguns, a rifle or two—even a pair of throwing stars once. But I'd never seen a sawed-off shotgun and with good reason—they were illegal in California. I pushed the gun back into place with a shudder. All weapons freaked me out, but guns were especially nerve-wracking.

In any case, there were no ghosts in the closet, so I continued on to the master bathroom. He had a good-sized shower and a jetted bathtub. The toilet paper roll hung with the paper on the top instead of on the underside, which meant Aaron probably wasn't a serial killer. No mold in the shower, either, which definitely meant black magic was afoot. I peeked inside the medicine cabinet. He had prescriptions for Xanax, Klonopin, Seroquel, Abilify, and Lexapro. I sighed and closed the compartment. I knew some of those drugs—Dr. Xena had prescribed me similar medication. It looked like Aaron was struggling with anxiety, mood disorders, and maybe even hallucinations or delusions. Well, that tracked. When I first told my doctor I was seeing ghosts, she put me on anti-psychotics, too. When I realized I wasn't imagining things, but no one believed me, she put me on anti-depressants.

Technically, I'm still supposed to take them, but I don't. Not because I'm cured but because I don't think the drugs were helping. Considering Aaron's pill bottles were all expired, I supposed he felt the same way.

From there, I wandered into the spare bedroom, which contained only a single bed and bedside table. No other amenities adorned the space. I checked the closet, which was empty. For grins, I even looked under the bed. Nothing hiding under there, either.

Further on, I peeked into the hall bathroom. "Any ghosts in here?" I whispered.

Only silence answered me.

I headed back into the living room, giving it a quick once over before moving into the kitchen. A half-eaten sandwich still wrapped in deli wax paper sat on the counter, along with a glass of water. There were no dishes in the sink, and no ghosts anywhere to be found. I walked back into the living room and settled into the couch. Aaron's expression was hopeful. "Well? What did you find?"

I jammed my thumb over my shoulder. "You've got an illegal firearm in your closet," I said. "I don't really care one way or another—I mean, it's your business—but if you get caught with that, it's several years in prison plus a huge fine."

Both brothers blinked at me. Then Cary said, "What are you talking about?"

Aaron, too, looked befuddled. "An illegal firearm? I don't—oh!" A wave of relief passed over his face and he laughed, shaking his head. "It's not real. It's a prop from a pilot I shot a few years ago. I kept it as a souvenir."

"You never told me about that," Cary said, still blinking.

Aaron shrugged. "Do you want me to tell you about all the dumb stuff I bring home? I ordered a package of underwear today from Amazon. And last week—"

"Hilarious," Cary interrupted with a roll of his eyes. Turning to me, he said, "Brothers, am I right?"

"I have no idea," I said. "I'm an only child. Also, all your meds are way overdue for a refill. If you call your doctor, you can probably get them to call in a prescription without going in for another appointment."

Aaron stared at me blankly, his cheeks coloring red. "I…yeah, I know. It's just—I'm not sure I should be taking them anymore. But I appreciate the advice."

Cary turned to his brother. "Did you stop taking your meds? Mom's gonna freak out."

Aaron clenched his jaw. "A few months back. I'm just trying to get a baseline for who I am without the medication. I'm *feeling* things for the first time. Anyway, can we talk about this later? Not in front of strangers?"

Cary was silent a minute, and then faced us again, clearing his throat loudly. "What else did you find? Relevant ghost-related things, I mean."

I blew out my cheeks and shook my head. "This house is clean. There are no ghosts here—not a single one."

Aaron looked down into his lap, shaking his head. "It just doesn't make sense," he said under his breath. He sank back into this chair and must have kicked the table because a tumbler of water fell over, spilling onto the carpet.

"I'll get a towel," Sloth said, climbing slowly to her feet and meandering into the kitchen.

While Sloth shuffled into the next room, I turned to Aaron. "Now is a good time to tell me what you've been experiencing," I said. "What makes you think this place is haunted?"

"A few things," Aaron began. "At first, it was just…I felt a presence. Like someone was watching me. I usually notice it around this time of night. Nothing concrete. Just a feeling. The hairs stand up on the back of my neck. My skin crawls."

I nodded. That sounded like standard paranoia and explained the bottle of Seroquel in his bathroom. Sloth returned with a towel in hand and placed it on the spilled water. "Is that all?"

Aarons shivered. "At first, yes. But then it progressed.

I'd wake up to find my things moved around. The TV remote, books, even my lounge pants wouldn't be where I left them. As you may have noticed, I'm a meticulous person. You might even call me a neat freak. I don't leave things where they don't belong. But more and more, I'd awaken to find my apartment a mess. Almost like a second person was living here. A second messy person," he amended with a wrinkling of his nose. "A few times, I even woke up to find a script I'd been rehearsing torn to shreds."

"Is it possible you were sleepwalking?" Gluttony asked.

"Anything is possible," Aaron admitted. "But I find that far-fetched. Why would it start now? Doesn't that kind of thing begin in childhood?"

"For what it's worth, I thought the same thing," Cary said. "I told him to get a camera and set it up at night, just to see what was happening."

Sloth shrugged. "Seems reasonable. Did you do it?"

"Not yet. Those cameras are expensive, and financially, I'm stretched so thin, you can see through me."

Cary grunted. "That's no excuse. You know Mom and Dad would—"

"I don't need Mom and Dad's help," Aaron interrupted. "I'm a grown man—it's past time to cut the apron strings. Besides." He turned to me and offered an abashed smile. "I really hoped you'd say there was a ghost. It would make things simpler."

"It actually wouldn't," I said. "Ghosts can rarely touch objects. It's even rarer that they can move things around. If you had a supernatural presence here doing that, it wouldn't be a ghost. Maybe a poltergeist. Maybe a wight. And I'm not sure you'd want to deal with something like that."

Aaron winced. "No, I suppose I wouldn't." He ran his hands through his hair, fluffing it out like a halo. "Maybe my doctors are right and it's all just in my head. Maybe it's paranoia or overwork. I've been working double shifts at the Grille for who knows how long. I'm so tired."

Sloth gestured toward the painting in the corner of the room. "Well, it looks like you have a good creative outlet, at least. That's important for managing stress. Though I can imagine that painting took an awful lot of work."

Aaron and Cary exchanged a glance, their expressions hardening. When Aaron looked back at us, the color had all but drained from his face. "The painting is the reason even Cary is convinced I'm not sleepwalking."

Gluttony leaned forward, resting his chin atop laced fingers. "Come again?"

Aaron looked at the painting, his expression verging on disgust. "I didn't paint that," he said. "I mean, I did. But not like that. I worked on that painting for weeks. I couldn't get the composition right, nor the colors. The whole thing was making me crazy. Then one morning, I woke up—the house was a mess. Food was left on the counter. My computer was on. Fresh paint was on my palette. And the painting...well, it was fixed. Every problem I'd had with perspective, lighting, color...they were gone. It was like Rembrandt sneaked into my house in the middle of the night and produced what I couldn't."

"It is a nice painting," Gluttony said.

"It's more than nice. It's amazing." Aaron blew out his cheeks, cutting his eyes at the artwork on the easel. "Do you know how frustrating it is to see your failure staring you in the face every day? Here you are, doing your best to create something meaningful that will get you the recognition you deserve, and then BAM—some ghost or whatever creates in one night what you couldn't do in weeks. It's so unfair."

I chuckled without even realizing I was doing it until I saw Aaron's eyes on me, his expression stern. "It's really not funny," he said.

"No, it isn't," I agreed. "I wasn't laughing about that. You just reminded me of my housemate, Envy. That's all."

Cary snickered. "You're perceptive. When we were kids, Mom and Dad could never praise me without also praising Aaron or he'd throw a fit." Turning to his brother, he added, "You still do that, you know. That's why things didn't work out with you and that girl you were seeing. You hated all the kudos she was getting on social media."

Aaron ignored Cary, turning his eyes back to the painting. "Sometimes I want to destroy it. Just so it stops mocking me. But I can never bring myself to touch it."

Just then, one of the containers holding Aaron's paintbrushes tipped over. Aaron cursed under his breath as he stood to right the bottle. "The floor in this apartment is slanted," he explained. "Stuff falls over all the time. But the landlord gave me a discount, so I'm not complaining."

A long silence stretched between us as Aaron rearranged his art supplies. Finally, Sloth said, "Aaron, isn't it possible someone's been sneaking in here in the middle of the night? It's an apartment complex, so any number of people might have a key. Have you considered that?"

"I have," Aaron said, "but that doesn't explain the presence I feel. Plus, wouldn't I hear them? Could anybody sleep through a ruckus like that?"

I ran through the drugs I'd seen in Aaron's cabinet. I saw no sleep medication, even though several of the medicines he was on sometimes produced insomnia. Similarly, I hadn't found any alcohol or recreational drugs when I'd been snooping around—err, investigating. Unless he slept like the dead, it was unlikely someone could break into Aaron's apartment without him noticing, especially if they made as much of a mess as he claimed.

Unlikely, but not impossible. After all, if a statue could vanish and reappear elsewhere, I couldn't write anything off completely.

"Aaron, can I go on a tangent here for a moment? I noticed something in your room. The article about the Star of the Sea. Is that a particular interest of yours?"

Aaron looked taken aback at the change in subject but responded with a half-hearted shrug. "No, not especially. I framed the article because they quoted my mother. She's the civil rights attorney mentioned toward the end who got angry about desecration or whatever she said."

"Oh, she really let the police have it," Cary put in enthusiastically. "She said if the statue had been inspired by a White woman instead of a Native woman, they'd be turning the city upside down to find her."

"Which is ridiculous," Aaron said. "At the end of the day, it's a mermaid. It's not exactly Sojourner Truth. The city just doesn't have the resources to go hunting for a statue."

"Odyssey does have a super high murder rate," Sloth agreed. "They have to prioritize."

Aaron nodded. "Right. Well, Mom wrote to various journalists expressing her displeasure. At the time, I found it embarrassing because I thought she was just drumming up business. But the more I thought about it, I realized she'd always been that way, especially about art. Whenever art funding gets cut in schools, she calls newspapers. Whenever there's talk of censoring an art exhibit, she calls reporters."

"She does have an outsized predilection for preserving art, especially here in Odyssey," Cary said with a smile. "If she weren't so smart, I'd say she let her obsession rot her brain."

"Maybe that's where I get it from," Aaron added with a grin. "Like mother, like son."

"Oh, don't start that again," Cary whined, throwing up his hands. "We're not rehashing that old chestnut."

"What old chestnut?" Sloth asked.

Cary rolled his eyes and gave Sloth a pointed look. "Nature versus nurture. Aaron and I are both adopted.

He likes to pretend my idiosyncrasies are inherited, while his—"

"I don't have any," Aaron interrupted playfully.

"Uh-huh." Again, Cary rolled his eyes. "But Aaron is right about one thing—Mom is like a dog with a bone when it comes to local art. When that statue initially disappeared, she went apey. But then it came back, and…Well, now Mom doesn't know what to think."

"Just like the rest of us," I muttered.

Gluttony turned to Aaron, his head tilted to the side. "How important is art to you? That painting, for example—just a pastime, or is it something more?"

Aaron blinked, his eyes flitting briefly to the painting in the corner. "How important is it?" He spread his hands out before him. "Well…painting is my life. It's all that matters."

Now, Cary cleared his throat loudly and chuckled, leaning forward in his chair. "Well, not everything," Aaron's brother corrected. "What he means is…well, you know. Everyone needs a hobby. But it's not everything. It's not as important as his career."

Nobody said anything for a moment. Then, Sloth said, "Aaron, only *you* know what's truly in your heart." She shot a quick sideways glance at Cary, her mouth quirking into a disapproving frown. "You have to follow your bliss, no matter where it takes you. Take me, for example. Just the other day, I met a wonderful woman while investigating the Star of the Sea. Tabitha Antoinette? Have you heard of her?"

Aaron's eyes widened, and he nodded with enthusiasm. "Oh, sure, she's been on some of my favorite shows. You met her? That's so cool. Did you take a photo with her? I hear she's even prettier in person."

"I didn't think of it, no," Sloth said. "But the point is —meeting her was a milestone. It changed me."

"Meeting celebrities really can do that," Aaron agreed, his expression wistful. "It's like they exist on another plane from us mere mortals. Wow, some people have all the luck. But good for you, though." He sounded only the tiniest bit jealous. "So will you, I don't know, start going to yoga or something?"

Sloth smiled, shaking her head. "No, I mean really changed me. She helped me rethink my priorities. In fact—I haven't told anyone this yet, so." She pressed a finger to her lips. "I've decided to leave the show to help her start a foundation that teaches women to reclaim their power."

All the air went immediately out of the room. I closed my eyes and sank back into the cushions. At the same time, Gluttony and Cary objected in concert, tripping over each other's words.

"What are you talking about?"

"What do you mean, leaving? Where are you going?"

"Can you do that? You can't do that! What will happen to the show?"

"There are *seven* deadly sins. Not six!"

"They'll cancel the show for sure. Think about what you'd be doing to everyone else's career. How can you be so selfish?"

Sloth twisted her hands in her lap looking crestfallen. "I appreciate that I'll be missed on the show," she began, "but you can't blame me for wanting to do what's right for myself."

"I ain't blaming you," Gluttony said. "I'm just…*surprised.* That's all." He looked at me, one eyebrow perched higher than the other. "You already knew about this, didn't you?"

I shrugged. "She asked me not to say anything."

"I'd seriously rethink it if I were you," Cary said. "The show really can't go on without you. And you'll be blackballed in Hollywood. No one will ever cast you again. If Tabitha thought for one second about what's right for you, she'd never ask you to break your contract. She's in the Screen Actors Guild, after all. She knows better."

"I'm not interested in an acting career," Sloth said with the slightest smile. "This was just something fun to do while I figured out my life. But it's not who I am. Not really."

"Well, you can't know that," Cary pressed. "It seems foolish—"

"That's enough," I interrupted. I pinched the bridge of my nose and sat forward. "Sloth can do whatever she wants. She's a big girl." I glanced at Sloth who seemed relieved not to have to defend herself. "Look, we came, we saw, there's nothing here. No ghosts." I turned to Aaron and offered what I hoped was a reassuring smile. "Whatever is happening with you isn't a haunting."

The out-of-work actor grunted. "I guess that should make me feel better. But it really doesn't."

"Well, we appreciate the hospitality, but it's getting

late." Gluttony stretched and climbed to his feet. "We should probably go."

Aaron nodded. "Right. Well, thanks for trying, anyway. I really do appreciate your time. And Sloth?"

My housemate looked up. "Yeah?"

"I wish you the best of luck in your new career. I wish I had the guts to go after what I love."

Sloth blushed and nodded but didn't respond. A few handshakes later, we were out the door.

seven

. . .

"Are you sure you don't want me to come with you? I can be packed and ready to go in just a few minutes."

It was morning, and Sloth and I were standing in the driveway as I prepared to make the 4-hour drive to Santa Barbara to meet with Arjun Singh. I threw my bag into the trunk and surveyed my things. I didn't need much; I only planned to stay one night—two at the most. I slammed the car trunk closed and turned around. Sloth was sipping a steaming mug of coffee, the morning breeze ruffling her hair. She was barefoot, clutching the lapels of her terrycloth robe in her free hand. The cuffs were stained with what looked like strawberry jam. Or maybe Kool-Aid.

I smiled and dug my hands into my pockets as I leaned against the trunk. "I appreciate the offer, but it's best if you stay behind. *Someone* has to try to break the statue case."

Sloth yawned and took a tentative sip of her brew.

"Gluttony and I are going to talk to the property owners at all the places the statue has appeared. Who knows—maybe they're all siblings, or they all poured pig's blood on the local reject at prom or something."

Knowing Sloth, I had a feeling that was a movie reference. But I'd never seen whatever movie she was talking about, so I ignored it. "That's a good idea. Also, maybe you guys can ask around about a significant Luis in Odyssey's history."

"Research historical relevance, check. Interview property owners, check." Sloth sighed dramatically and reached for a pigtail. I thought she was going to munch the end like she often did, but instead, she tossed it back. "I know we have to work on our case, but I've never been to Santa Barbara, and it sounds like fun. And I'm just saying—I'm fantastic company on road trips, you know. I like a wide variety of music. If you prefer podcasts or audiobooks, I can recommend at least a few dozen I think you'd like. And if you *do* get a clue about what happened to the commune and your family, I'm also great at thinking out loud and solving mysteries. And don't forget, Pride—this may be the last mystery I get to solve."

The front door opened, interrupting my impending objection. Craig struggled through with an equipment bag in tow. He waved as he stumbled through the door, flashing us a goofy smile. "I've still got one more bag in the house," he called, dropping the pack on the porch. "I'll be right back."

Sloth turned to me, her lips drawn in a frown. "I can't believe you're taking Craig and not me."

"Well, that wasn't exactly my choice. Tricia's not happy with our progress on this task *or* that I haven't looked into the commune thing. And since *Sinful House* is the only shelter and paycheck I have…"

The front door flew open again, and Craig emerged with a duffel bag over his shoulder. He opened the trunk, threw the bag inside, and then returned for the camera equipment, which he handled more delicately. "Who's driving?" he asked.

"I always drive." I dug the keys from my pocket and headed to the driver's side door. "Except when Wrath doesn't let me."

"You shouldn't let him boss you around," Craig said, shaking his head. "It sets a bad precedent."

I didn't respond to that. I didn't know what precedent I was setting, and Wrath didn't boss me around, anyway. But it seemed petulant to say so, so instead, I said, "Do you have everything? Are we ready to get this show on the road? Literally?"

Craig shot me a peace sign as he slid into the passenger seat. Sloth sidled up beside me and gave me a one-armed hug, keeping her coffee as far away as she could, which I appreciated. "Have a safe trip," she said. "And try to have fun. And good luck! Don't do anything I wouldn't do!"

There were plenty of things Sloth wouldn't do that were actually pretty important to me, like picking up after myself and doing my laundry regularly. Still, I returned her hug and then slid into the car. A few minutes later, we were on the road.

Four excruciating hours and two stops at In-N-Out

Burgers later, I was finally ensconced in the privacy of my own room. If you've never had the pleasure of traveling in a compact car with a loquacious cameraman with diabolical taste in music, I have to say, I can't recommend it. I don't usually like to speed, but driving 10 miles over the speed limit was the only way to shorten the term of my torture. By the time we reached the hotel, I was a frazzled ball of nothing but nerves.

Now, I was stretched out across my queen-size bed, remote control in one hand and a milkshake in the other. I was about to unwind by binge-watching bad television when there was a knock at my door.

I growled as I sat up. I'd just spent several hours in the car with Craig—I didn't think I had it in me to spend another minute with him. And if he was going to ask to borrow deodorant or toothpaste, I was really gonna let him have it.

I went to the door and rested my hand on the knob. Then I looked through the peephole because I'm not a psychopath. But when I saw who was standing on the other side, I took back my previous sentiment. I would have vastly preferred Craig the Cameraman.

With my breath held, I opened the door. Lust stood in the doorway, hands jammed into her hip pockets. She was wearing a pair of slim-fitting joggers and a lilac crop top with an old pair of canvas running shoes. On anyone else, the outfit might have looked slovenly. But Lust looked divine.

When she saw me, her face lit up, and she smiled and tossed her dark hair over a shoulder. "Oh good, you made it," she said, a hand pressed to her chest. "I've been obsessively checking the time for the past hour." She paused, her smile faltering only a little. She lifted her chin and asked, "Is it okay if I come in?"

"Come in?" I blinked back my confusion, brow wrinkled. "What are you even doing here? How did you know I was—"

Realization hit me like a tsunami, and I crumpled against the doorframe, pressing a hand to my forehead, mortified at my stupidity. "Tricia set up my meeting with Arjun," I said with a dry chuckle. "She also booked this room. Let me guess." I poked my head through the door and looked up and down the empty hallway. "Your room is just next door?"

"Two rooms down, actually," Lust corrected with a nervous laugh. "So can I? Come in?"

She didn't wait for me to answer. She angled her body to slip past me and stepped inside. After giving the room a quick once over, she flopped down on the foot of my bed and folded her hands in her lap. "Seriously, Pride. We need to talk."

"We need to talk" are four words you never want to hear from your partner, boss, or doctor. Lust wasn't any of those things, but I still felt like dying as soon as she spoke them. Instead, I pulled a chair out from the desk and sank down, dropping my chin into my hands.

"You drove all the way out here for this moment," I said. "So I guess it would be rude if I said I was just in the middle of *The Real Housewives of New York*."

Lust dropped her gaze into her lap, her lips folded beneath her teeth as she twiddled her thumbs. Finally, she took a deep breath and looked up, her eyes as wide and round as a doe's. "Let me start by saying this whole thing has gotten way out of hand, and I never intended to hurt you."

I let that phrase hang in the air between us before I asked, "What whole thing?"

Lust sighed and ran her fingers through her hair. "You are *not* gonna make this easy on me, are you? I guess that's fair. I guess I deserve that." She looked around the room, her eyelashes fluttering. I couldn't tell if she was trying to be seductive or trying not to cry. Not that it mattered. I didn't like either possibility.

"Tricia gave me some advice when I first came on the show," she explained. "She said viewers would naturally be attracted to me, and I would easily become the fan-favorite. In fact, she and some of the other producers had already decided I would be the winner long before we ever started filming."

That was news to me. "How can they decide that? Are the votes *rigged?*" I stared with my mouth agape. It seemed ridiculous to get upset over something like this, but this revelation really bothered me for some reason. "If they've already decided a winner, then why does Tricia waste our time every week with—"

"It's not rigged," she interrupted. "Not like that, anyway. It's all in the editing, Pride. The network can make each of us look however they want. All they have to do is show the viewers a carefully constructed version of each housemate. Anyway, Tricia said the network was betting on me to make the show a success. But to clinch the deal, I couldn't rely just on my looks or personality. I needed to bring the drama. And preferably, I needed a relationship." Her face flushed red and damp, and she tore her gaze away, her voice wavering. "She didn't tell me *who* I needed to set my eyes on. She just gave me some general advice. She said it would be smart to choose the most vulnerable person in the house. And… I'm so sorry, Pride, but at the time, I believed the most vulnerable person was you."

I didn't know what to say to that, so I said nothing. The truth was, I was feeling a lot of different things. Anger, disbelief, humiliation. I never thought Tricia Woodward or anyone else at the network was my friend or anything. But I at least thought I was getting a fair shot.

It hurts to get your rose-colored glasses knocked off without warning.

"In the beginning, when I first started flirting with you? It was an act," she admitted. "I was just doing what Tricia told me to do. I was bringing drama into the house, and since we were partners, I used our on-screen time together to build up chemistry. But then something happened. At some point, I started to have actual feelings for you."

I recrossed my legs and sat back in my chair. I didn't know how I was supposed to feel about any of this. "Actual feelings for me? Was that before or after you started cozying up to Greed?"

Lust pursed her lips and rolled her eyes. "My interactions with Greed were all for the cameras," she said. "Aside from you and Wrath, Greed's the only person who succumbs to my wiles. And if you think I'm flirting with Wrath, you're nuts. Even I have my standards." She snorted and tried on a smile. When I didn't return it, she plunged on. "Pride, we're the Seven Deadly Sins. They cast me as Lust. I have a part to play, and I was playing it!"

"Well, how do I know you're not just playing a part now?" I asked, exasperation making my voice sharper and louder than I intended. "How can I believe anything you say? How do I know you're not just using your siren abilities on me to make me do what you want?"

I stopped ranting long enough to see that Lust looked as though I had just slapped her in the face. "How dare you?" she whispered. "I promised I would never use my talents against you. And I'm a lot of things, but I'm not a liar."

"You *just* admitted you were lying about your feelings for me!" I thundered. "Lust, do you even know what you're saying? Do you hear yourself? How do you think any of this makes me feel?"

Lust's cheeks blazed red hot, and her nostrils flared. "You can feel or not feel whatever you want," she shot back. "I'm just trying to be honest with you. I've wanted to come clean about all this for a while now, but every time I try to talk to you, you find an excuse to get away from me. That's why I'm here now. I begged Tricia to get me a room here in Santa Barbara so you and I could spend time together. Alone. And really get to know each other."

I said nothing for a while. I was hyper-aware that we were alone, and she was sitting on my bed. What I didn't know was how I felt or what I wanted. Two weeks ago, I was sure I was done with Lust. But had that even been real? Or was I just putting on a brave face because it hurt too much to accept that she'd rejected me?

I steepled my fingers beneath my chin and narrowed my eyes in the dim light. "So, you're here to mend things between us. That's your story?"

"Yes. And it's not a story."

I chuckled grimly, shaking my head. "Are you sure? Because if you come clean now that you're just here because you found out Craig was filming this whole shebang and you wanted air time, I won't hold it against you. But if I find out later—"

"I'm not here about the Sam Lovelace thing," she said, her voice rising. But just as quickly, she huffed and backed down. "At least, not in the way you mean."

"In what way, then?"

"I know how little you pretend to care about the vanished commune," she began, her voice suspiciously steady. "And I know you claim that discovering what happened to your parents doesn't matter to you. But I also know that no matter what Tricia or the network threatened you with, you wouldn't be here if you weren't curious. You wouldn't have come all this way if you didn't want to know. I want to make sure you get all the answers you deserve." She lifted her chin and squared her shoulders, something like fire smoldering behind her eyes. "Even if it means I have to use my charms on Arjun. Hopefully, it won't come to that. But I'm ready if it does."

I grimaced and shook my head. "That won't be necessary. So, you're really here to help?"

My housemate stood and moved closer to me, and I had to fight the urge to shrink away. She was creeping into my bubble, and I really didn't like that. Still, she smelled of laundry soap and citrus and mint, and her nearness wasn't entirely unpleasant. She brushed the tips of her fingers along my cheek. "To help you, yes, but also…to see what there is between us. To see if maybe we should give this thing a real shot."

I blushed hot and pulled away, getting to my feet to put some distance between us. "All right," I said. "I'll take you at your word. Let's get through this appointment with Arjun, and then we'll see…" I shrugged. "…What there is to see."

Lust was still a moment, then she, too, climbed to her feet. "I have something for you."

She reached into a pocket and withdrew a small, black object that fit in her palm. She held her hand out and unfurled her fingers. "This is for you—if you'll have it," she amended. When I didn't move, she pushed her hand forward. "Go ahead. Take it."

Gingerly, I plucked the object from her hand. It was long and thin, made of some combination of black metal and plastic. It looked like a small smart watch. I dangled it before my face, gripped between my thumb and forefinger. "What is it?"

"It's a digital mood bracelet," she said. She was smiling, but her lips trembled, like maybe she was nervous or shy. I couldn't tell. "But it's not…I mean, it doesn't show you *your* mood. It shows you mine."

She held her hand before her face, fingers spread. On her middle finger she wore a matching black ring with a glossy domed surface. A shimmer flashed across the dome, its face glowing a soft, iridescent blue. "This is a digital mood ring. It monitors things like my body temperature and heart rate and assigns a mood based on those bioelectrical readings. Or something." She smiled, still awkward, but with growing confidence. "Anyway, your bracelet is a receptor. You can check it any time and see my mood. Go ahead. Try it."

I eyed the bracelet warily. I wasn't a gadget person, and I was much less a jewelry person. But I was a *curious* person, and I was interested to know why Lust was giving me the adult version of a friendship bracelet. I laid the device across my wrist and adjusted the clasp. As the bracelet warmed up on my skin, a message flashed briefly across the screen: "Hello! Currently, your partner is feeling…" The words faded away and the surface lit up with a soft indigo glow that matched the color of Lust's ring. Then the screen said, "Learn more about what the colors mean on our website."

"You're feeling blue," I said, dropping my arm to my side.

"It's not literal," she said, tittering softly. "And I know the default language calls me your partner. But you can change it once you set up a profile on the website." She held out her hand and admired the gadget on her finger. "Blue doesn't mean sad—it means nervous, anxious, or uneasy."

"Why are you nervous, anxious, or uneasy?" I asked.

Lust chuckled and dropped her hand. "Because I'm baring my soul to you, and I have no idea how you really feel about me."

"That's because *I* don't know how I really feel about you, Lust. Sometimes I don't know how I feel about anything."

"Sorry, I'm not phrasing this right." She twisted her hands together at her chest, chewing on her bottom lip. "Wear that for a little while. A week or two. See how it makes you feel. If seeing my emotions makes you feel comfortable, connected, or, like, warm…well, maybe that means there's something between us. But if knowing what I'm feeling makes you feel annoyed or bored…then maybe it means we're not meant to be together. I'm just saying maybe wearing the bracelet will help you know your own feelings. Kind of like doing a coin flip."

I frowned. "Coin flip?"

"You know. You flip a coin because you're undecided about something, but secretly you're hoping the coin comes up heads or tails and then you realize how you felt or what you wanted all along."

That sounded slightly ridiculous, but I didn't bother to say so. "So, the bracelet just mirrors what your ring is doing? That's all it does?"

"You can set it to do other things," she said. "You can set it to vibrate if my ring turns certain colors. Basically, it notifies you if I'm feeling sad, angry, or…" She winked. "…Lustful."

"Got it," I said. I glanced down at the bracelet and felt a pang of…something. I wasn't sure what a normal person would want with a bracelet like this, but for someone like me? It could be a game-changer. A device that told me in plain, simple language how another person was feeling could be the answer to my low emotional IQ. Now if only I could get one for every person I ever had to interact with. "Thanks for the gift. But um, not to be rude but…" I gestured to my bed. "I'd like to have a nap. Alone."

Lust nodded and opened the door, stepping into the sunlit corridor. A ray of light fell across her face, lighting up her eyes like magic. "I'll see you in the morning," she said. She walked the distance of two rooms down the hallway, opened her door, and was gone.

eight

. . .

I had never been to an art collector's house, and when we pulled up to Arjun Singh's place, I was surprised to find he didn't live in a mansion. The house was relatively modest, nestled at the end of a quiet cul-de-sac on the edge of town. The lawn had recently been mowed, and a neatly trimmed hedge lined our walk to the front door.

Craig the Camera Guy followed Lust and me as we walked up to the house. Butterflies fluttered mercilessly in my stomach. I wasn't sure why I was nervous. In my time on the show, I'd been in way more awkward situations. But on the other hand, I'd never faced the possibility of finding out something about my heritage, either.

I must have been standing there for longer than I thought because when Lust poked me in the shoulder, I jumped at her touch. She smiled and tilted her head to the door. "What are you waiting for, Freak Show? Ring the doorbell."

I glanced back at Craig, who made a shooing motion with his hand. *Here goes nothing*, I thought, turning back to the door. With my breath held, I rang the doorbell.

Immediately, the door opened, and we were greeted by a man in his late 50s, with smooth, nut-brown skin and silky salt-and-pepper hair tied away from his face in a low-hanging ponytail. He wore perfectly pressed chinos with a navy-blue sweater. A polished pair of cordovan penny loafers completed the look.

"Well! You must be Pride and Lust!" His smile took over his whole face, lighting it up from inside as he looked rapidly from Lust to me and back again. He looked like he'd just won the lottery. "Don't make me guess. Who is who?"

Lust extended her hand and smiled warmly. "I'm Lust," she said. "It's nice to meet you."

Arjun accepted and gave Lust's hand a perfunctory shake. But the whole time, he was looking at me. I felt my face flush hot as I cleared my throat and extended my hand. "I'm Pride," I said. "And that's our camera-man, Craig. Just act like he isn't here."

Arjun shook my hand vigorously, lips smacking as though anticipating a delicious meal. "I can't believe I'm actually meeting you face-to-face," he cooed. "I've been following the story of the lost commune for years, just like everyone else, I suppose. What a bizarre tale, truly. Though for the past several years, I have heard little about it?"

He said it as a question, so I offered a wan shrug. "I

guess there hasn't been anything new to report," I said. "It's kind of a cold case."

Arjun's eyes twinkled as his smile grew impossibly wider, the apples of his cheeks shining pink with joy. "But today might change all of that, am I right?" Suddenly, he blinked and shook his head, stepping to one side. "I'm so sorry. Please come in. I've never met a celebrity before, and I guess the shock of it knocked my sense of hospitality right from my brain. Please, please, come in."

We followed Arjun into the house, and as soon as he closed the door, I was rendered speechless. From the street, the home was unassuming. But inside the house was a different story. Art decorated every surface. Paintings and framed photographs covered every inch of wall, from the floorboards to the crown molding overhead. The tables were cluttered with handcrafted journals, lacquer boxes, and ornately carved statues of various shapes and sizes. Antique bookcases housed a variety of delicate tchotchkes, from tea sets to Lladro statuettes. I ambled through the room, marveling at the collection.

"It's been a long time since I've had visitors," Arjun explained as he guided us into a sitting room. "My wife passed away some time ago, and I'm afraid I became something of a hermit afterward. No, please don't bother with condolences," he said with a friendly wink. "Life goes on, and I have adjusted quite well, thank you. Still, I've lost some of my good manners." A bashful grin punctuated his words. "But now that I have you here, can I get you something to drink? Perhaps a cup of tea? Or perhaps something stronger? I know how you young people are."

"Tea would be awesome," Lust said, settling down on a lovely but uncomfortable-looking velvet chaise. "Thank you. Is it too much trouble to ask for cream and sugar?"

"Not at all—I take mine the same. And you?"

I shook my head, nose wrinkled. "I don't like tea," I said, sitting down next to Lust.

Arjun chuckled good-naturedly and moved into another room. When we were alone, Lust sighed and gave me a pointed look. "If someone offers you tea, just accept it," she said.

"Sloth already told me this," I grumbled. "But I don't see why I should put anyone through the trouble of making a drink I don't even like."

"It's more trouble if you refuse," she continued. "Because then your host has to ask if you'd prefer something else."

I nodded toward where Arjun had stood only a moment ago. "He didn't," I pointed out.

Lust sighed. "You're *really* not very good at the social niceties, are you?"

That was the understatement of the century, and I hardly thought Lust needed me to confirm it. A few minutes later, Arjun returned carrying a tray with a porcelain teapot and teacups with saucers.

"I hope Earl Gray is all right," he said, pouring steaming water into the teacups. "It was my wife's favorite. It's the only thing I buy now."

"I'm not picky," Lust said, dunking a bag of tea into

her cup. "Thank you. So! Arjun, I'd love to hear your story. How did you begin collecting art?"

Arjun took a seat in a Queen Anne chair across from Lust and balanced his teacup and saucer on a knee. "My wife Bhumika got me into it," he explained. "Both her parents were art historians, and she grew up with a healthy appreciation for all kinds of art. When we met, I was a dumb jock. You wouldn't know it to look at me now, but I was quite athletic in my youth. But as is often the case, when one meets a young lady he would like to woo, one learns to appreciate her interests. Whether that appreciation is genuine in the beginning, well…"

He let his voice trail off with a chuckle, and I felt my face flush hot. "I know exactly what you mean," Lust said. And though I couldn't be sure, I thought I detected a note of mockery in her voice.

I snapped my head to look at her, but she didn't take her eyes from Arjun. Still, I saw the way her lips quirked like she was trying to hold back a smile. So, she *was* making fun of me.

Not long ago, when I thought Lust was into me, we'd gone on a date to an art museum. I didn't care a thing about art, but she did, and I wanted to do whatever would make her happy. Maybe it had been an obvious, boneheaded thing to do, but going to that museum was the reason I was sitting here now.

I'm not saying there's such a thing as fate. But maybe there's something to that whole "follow your heart, and it will lead to where you're meant to be" thing.

My therapist, Dr. Xena, would have a field day with that one.

"Anyway, shortly into our courtship, my wife took me along to an estate sale. And the things I saw in that house changed me forever. It wasn't just art, though. There was a feeling about that place. I almost want to use the word haunted, but that has such a negative connotation. It didn't feel sinister. It merely felt alive with spirit, as though something more than human inhabited that space." He paused and tittered, his eyes downcast. "I suppose that must sound silly to you," he said, almost under his breath.

"Not at all," I said. And to my surprise, I meant it. "I mean…I've never experienced that myself, at least not the way you describe it. But I can see and talk to ghosts. And they're not usually sinister. They're just echoes of a life that ended too soon. And in some ways, the ghosts I meet feel more alive than some people I know."

I could feel Lust's gaze on me, but just as she had pretended not to see me looking at her, I pretended not to notice her now. I didn't have more to say about this topic, anyway. Elaboration wasn't my strong suit.

Luckily, Arjun didn't prod. "Then you understand," he said with a smile. "After that day, I started researching art on my own. Going to estate sales, even yard sales. Goodwill, too. Nothing was off-limits. I didn't even know what I was looking for, but I was looking, and that was an important first step. But in point of fact, the first painting I ever bought was that one." He pointed to a large painting over the fireplace, a jester juggling before the court. He chuckled wryly. "Don't hold it against me. My taste has improved over the years." Arjun took a sip of tea and readjusted in his seat. "May I ask you something?"

I shrugged. "You can ask."

"Would you tell me about the incident that brought you here? Your producer wasn't very forthcoming. But I understand there was an incident with a medium at a séance?"

I nodded. "You know the medium Andromeda Clark? She was hosting a séance, and something came over her. Her whole body and face changed, and she said, *'Find Sum of All Prophets on vinyl. Start there. That's where you began.'* And as if that weren't creepy enough, then she looked right at me and said, *'Sam said this might happen.'* And…Then it was over."

Arjun nodded. "Sam being Sam Lovelace, I presume?"

I nodded. "That's what I think, yes."

Our host paused for a long while as he studied my face. Finally, he said, "There's more to this story, though, isn't there?" His lips twitched, his head cocked mischievously to one side. "It's all right. You can tell me. It wasn't just the words she used that interested you, was it? There was something more."

I swallowed around the lump in my throat and dropped my gaze into my lap. I'd only told one other person why the séance had moved me so—and that person was sitting beside me on the chaise. If I spoke the truth now, in front of the camera and all of TV-watching America, the relatively simple life I'd led until now would fly right out the window. My life would be overrun with reporters, documentarians, writers, and all kinds of fame seekers looking for an exclusive interview with the Lone Survivor of the Vanished Sam Lovelace Commune.

I'd never wanted that notoriety. I still didn't. But I didn't drag Craig the Cameraman all this way just to let Tricia and the network down now.

I lifted my chin and gave a stiff nod. "It was her voice," I said. "The voice that came from Andromeda's body wasn't her own. That itself isn't unusual in a séance. But what was strange was…" I gulped and closed my eyes. "I recognized it. Something deep inside me reacted to that voice. And I know this is gonna sound crazy because I was an infant when the art commune disappeared, but…I recognized that voice. It was my mother."

Arjun said nothing for a long while. Then he steepled his fingers beneath his chin and winked. "It really isn't that strange. We spend nine months listening to nothing but the rush and gurgle of our mother's heartbeat against the ebb and sway of her voice. That heartbeat, that constant metronome ticking out the seconds until we slide naked and afraid into the world, that's *life*. And against that pulsing rhythm is the sweet melody that gives us the strength to venture into the world—for the hope of warm arms around us. For the hope of meeting the voice that has been our lone companion for oh, so long."

I looked away, blushing furiously at his words. That kind of cockamamie New Age nonsense was not in my wheelhouse, and I got a serious case of secondhand embarrassment hearing that drivel coming out of his mouth. And yet, there *was* something to those words, wasn't there? After all, I *did* recognize the voice. I don't know if it gave me the strength to be born or not, but I guess I couldn't completely count out the possibility.

Man, living in Odyssey had really done a number on my worldview.

Arjun placed his saucer on the table and clapped his hands together. "Well! I don't suppose you came all this way to listen to an old man blather on philosophically, did you? Forgive me, I get carried away sometimes. That said, I appreciate your sharing with me, Pride. From the look on your face, I can see it wasn't easy for you. Shall we go see the piece, then?"

We got up and followed Arjun through the house. He led us down the hallway, through the kitchen, and out through a side door. "It's just out here, in the garage." We padded over to a detached building with no windows, where Arjun unlocked the door and flipped on the light switch.

Technically, I suppose it was a garage in the sense that the original builders intended it to house cars. But in reality, it was one of the most outrageous mancaves I'd ever seen. A polished billiards table occupied the middle of the room, with an ornate chandelier glittering from above. He'd built a custom bar into one end of the room. At the other end was another collection of various musical accouterments. I saw a vintage jukebox, at least a half-dozen turntables, and boxes and boxes of records.

All of that was breathtaking enough. But there, mounted above a refurbished 1950s console, was the art piece we'd come all this way to see. It was about 35 inches high by 75 inches long. The background was constructed entirely of vinyl records without labels. Then the artist painted a scene onto the albums. A group of faceless people was being attacked by gruesome spirits while a robed wise man in the corner counted out his money, ignoring the others in distress.

"Sum of All Prophets," Arjun intoned as he gestured at the painting. "It's such a strange piece, isn't it? It's rare to see a painter with such obvious talent choosing an unconventional surface medium. I often wonder what went through this artist's mind when they chose to paint vinyl records. For a while, I actually considered deconstructing this piece, if you can believe it."

Lust looked over at our host, her eyebrow quirked quizzically. "Deconstructing it? For what?"

Arjun chuckled. "Besides my obsession with art, I'm also quite the music aficionado. And I can't help but wonder what record albums the artist used to construct this piece. I didn't take it apart because Bhumika convinced me that after all the layers of lacquer and glue, the records were undoubtedly unplayable. Still, I will always wonder if there's a secret message encoded here. When I look at this piece, I always ask myself, did she choose these albums for a reason? If I knew the music represented here, would I glimpse the artist's soul?" He chuckled and gave a self-conscious shrug. "Probably not. But a man can dream."

I stared at the painting, taking it all in. Before now,

I'd only seen a thumbnail of the image, and I didn't find it very impressive. But up close, it sent shivers down my spine. Something about this painting felt eerily intimate and impossibly familiar. I'd never seen it before, yet I felt I knew every brush stroke like I knew my own reflection.

"I don't suppose you'd be willing to sell this piece?" Lust asked suddenly.

Arjun folded his hands before him and gave Lust a rueful shake of his head. "I'm sorry. I can imagine what this piece might mean to your friend here, but I'm afraid I can't let it go. Not for any price."

Lust took a step nearer to Arjun and rested a hand on his elbow. I felt my skin pimple over as I realized what she was about to try. "Lust—"

"Don't you want to reconsider?" she asked, ignoring me. The subtle change in the timbre of her voice confirmed what I already feared. She was trying to use her siren ability on Arjun to make him sell us the painting.

Arjun stammered and blinked, turning his gaze from Lust to the painting and back again. He looked like a deer caught in headlights, with no idea what was happening. Disgruntled, I slapped Lust's hand away and worked myself between them. "That's not necessary," I growled. "Please, don't."

Lust hesitated a moment before flipping her hair over her shoulder. "I had to try," she said.

"You're welcome to photograph it if you like," Arjun said, oblivious to what had just transpired. "And I can tell you what I know about it if that will help."

"What do you know about it?" I asked.

Now, Arjun laughed. "Not much! I bought it from a man liquidating his estate after he went bankrupt. Like me, he was long interested in the Sam Lovelace commune. I understand the commune was trying to use art to channel entities from beyond. To touch the spirit world as it were. Is that right?"

I nodded. "Yeah. They were into weird hippie stuff like that."

Arjun smiled. "After the commune vanished, the city seized some of the art, though unfortunately, not much was left. Investigators found a barn filled with the burned remains of sculptures, paintings, photographs…art of all kinds had been destroyed. And what little survived the fire was vandalized or stolen. Thankfully, this piece endured, though I'm unsure how it ended up in a private collection. But now, here it is. And here you are."

I nodded, readying my hand to snap a picture of the painting. However, instead of photographing the artwork, I took a tentative step toward it. "Can I touch it?" I asked.

Arjun sucked in a breath, concern written plainly over his face. "I'd rather you didn't," he drawled. "The oils in the skin, you see…"

"I understand. It's just that sometimes when I touch people, I see things."

Arjun's frown deepened. "But this painting isn't a person. It's a thing."

"I know. But I can't explain it. I just think if you let me touch it…"

For a moment, Arjun said nothing, studying me as

he had in his parlor. I couldn't read his expression. Finally, he nodded with a flick of his wrist and said, "You can touch the bottom there, on the underside of the album. But please try not to touch the face of the painting. I would hate for anything to happen to it."

Gingerly, I stepped toward the artwork. I didn't know what I hoped to accomplish. Arjun was right— touching objects and touching people were not the same thing at all. I didn't have psychometry. Nothing happened when I touched inanimate objects. And yet, I felt called to this painting in a way I couldn't explain.

I reached out and let the pads of my fingers brush lightly against the underside of the records. As soon as my skin met the vinyl, I gasped. Thousands of images flashed before my eyes: people, buildings, abstract shapes, light, skylines, mountains. Hands holding a paintbrush. A man's face in the dark, smothering me with kisses. A museum.

A fire.

Nothing was clear or defined, and the jolt of information that struck me left me lost for words. Even my breath left my lungs, and I stumbled, dizzy on my feet as the data zapped me and then, suddenly, was gone.

I snatched my hand away and held it tight against my chest, my breathing shallow and fast. I felt the blood leaving my brain as my vision swam.

"I need some air."

I tumbled from the house into the open air, gulping down huge lungfuls of oxygen. I leaned forward, hands on my knees as the world slanted and slowly straightened. I stood, digging my knuckles into my eyes, trying to regain my bearings.

What had just happened?

I found my way to the patio and fell into a porch swing. I closed my eyes, trying to conjure the images that had raced through my mind, but there had been so many. Too many. I felt like my brain would explode.

Had I just seen my mother's memories? Whatever the images were, they were already fading. In a few more minutes, they'd be gone completely. I wasn't sure whether that was for better or worse.

I was probably outside only 10 minutes when Arjun approached me on the patio. He was carrying an envelope yellowed with age. He sat beside me and placed it on my lap.

"That came with the painting," he said. "It was originally affixed to the back. It was still sealed with lacquer when I discovered it, so I believe I am the only person who has ever read its contents. It was perhaps a sin to go at it with solvents like I did—I risked damaging the painting. But I had to know what it said." He began rocking the swing with his toe. The gentle back and forth produced a breeze that felt good on my overheated skin. "As you'll see when you open it, I've read this letter many, many times. It's rather creased with age, and the ink has begun to fade. But I assure you, it's still quite legible. I don't know what good it will do you," he admitted. "But it belongs with you. I know that now. I can't sell you the painting, but that letter… well, it belongs with you."

I turned the envelope over in my hands. There was

no inscription on the front. Part of me wanted to rip into the letter then and there. But a little voice in my head whispered that I should read it in private. I slipped the envelope away and smiled. "Thank you for everything," I said. "We should probably get going."

We said our goodbyes and returned to the hotel. Lust tried to come back to my room with me, but I put the kibosh on her advances. Craig wasn't as easily dissuaded, however. "Do you know what the network will do to me if I don't film your reaction as you read that letter?" he said. "I'd lose my job."

I couldn't very well walk around with Craig's unemployment on my conscience. So, we set up the room as best we could, and then I sat on the bed to read the letter to myself on camera.

I pulled out the letter, turning it over in my hands before finally opening the envelope and retrieving the paper. Carefully, I unfolded it.

The letter was written in elegant penmanship in blue ink on white paper that hadn't aged well. I stared at it a while without reading, merely taking it in. A buzz hummed down my spine, and a strange feeling came over me. I had an odd moment of déjà vu, but I'd never been to this hotel, never held an old letter in my hands.

And yet everything about the moment felt like I'd lived it before.

I swallowed, took a breath, and began to read.

When I was through, I put the letter away and called Paola Barbosa.

———

"Hello?"

I recognized the caretaker's voice immediately. "Claudia. It's me, Pride. May I speak with Paola, please?"

I heard her sharp intake of breath. "Just a minute."

A moment later, I heard a slight wheezing on the other end, followed by Paola's accented voice. "If you're calling, I expect you have something for me, after all."

"I saw an art collector today," I began. "Are you familiar with the painting *Sum of All Prophets?*"

"I'm not. Please elucidate."

"An artist from the commune painted it before she vanished," I said. I guess I didn't need to add the before she vanished part. I suppose that was implied. "Anyway, Arjun—the collector—discovered a letter stuck to the back of the painting. He wouldn't let me keep the art, but he let me have the letter. I've just finished reading it, and I thought…well, you said you wanted me to tell you something about the commune no one else knows. This letter might be that something."

Paola sniffed. "I'm listening."

I drew in a breath. "It's a letter from the artist to her child. No names are used, though, so I'm not *sure* who the recipient was supposed to be. But I think…maybe…"

I heard the grin in her voice when she said, "You think perhaps it was written for you."

I sighed and nodded. "I know how that sounds. Believe me. I feel like I should check myself into the looney bin just for thinking it. But yes. I think it's a letter from my mother to me. However, I'm not sure how to interpret it. Some of what she says is unclear."

"Unclear how?"

I hesitated. The truth was, the letter wasn't really unclear at all. But if I was reading it right, the narrative we'd all come to believe about the commune might not be accurate. "Maybe you'd like to read it for yourself," I said finally. "That's what you want, isn't it? You wanted new information no one else has. Well, this is your chance."

I heard movement on the other end—the rustling of clothes, the squeak of a chair as she readjusted herself. I wished I could see her face. Was she smiling? Had she anticipated this? Was she about to hyperventilate with absolute elation? Finally, she said, "Meet me at my home tomorrow. Bring the letter. Don't be late."

She disconnected.

Craig had gone, so I put the phone away and stretched out on the bed, staring at the ceiling. I replayed the contents of the letter over and over, my heart rate picking up each time. And not just because of what the letter said—but how I ended up with it in the first place. If I hadn't been at that séance with Andromeda, I wouldn't have heard the message telling me to come find the painting. And I wouldn't have been there if I hadn't been investigating Tamora Preston's catfishing case. And I wouldn't have been doing that if I hadn't been cast on *Sinful House*. And I wouldn't have been on *Sinful House* if Shayda hadn't broken up with me. And she wouldn't have broken up with me if I'd had a normal person's brain and hadn't missed her sister's wedding.

Well, she probably would have broken up with me, eventually. I'm not sure I'm really relationship material. But you see where I'm going with this.

A series of events that could have easily not happened led me to this moment. A breakup, potential homelessness, the random luck of appearing at a séance…all those things led me here, to this moment, which had just clued me into something that could potentially change my life.

That sounds dramatic. But that's really how I felt lying there. Who was my mother, really? What were those hippies really doing in the middle of nowhere?

Lying on a hotel bed in Santa Barbara wouldn't bring me any closer to these answers, and I had no reason to stay any longer. So I got up, packed, rounded up Craig and Lust, and before the clock struck midnight, the three of us were back in Odyssey.

nine

. . .

Paola Barbosa lived at the end of a cul-de-sac on a shaded avenue in San Diego. The house looked cozy from the outside, with a covered porch and an attached garage. A cat lay on the lawn, grooming itself in the sun. I parked the car and turned to Gluttony. "Is this the right address?"

Gluttony checked the notes I'd given him at the house. "4590 Butternut Avenue. This is it. But before we go in…" He pulled out his phone. "Let me tell Sloth we're here. I feel weird doing this without her."

I waited while Gluttony tapped something into his phone. I hadn't wanted to come out here without Sloth, either. But she said her stomach was bothering her and asked if she could take a personal day. I thought it was nuts for her to ask this. If people need a day to themselves, they shouldn't have to ask for it.

Anyway, Gluttony and I were on our own.

When Gluttony finished his message, we hauled ourselves from the car with Craig in tow. We shuffled up to the front door, past the cat who eyed us with typical feline suspicion, sparing not so much as a meow when Gluttony psspsspss'd at him. The big man pointed a finger in the kitty's direction. "You the reason I don't like cats," he said. "You ain't friendly, you don't play catch, and you put your nasty behind on the kitchen counter."

The cat made no reply, resuming the licking of his lustrous coat.

I rang the doorbell.

The door opened, and a short, fat, frazzled-looking woman met us. She was twisting the crucifix that hung from her neck around a chubby finger. "Can I help you?" she asked.

Somewhere behind her, a voice shouted. The words were indecipherable, but the person shouting them sounded angry. I heard breaking glass. The woman at the door flushed, gave an almost imperceptible head shake, and pressed her lips into a line. "Now isn't a good time," she said.

Gluttony and I exchanged glances. "Uh, hi," I stammered. "I'm Pride. This is my partner, Gluttony. We have an appointment with Paola today?"

The woman cursed to herself and stepped outside, pulling the door to without fully closing it. A sliver of light fell through the gap. "I'm so sorry. I'm Claudia. I meant to call you earlier, but time got away from me, and... Well, I'm afraid Ms. Barbosa can't see you today. She's not in an appropriate state for visitors."

Behind the closed door, I heard the thud of something heavy falling to the ground, followed by a piercing wail.

Gluttony's brow furrowed as he tried to peer around Claudia's ample form. "Uh…is everything okay in there? Do y'all need any help?"

Another thump came from inside the house, then another, followed by a crash that sounded like dishes smashing to the floor. The color drained from Claudia's face, and she shook her head, glancing over her shoulder. "We don't need help—at least, there's nothing you can do. This must run its course. No, please don't worry. This is not unusual. She's just having an episode. But, it might be better if you came back tomorrow. I'm so sorry you came all this way just to be turned away. But I hope you understand."

Again, we heard a crash inside the house, followed by shouting in a foreign language and then hysterical crying. Claudia crossed herself and backed into the house. "I'm so sorry. Come back tomorrow."

And with that, Claudia slipped back into the house, closing the door in our faces.

We stood on the stoop a little longer, listening. I don't know what we planned to do—we weren't cops. It wasn't like we could wait for a sign of distress and then burst our way in, shouting probable cause.

Eventually, we returned to the car, passing the cat who merely watched us unblinkingly as we skulked by.

I had barely turned the ignition when Gluttony said, "I don't feel right about this. Those women need help."

I leaned my head back and heaved a sigh. "Whether they do or not doesn't matter. We offered and were rejected. From the way Claudia talked, this happens with some regularity. I'm sure she has it under control."

"That's how you want to leave it? It's under control?"

"Gluttony's right," Craig put in. "Maybe we should call the police."

"Now hold on, I didn't say that," Gluttony said, holding up a hand in objection. "I see no reason to bring people with guns into this."

"Claudia doesn't appear to be in immediate danger," I agreed. "Police would just…make everything worse."

"Maybe we should alert a neighbor." Gluttony was already lugging himself from the car. "I'll just be a second. Just want to tell someone to keep an eye out."

Gluttony rang the doorbell at each of the houses on the cul-de-sac, but no one answered. Finally, he got back in the car with a shrug. "I tried. That's the best I can do. I saw a 7-11 on the way out here. Let me run in and get some snacks for the drive home."

I gaped at him. "It's a twenty-minute drive."

He grinned. "That means I can get in at least two cinnamon buns. Maybe a Ding Dong if I time it right."

By the time we got back to Sinful House, it was approaching dusk. I was fantasizing about an evening jog on the beach when I saw someone crying on the stoop. Her face was buried in her hands and her hair was covered by the hood of her sweatshirt, but I could tell from the stains on her sweatpants that it was Sloth.

I got out of the car and slammed the door. At the sound, she looked up, her face red and splotchy, tears streaming down her face. I ran to her. "Sloth? What's happening? Are you okay? What's going on?"

Snot dripped from my housemate's nose as she

shook her head, fat tears running down her cheeks. "I just heard the news," she said through her sobs. "He completely snowed us. He completely snowed *me!*"

Dread roiled in my stomach, and I sat beside her, clutching her knee and shaking her gently. "What signs? Sloth, tell me what happened."

"We should have known something wasn't right when we showed up to the apartment and everything was so…perfect. No sign of a haunting. And that outlandish story about the painting? We should have seen right through him!"

"Sloth, what are you *talking* about?"

"And why did he want all of us there in the first place?" she continued. "Well, it's obvious, Pride! He wanted witnesses. He wanted us to *see* how disturbed he was. I should have asked questions. I should have done *something!* And now she's dead!"

I moved my hand to her back, rubbing between her shoulders, trying to comfort her. "Who, Sloth? Who's dead?"

Now, Sloth emitted a terrible sob, her shudders redoubling. "Tabby! Tabitha Antoinette's been murdered. And the police have arrested Aaron for the crime!"

I led Sloth back into the house, where I settled her on the couch and fetched her a glass of water. I pressed it into her hands, and she drank it greedily, rivulets dripping from the corners of her mouth. She wiped her chin with the hem of her shirt and sucked in a lungful of air. "I can't believe this is happening."

I sat down next to her and leaned onto my knees.

"So, what happened? How did they make an arrest so quickly? The Odyssey police aren't exactly known for their investigative prowess."

Sloth sniffled. "It's been all over social media. There's camera footage of him…dragging her body…" Sloth's chin wobbled, and I thought she might begin sobbing again, but she collected herself, wiping feverishly at her eyes. "A neighbor's doorbell camera caught him on video dragging her body out of the front door of her vacation rental onto the street and then…and then he just…he just *left* her there…!"

I frowned. "Well…that's understandable. Dead bodies are actually really heavy."

But that was apparently the wrong thing to say, because Sloth burst into tears again. I put an awkward arm around her shoulders and tried to pull her close, but she wasn't having it. She slammed her fists against her thighs and thundered, "I don't want to be comforted! I want *justice*, Pride!"

"It seems you're not the only one."

I looked up to find Greed sauntering into the room, an oily smile on his lips. He was wearing a silk housecoat open at the chest, his hair wet and combed away from his face. He looked like he'd just come off the set of a cheesy adult movie. Not that I'd know anything about that. "Oh, you haven't heard? Now, that's just sad."

I grit my teeth and shot Greed a look. "Do you mind? We're kind of in the middle—"

"Well, I assumed you already knew since it pertains to your case. Though, from what I hear about the progress you've made, I guess I shouldn't be surprised you're the last to know."

I really didn't want to give Greed the satisfaction of professing my ignorance, but I needed to know what he was talking about. I was ready to swallow down my pride and ask the question, but Sloth beat me to it. Luckily for me, she didn't have an ego. "Last to know *what?*" she asked.

Greed smirked. "Guess who isn't standing outside Julio's boutique anymore?"

I blinked. "Wait…really? The Star of the Sea is gone?"

"No, not gone. She's moved again. And guess where she is now?"

I got to my feet, hands spread before me, pleading. "Greed, I'm not remotely in the mood for guessing games. Where is she?"

From another room, I heard Wrath shout, "For crying out loud! Television, show the news."

The television flickered to life, and a news program came on the screen. In it, a reporter stood on the street gesturing to the crowds behind her. "And in an unprecedented turn of events, the Star of the Sea has appeared on the pavilion just outside the Odyssey Courthouse. As has now become customary of the wandering statue, she has once again changed her appearance. And this time, it looks like the mermaid means business."

The reporter disappeared from view, and now an image of the statue filled the screen. When I saw her, I gasped.

The Star of the Sea was blindfolded, her expression

unreadable. She held a sign above her head that read, "Aaron Burton is innocent."

"Holy cannoli," I breathed, eyes wide as I stared at the scene. "Sloth, do you see this? Where's Gluttony? This is the first time the statue has done anything like this. This has to be a clue! Sloth, are you listening? Sloth?"

But Sloth wasn't listening. Her face buried in her hands, she wailed, "What kind of person would hurt a shining soul like Tabitha Antoinette?!"

I thought the "shining soul" thing was a bit much even from Sloth, but it was an important question. Assuming the statue was right about Aaron's innocence —which was a big if—who would benefit from taking out a second-rate actress?

And more importantly—at least for my case—why was the statue proclaiming Aaron's innocence?

Almost as quickly as the question came to me, however, I felt an overwhelming sense of ickiness. Here's why:

1. I might not be a Tabitha Antoinette fan, but the woman was dead. Was I really so callous that my first concern was whether it might lead to a break in my case? Obviously, the answer was yes, which bothered me more than a little.
2. Clearly, I needed to talk to Aaron. You didn't need years of detective experience to figure that one out. But the cops had him in

custody. They'd never let me interview
him…

3. …Unless I begged for a favor from someone
    I really didn't want to be indebted to.

I turned to Sloth and gathered her hands in mine.
"Sloth, I can only imagine how you feel. I know how
important Tabitha was to you." I wanted to add something more, but the condolence stuck in my throat like
glue. The truth was, shamefully, part of me was relieved
that Tabitha was dead. I know how horrible that sounds,
but if I can't be honest, what's the point? With Tabitha
murdered, maybe Sloth wouldn't leave the show. Maybe
I'd get to hold onto my friend a little longer.

I rose to my feet. "I need to talk to Gluttony. I have
an idea for how to move forward. Where did he run
off to?"

"Kitchen," Greed said, pointing. "It's almost dinner-
time. Well, good luck with your case. I predict you'll
need it."

Greed chuckled as he slithered out of the room, and
I had to bite my tongue from making a nasty remark.

Sometimes, being the adult in the room is a giant
buzzkill.

ten

. . .

I called Cameron Realty first thing the next morning.

I didn't want to make this call, but I *did* want to get to the bottom of whatever was going on with that statue, and Portia Cameron was my best bet. She was the only person I could think of who might have both the power and a vested interest in helping me get face time with Aaron Burton.

"It's a beautiful day at Cameron Realty. How can I help you today?"

I cringed at that ridiculous greeting. "I need to speak to Portia, please. This is Pride, and it's important. I already tried her cell phone, and she's not answering."

The receptionist on the other end sighed. "She's not here, unfortunately. She's doing her civic duty at City Hall."

I frowned, my brow wrinkling. "What civic duty?"

"Well, with the mayor in jail and the city manager dead, Portia is next in line to run Odyssey's government. So, she's acting as interim mayor until the emergency election, which she also plans to win, of course. And as mayor, she's trying to mitigate the poop storm this whole statue thing has caused. And you *know* how Portia feels about anything supernatural, including traveling statues."

I grimaced. Portia Cameron was one of Odyssey's wealthiest and most powerful people, and she hated the supernatural. In fact, her mayoral campaign was based on weeding out the town's paranormal elements to make Odyssey a safe haven for business development.

"Oh." I shrugged. "Then I guess I'll just run over to City Hall and talk to her in person."

"Good luck with that," the woman chortled. "Haven't you seen the news? The City Hall-Courthouse complex is crawling with onlookers, tourists, security, you name it. They're not letting anybody in the building except a skeleton crew of government officials. Things have turned into a circus."

Well, that put a real damper on my plans. It sounded like I wouldn't be able to get a meeting with her, let alone wrestle a favor from her.

Unless…

"All right. Thanks for your help." I disconnected and dialed a second number. A woman answered.

"Hi, Peyton. It's me, Pride. Do you remember me?"

Peyton choked out a laugh. "Um, of course I remember you. You can't exactly forget the person who rescued you from your kidnappers. It's good to hear from you. Are things going well with the show? Are you winning?"

"Definitely not," I said. I'd never been one to mince

words. "And, actually, that's why I'm calling. I need a favor." I blushed and cleared my throat. Just because I knew it had to be done didn't mean I didn't feel like a schmo for doing it. "Can you meet me at the courthouse in, say, 15 minutes?"

"I *can*," she drawled, "but why? What's this about?"

I closed my eyes. *Here goes nothing,* I thought. "I need you to pretend to be Portia to get me past security. I need to speak with your sister. It's important."

Peyton was quiet a minute. Then, a burst of laughter came over the phone. "You want me to fake being Portia? Of all the things! I suppose we can try it, but I haven't done that whole 'twin swap' thing since we were kids! Do you think it'll work? I mean, she's already over there. In the building. Won't they know I'm not her?"

"I doubt it," I said. "From what I saw on the news, it's utter chaos out there. It's totally possible Portia could have slipped out without anyone noticing. The only question is: do you know what she was wearing this morning, and can you reproduce it?"

Peyton giggled, and I heard the smile in her voice when she said, "Oh, I've got this. Meet me on the pavilion in fifteen."

She hung up.

Twenty-five minutes later, Gluttony and I were weaving our way through a crowd of onlookers searching for Peyton. We finally found her wearing over-sized black sunglasses pretending to read a newspaper. When she saw us, she threw the paper aside. "There you are," she said, breathless. "I wasn't sure how much longer I would make it out here."

Peyton was wearing a fitted gray suit with an icy periwinkle silk shell. It was a little large on her—she had recently been rescued from depraved kidnappers who hadn't taken the best care of her, and she'd been rail thin when we'd found her. She'd filled out some, but she still wasn't as athletic as Portia. I thought she looked close enough, though.

"Why's that?" I asked. "And what's with the celebrity glasses?"

Peyton motioned with a lift of her chin to a man amassing a crowd of his own on the other side of the street. He was shouting something unintelligible into a bullhorn. But when I realized who it was, I laughed.

"Is that Dewey Delaney? The mermaid preacher guy?"

"In the flesh," Peyton sighed. "We all thought he was a nuisance when he was just the local religious zealot. But now he's really upped the ante. He's running for mayor."

I couldn't help it. I laughed again. "That guy's running for mayor against your *sister?*"

"I know," Peyton said, still watching Dewey across the pavilion. "It's absurd. But what's even more unbelievable is that people seem to like what he has to say. I hate to admit it, but my sister may have an actual fight on her hands."

I squinted into the sun to get a better look at Dewey. Today, he was wearing a neon orange bowling shirt, green plaid golf pants, and a pair of electric yellow glasses. As shocking as his outfit was, though, it wasn't the strangest thing about him.

"Peyton," I drawled, "is he wearing a hairpiece?"

Peyton jabbed me in the side with her elbow. "You noticed that, too? I may have to vote for him just because of his sheer audacity."

Dewey was still shouting animatedly into the bull-horn. While I couldn't make out most of what he said, I definitely heard him finish off with, "…and erase the Witch of Babylon from the face of Odyssey if it's the last thing I do!"

Gluttony turned to Peyton. "The Witch of Babylon?"

Peyton frowned. "He means my sister. Crime and villainy are on the rise in Odyssey. Everyone knows that."

"Sure," I agreed, "but what's that got to do with Portia?"

"Not a thing. But it's politics, Pride. It doesn't have to be based in reality. Anyway, he also says the police department has the wrong man in custody, and the real killer is still on the loose. And of course, he blames my sister for that, too."

Gluttony grumbled and pulled a lollipop from a pocket, unwrapping it noisily. "What makes him think Aaron's innocent?"

Peyton smirked and jerked her head in the general direction of the statue causing all this ruckus. "The Star of the Sea said so. And as far as Dewey's concerned, that's the final say on the matter."

Gluttony stuck the candy in his mouth and smacked his lips wetly. "You ask me, the guy's got a few screws loose."

"People get weird when running for office," Peyton said. "Though I guess Dewey's been weird from the beginning. Anyway, let's get inside before this mob tries to kill me."

Peyton guided us through the crowd to the front steps of City Hall where a dozen camera crews had already set up shop. I had a feeling it was going to be a hectic news week in Odyssey.

As we approached the building, a uniformed man gave Peyton a once over, squinted his eyes, and said, "You're slumming it with the riff-raff today?" His gaze drifted to me, an unfriendly smile on his mouth. "I know who you are. You're from that show. I haven't voted for you, not once. I'm voting for that other one. That *hot* one."

I smiled and gestured with a tilt of my head toward my lollipop-sucking teammate. "And I'm sure Gluttony appreciates your vote!"

The man stammered, red-faced, preparing his objection. But Peyton pushed us through the door, relieving him of any chance to reply. "Don't make a scene," she said, half laughing. "They'll definitely toss us out if they realize I'm not my sister. Can you go to jail for impersonating a city official?"

She didn't wait for an answer, though. She quickened her pace as she guided us down the hall. "Portia's holed up in here."

I opened the door to find Portia draped over a chair behind a large desk covered with scattered papers. Her head lolled back, and her eyes were closed. She didn't open them when she said, "I thought I said I didn't want to see anybody for at least another twenty minutes. Do I need to ask the police chief for a security detail?"

I frowned. "I don't think that will be necessary."

Portia's eyes shot open, and she sat up, folding her hands on the desk. Her face was pinched, and her nostrils flared. Portia and I weren't exactly friends, so I wasn't surprised that she wasn't happy to see me. Her expression softened when she saw her sister, but only for a moment. Because when she saw what her sister was wearing, she said, "Peyton. You didn't."

"I didn't have to say anything!" Peyton exclaimed with a smile. "That police guy outside just let me right in."

"We haven't done that since we were kids! How did you even remember what I was wearing?"

Peyton grinned. "Photographic memory?"

I glanced from Portia to Peyton and back again. They really did look identical. Both women wore blood-red lipstick, their platinum hair pulled into a severe bun at the nape of their necks. The only difference between them was that Portia wore a white shell beneath her gray suit instead of Peyton's pale blue.

"You'd think these idiots would remember I have a twin and ask for identification," Portia grumbled, adjusting herself in her seat. She heaved a heavy sigh and leaned her head to one side. "I suppose it's too much to hope that this is a friendly visit? Please tell me at least one of you brought lunch."

To my surprise, Gluttony stepped forward and shrugged out of his backpack. He eased down the zipper and withdrew a white paper sack, which he tossed on

Portia's desk. "Chicken salad on rye," he said with a bashful grin. "Extra mayo."

While I was busy making gagging sounds (I mean seriously, extra mayo was an affront against humanity if you asked me), Portia tore into the bag, retrieved the sandwich, and practically melted as she bit into it. Her eyes closed in ecstasy. "Okay," she said through a mouthful of extra slimy chicken salad. "You can stay. The rest of you, see yourselves out."

Even I knew that was a joke, so I sat in one of the chairs before the desk. Gluttony took the other one. "Portia, we need to talk to Aaron Burton."

Portia's shoulders slumped, and she swallowed. "You know that's impossible, right?" She took another bite of her sandwich. "He's been arrested for murder." When I didn't respond, Portia dug around in the bag for a napkin. She found one and pressed it daintily to her lips. "Did you hear me? *Murder.* Your friend Aaron hit Tabitha Antoinette in the back of the head with some kind of bludgeon. So."

"He isn't my friend," I said, my voice weary. "But it doesn't matter. It looks to me like you've got a number of problems on your hands. You've got Dewey outside screaming to anyone who will listen that your administration has the wrong guy in custody. You've got a supernatural statue saying the same thing. Tabitha's murder—or, at least, Aaron's arrest for it—is obviously important to the statue. If you let me talk to Aaron, we might be able to find out why and kill all these birds with one stone."

Portia snorted and waved a hand dismissively. "The

statue is the least of my problems. I've got half the city camped outside listening to an angry mermaid preacher who's calling for my head on a platter. Last I heard, he was up two points in the polls! So unless you can solve *that* issue, we have nothing more to discuss."

"What's Aaron saying about the murder?" Gluttony asked.

"Nothing," Portia sighed, deflating. "Nothing at all. On that matter, he is as silent as the grave."

I gave Portia my best Cheshire Cat grin. "Well, then I guess it's your lucky day. I think I can get Aaron to talk. He trusts me."

That got Portia's attention. I saw her eyes flick to her sister as if seeking confirmation that I wasn't lying through my teeth. But then she recovered, recomposing herself and asking, "How do you even know him? You've been in my town half a minute. How many murder cases have you been involved in already?"

"Portia, I brought your sister back to you," I reminded her. "Are you *really* going to turn against me now?"

The interim mayor glanced furtively at her twin, and I saw some of the fight go out of her eyes. She slumped and blew out her cheeks. "So you think you can get Aaron to talk, do you? I have to admit, it would be helpful if you could. He's not saying much beyond 'I didn't do it.' He isn't even saying how he knew the victim. Then again, I notice you aren't telling me how you know *him* either."

"He asked me to look for ghosts in his apartment," I said. It wasn't Portia's business how I knew Aaron, and I usually wouldn't divulge that information. But if cooperating with her got me what I wanted, I'd play 20 Questions for as long as I had to. "I didn't find any, if that was your next question."

A shadow of a smile flickered across her lips, and she dipped her chin. "All right. So you think you can get Aaron to recount what really happened the night of Tabitha's murder. If you got a confession out of him, I'd be eternally grateful."

The last thing I was interested in was Portia's gratitude, but I played along anyway. "Yeah, well. So, when can I see him?"

Portia shrugged. "You can't. Even I can't see him. But I can get you his interview video. I'll send it to your phone."

I blinked. "Can you *do* that? I mean, legally?"

Portia barked out a laugh. "Do you *care?*"

I hesitated, considering the question. "No, I guess not. Okay. If that's the best you can do."

Portia smiled, but it didn't quite reach her eyes. "It's the best I can do. Now, if you'll excuse me, I have a mountain of paperwork to attend to, a campaign to run, and a murder trial to dig my way out of. And you." She turned her attention to her sister, pointing a sharp, slender finger. "Stop pretending to be me. Go home and stay out of trouble. You know I get physically ill when anything happens to you, Peyton. It makes me irritable and foul. We are two of a kind, you and I. That said," she dropped her twin a wink. "You do look great in that suit. Call my tailor and make an appointment. You should have your own."

We were halfway out the door when Portia called out, "Oh, one more thing. Solve your case already. Get that eyesore of a statue out of my hair. Silence her and put her back where she belongs. If she's still running amok in a week, I'll have your necks."

We left the building.

eleven

· · ·

An hour later, I was back at the house, foraging for something to eat, my head stuck in the refrigerator when my phone pinged. It was a video from Portia.

I ran upstairs to find Sloth and Gluttony. Sloth wasn't home, but she'd left a message on the whiteboard outside her room. It said, "Gone to a cuddle therapy session. I won't be home for dinner. Please don't wait up. Thanks."

I sighed and leaned my forehead against Sloth's door. It was good that she was getting some therapy. She was clearly dealing with a lot—first Eleanor's murder and now Tabitha's. But I'd be lying if I said I didn't feel a teeny bit abandoned.

After a minute of feeling sorry for myself, I walked into Gluttony's room, phone in hand. I dangled it before him, wearing a wry smile. "Guess who's in my inbox?"

Gluttony grunted. "Portia sent you that video already?"

I nodded. "I thought we'd watch it together. I tried Sloth's room, but…"

"Yeah, she's out cuddling strangers." He paused, staring off into the distance. "Do you think that's weird?"

"What? Cuddling strangers?"

"Yes," he said. "Do you think it's weird to pay money to have someone snuggle with you? Because to me, it sounds nasty. Like using the blankets they give you on an airplane. Do you have any idea how covered with germs those things are? You ever see a stewardess wash a blanket?"

"I think they're called flight attendants now," I said.

"What they're called is *nasty*," he repeated.

"Gluttony, just the other day I *saw you* eat Greed's leftover french fries right out of the trash," I said, exasperated. "That's way worse than cuddling with a stranger!"

"No, that's different." Gluttony wagged a finger in the air. "Them french fries was still in the box! They hadn't touched any garbage. Greed threw away perfectly good fried potatoes, and I was still hungry! Why are we fat shaming the kitchen witch?"

I prepared my mouth for an argument, but then realized my interest in this conversation couldn't get any lower. "Yeah, it's weird," I said finally. "Now let me Airplay the video to your computer. We can watch it on the monitor."

I selected the first video Portia sent me, titled "Doorbell Camera footage." I hit play.

A grainy, low-contrast image swam into view. I saw a

street lined with modest-looking houses and mid-range cars. A middle-class neighborhood. Nothing fancy, but cozy. Nice. The kind of place you raise your kids. It was early morning, and the street was still.

Then, a house on the other side of the street stirred. Its front door opened, and a man poked his head through the doorway. He ducked back inside only to reappear a moment later with his back facing the camera as he hauled something through the entry.

I already knew what was coming, but I still gasped when I saw it. His hands were hooked underneath Tabitha's armpits as he dragged her through the front door. She wasn't moving. I couldn't see anything visibly wrong with her—no gunshot wounds or blood or anything that obvious. But then I remembered Portia said she'd been murdered by a blunt object.

He hauled her into the front yard. Her skirt caught on a bush, and he gingerly fingered it free before resuming the exercise. He got her halfway across the grassy yard when he suddenly stopped and dropped the corpse. He stood up straight and looked around frantically as if he'd heard something. Then he looked down at the body he'd just hauled from the house, and his hands flew to his face as he stumbled backward, catching his own feet as he tumbled to the ground. He clawed away from the body, scrambling to get his bearings. And once he was on his feet again, he ran off. Tabitha lay motionless on the grass, and the front door remained open, swaying with the breeze.

The video ended, and Gluttony whistled, shaking his

head. "What on earth was that about?" he asked. "What was he trying to do? Get rid of the evidence?"

"That's what it looks like," I said.

"But why leave her on the front yard? And why did he look startled?"

I shrugged. "Maybe something spooked him." I gestured toward the video. "That's the problem with these doorbell cams. No audio."

"And that was for sure Aaron, right?"

I nodded. "Sure looked like him."

Gluttony grunted something noncommittal and waved his hand. "Okay, play the next video. The interrogation."

I hit a button on my phone, and a second later, a low-quality video flickered to life on Gluttony's monitor. It was an image of Aaron alone in an interrogation room wearing a faded gray jumpsuit. He sat at a desk with his elbows on top, his leg bouncing nervously below. He looked up, and a second person entered the room.

"I'm Detective Nicki Wilkes," the woman said. She was short, with curly red hair and a badly fitting suit. She sat down across from Aaron, crossing her legs and folding her hands atop her knee. "So, you're the guy who murdered Tabitha Antoinette."

Aaron fidgeted and ran his hands through his hair. He leaned away from the table, giving his head a decisive shake. I thought he was about to ask for a lawyer, but he said, "I didn't kill anyone."

Detective Wilkes gave a fake smile, her head tilting

provocatively to one side. "We saw the footage, Aaron. *You've* seen the footage. How do you explain it?"

Aaron said nothing, turning his head away and closing his eyes.

"I tell you what." The detective adjusted in her seat, her expression growing softer. "Let's back up. How did you know Ms. Antoinette?"

"I didn't."

"You didn't know her at all?"

Aaron hesitated, a shadow of doubt passing over his face. "I mean…not personally. I know *of* her from television and whatnot. We're in the same industry. I mean, we're both actors, but no, I don't know her."

The detective studied Aaron's profile in silence. Then she said, "Can you tell me what happened that night, Aaron? What were you doing at her house?"

Aaron gazed at the wall, his posture betraying nothing—not fear, not guilt…nothing. When he spoke, his voice was almost monotonous. "I wasn't there. I couldn't have been. I was asleep."

"Do you have an alibi? Anybody who can corroborate that?"

Aaron huffed. "No, I live alone. But it wasn't me. I wasn't there."

Wilkes patted her hair, sighing. "Is that really the story you want to go with, Aaron? You realize we found the weapon at the crime scene, right? It has your prints all over it."

Aaron stared blankly at the detective. "Weapon?"

The detective nodded. "Yes. Your rifle. The AK-47."

"What—?" Suddenly, Aaron laughed, though I

didn't see anything funny about the situation. "You mean the *shotgun?* It's not even real. It's a prop."

Wilkes smiled. "Oh, well, it was real enough to hit her in the back of the head with, wasn't it?"

Aaron stammered, his face going white as a sheet. "Detective, I don't know anything about that. I'm not a violent person. I don't even know Tabitha Antoinette. If the shotgun has my prints on it, that's because it belongs to me, not because I used it to bash that woman's head in that night. *It wasn't me. I wasn't there.*"

"Oh, come on, now, Aaron! Let me help you, okay? Your story is implausible. No, it's *absolutely bonkers.*"

I saw how Aaron tensed, and my heart went out to him. Nobody likes to be called crazy, but especially not people with medicine cabinets filled with mood altering drugs. "Crazy" was likely a stigma he'd been saddled with for a while. Whether the detective knew she'd hit a sore spot or not, I couldn't tell. She dropped her voice a few decibels and leaned in. "Nobody will ever buy your Looney Tunes 'I wasn't there' tale. So why don't you just tell me what happened, and maybe I can help dig you out of this mess."

Aaron looked away, trembling and chewing his lips. "It wasn't me."

"Come on. It's *you* on that video dragging—"

"It's someone who looks like me," Aaron said, suddenly animated. He was looking at the detective with his eyes wide, hands pressed against his chest. "Isn't that possible? I'm adopted—how do we know for sure this isn't a twin or something?"

A smile twitched over the detective's lips. "A long-lost

evil twin theory? You want to plead 'separated at birth?' That's really what you want us to work with?"

Aaron looked away again, swiping quickly along his cheek. "I don't know what to tell you, Detective. It wasn't me. I didn't know Tabitha Antoinette. I had no reason to be at her vacation rental that night. And I certainly never laid hands on her, let alone—"

The door burst open then, and an older woman with sleek, dark hair and an expensive-looking suit strode into the room. "You've got some nerve, Detective Wilkes," she spat without even glancing in the detective's direction. She marched to where Aaron sat and stood before him, hands on her hips. "Really? Talking to the police without your lawyer present? Have I not raised you better than this?"

Aaron tilted his face upward and smiled softly. "Hi, Mom," he said. "I should have known you'd come."

The video ended there.

I looked over to Gluttony, eyebrows raised. "Well? What do you think?"

My housemate puffed out his cheeks and blinked rapidly. "I think your boy is crazy," he said.

I bristled. "Why? Because of the medication I found at his house?"

Gluttony barked out a single laugh and waved at the now-black monitor. "Drugs is the most *not*-crazy thing about this man, Pride! Did you just watch the same videos I did? We *saw* that man drag that woman's body out that house and leave her on the front lawn. And yet he's sitting there talking about he didn't know her, he wasn't there…your boy even brought a *long lost evil twin* into the story. And couple all that with his haunted apartment claim? Yeah! I think that man's nuts!"

I had to admit, it was odd. The footage was taken from the other side of the street, but it was pretty clear—the man on the law was definitely Aaron Burton…

…or at least someone who looked *exactly* like him.

I turned to Gluttony. "Did you notice there's no footage of Aaron going into the house? Just him leaving?"

Gluttony frowned. "Now that you mention it…is that weird?"

"It just means something is missing," I said. "We don't know everything. We need to know what Aaron was doing at the house. Aside from their jobs, what could connect him to Tabitha Antoinette?"

"No way to know," he said. "We'd have to ask him."

"Well, you heard what Portia said," I drawled. "We can't. So, we need to talk to people who know him well. The brother, for a start. Then…a lover? A best friend? We need to find them. We need to learn who Aaron Burton really is."

"Well, right now, we need to talk to Paola," Gluttony said, glancing down at his watch. "We should have already left. But if we leave now, we'll have time to stop by Burger King on the way."

I stared at Gluttony, my eyes wide as saucers. "You're kidding me, right?"

But Gluttony grew serious when he said, "Look, you know I don't never joke about food. Now let's go. I feel a Whopper with my name on it."

twelve

. . .

This time, when we arrived at Paola Barbosa's house, all was quiet. Claudia once again met us at the front door and ushered us in, all smiles and hospitality. "Can I get you something to drink? Perhaps a cold lemonade?"

"And cookies if you have them," Gluttony said, rubbing his hands together. "That would be great. Thanks so much."

Claudia led us into the living room where a woman was waiting for us. She sat in a wheelchair with a red blanket thrown over her knees. She looked just as I'd pictured her—small, thin, with sharp, bird-like features, a pointed chin, small, intense eyes, deep creases permanently crisscrossing her forehead.

When she saw us, she smiled and raised a twisted, arthritic hand. "Well, if it isn't the intrepid investigators." Her voice was rich and sweet, a strong contrast to her hard facial features. "Thank you for returning. Please, sit. Claudia, refreshments, please?"

We took our seats as Claudia bustled from the room.

"So." Paola adjusted in her seat and brought her hand to her throat, fingering a thin gold chain. "I understand you were here yesterday, yes? But Claudia had to send you away because I was indisposed?"

I blushed and looked down into my lap. "It wasn't a problem," I said. "Things happen."

"Of course it was no problem for *you*," Paola said with a sharp laugh. "*You* weren't the one indisposed. Oh, yes, you had to drive here and back for no reason, but you *can* drive, eh? My driving days are long behind me."

If anyone else had said that, I might have thought they were trying to win my sympathy, which is a losing cause because I don't really have sympathy. It takes too much effort to feel someone else's emotions besides my own. But when Paola said it, it didn't feel calculated. She was just stating a fact. "Do you leave the house much?" I asked.

"No. But that's by choice. Don't you go feeling sorry for me."

"I don't," I said. "Leaving the house is overrated."

Paola chuckled. "I agree. I have everything I want right here. Well." She leaned forward, her eyes glinting in the sunlight. "Almost everything. Now. Enough about me. You said you have information for me, isn't that right? Well? Don't keep a girl waiting. I'm not getting any younger."

I reached into my backpack and retrieved the letter I'd received from Arjun. I handed it to Paola wordlessly and held my breath as she read.

Here's what the letter said:

"My dearest Pride and Joy,

They say that to be a mother is to forever walk around with your heart beating outside your body. I don't know if that's true, as you are my first child and you're not here yet. For now, you're safe in my belly, and nothing can harm you. But one day, you will be in the world—exposed, naked, vulnerable. Sadly, I shall not be here to protect you from it. My heart will never beat outside my body. Or at least, not for long.

I'm sorry I can't explain it better. But you were never supposed to be here, and you cannot go where the rest of us are headed. I understand now why you were forbidden. I wish I had made different choices, and now you will pay the price for my imprudence. I'm sorry about that. But I know you will find a way to exist in the world, even thrive. That's what people do. We persevere. We survive. We flourish. But this world is harsh, and I am soft. Perhaps my next passenger will find a way to make us more compatible. I pray for it.

One day, you will find me. We are leaving you behind, but not without the gifts you'll need to return home. By and by, the whole history of who you are will be laid bare. And won't that be such a Joy?

With love always,

Mother."

Paola must have read the letter several times because she sat there holding it far longer than I expected. But when she finished, she looked up, unsmiling. "Do you know what this is?" she asked.

I shrugged. "It sounds like a suicide note."

Paola looked down at the letter, trembling from the tremor in her hands. "Oh, no, you misunderstand," she whispered. "That's not what this is. This is a Dear John letter."

I frowned. "So, my mother was breaking up with me?"

Paola tutted. "Don't be foolish. She wasn't breaking up with *you*. She was breaking up with the world."

I glanced over at Gluttony. His skewed frown and unblinking eyes mirrored how I was feeling—he wasn't buying it. "If you don't mind me saying so, that sounds like a difference without a distinction."

"That's because you don't understand artists," Paola snapped.

At that moment, Claudia returned with a tray of cookies and lemonades. She passed them out and then vanished the way she'd come. "What do you mean by that?" I asked.

Paola heaved a sigh and returned the letter to me. "The woman who wrote that letter didn't want to die. She wanted to escape so she could truly live. This line about finding compatibility—she wanted to live peacefully in the world. She prayed for it." She clucked her tongue. "Though admittedly, I don't know what to make of the 'next passenger' business. Perhaps another pregnancy?"

I glanced at Gluttony for some help deciphering this, but he just shrugged his big shoulders and stuffed a cookie into his mouth. I looked back at Paola and said, "Regardless, this letter turns everything we thought we knew about the commune on its head. In her article, Anne Lovett said everyone vanished suddenly—plates were filled with food, clothing was still in the washing machines. Like they didn't plan to leave. But this letter— this sounds like my mother knew something would happen. Something that would take her and the whole commune away from this world—and from me."

For a while, Paola said nothing. But then she lifted her blanket and grabbed the wheels of her chair, directing herself to a bookshelf where she plucked a framed photo and stared at it, smiling. Then she came to where I sat and pressed the picture into my hands.

The photo showed a man and a woman wrapped around each other in front of Niagara Falls, their faces pressed together like bookends. The woman's hair was disheveled; the man sunburnt. They were both smiling like they hadn't a care in the world. After removing about 40 years from Paola's face, I recognized her as the woman in the photo.

And the man? Well, he was unmistakable.

The man was Sam Lovelace.

"Sam and I were best friends," she began, smiling as she moved back toward the couches where Gluttony and I were still staring at the photo. "We met in art school, of course. We were inseparable. I loved him very much, though the feeling was not exactly reciprocated. At least, not the way I wanted."

"He loved you as a friend," Gluttony said, reaching for another cookie.

"That's right. Youth, however, is full of wondrous optimism, and I believed I could make Sam love me. I prayed for it. I did even more than that." She chuckled until the laughter turned into a rasping cough. "So, you can imagine my consternation when Sam explained that he was gay. He'd never had any interest in women. I was heartbroken, but that was only the first time Sam emotionally devastated me. The next time would be a few years later when he went off to start his commune and refused my plea to come along. We had a huge fight about it, and then he was gone. I never saw him again."

That stopped my heart, and I looked up from the picture, blinking rapidly. "He wouldn't let you join? Why not?"

Paola paused for a long while, taking the photo from my hands and replacing it on the shelf. "He had his reasons. But that's why your story is also my story, you see. You were left behind by a mother and father. I was left behind by my dearest friend. And although I've had my fair share of misery, I've never since experienced anything quite like that loss. That's why I asked you to bring me information. It's not closure exactly. But it's something."

We sat in silence for a moment. Then I asked, "What do you think happened to them? Everyone has their pet theory. What's yours?"

The old woman grinned. "I used to think they accidentally slipped into another dimension. Or perhaps were *taken*. But after reading that letter, I suppose they went willingly."

"Taken into another dimension?" Gluttony leaned back in his seat and shook his head. "Like in *The Twilight Zone?* Why don't more people believe they were kidnapped by a Mexican cartel? That seems much more likely than stepping into another dimension."

I thought Paola might make a snappish remark in reply, but she merely lifted her shoulders in a wan shrug. "Perhaps for you. You live in a reality where cartels are a more likely threat than worlds beyond. Me? I know better."

Our host licked her lips and propped her elbow on the chair's arm, her head twisted to one side as she thought. "I was raised by my aunt. She was eccentric. She chanted spells and danced magic, and I grew up thinking that was normal. I thought everyone knew to spike a man's drink with rosehip oil to make him love them. I thought it was common practice to bury silver under a tree to bring wealth into the home. I thought nothing of laying nightshade at the doorstep to keep out bad luck."

At the mention of spells and magic, Gluttony actually put down the handful of cookies he was holding. "Yo, hold up. Did you know I'm a kitchen witch myself? I never met another practitioner of the art." He said this like he was handing out degrees at a hoity-toity college commencement ceremony. "Are you…are you a witch as well?"

The sculptor winced and waved a hand like she was trying to dissipate a foul odor. "I don't like that word. It sounds fanciful and droll. But I cannot deny that strange things happened to me that did not happen to others. If I had a bad day, it would begin to rain, even if there wasn't a cloud in the sky. When I was happy, the smell of roses wafted from my skin like perfume. And more than once, my anger caused all the electricity in the house—sometimes the whole neighborhood—to go out like *that*." She snapped her fingers with a sly smile. "But I can see you are still skeptical. So, perhaps you'd like a story about the time I was young and silly and fell in love with a neighbor boy. And then you can decide for yourself if I am what I say."

She smiled and sniffed, lifting her chin and squaring her shoulders. "He was a year or two older than I. We shared nothing in common—no friends, no classes, no hobbies. Yet I swooned over him. I couldn't eat for want of him. And then, one day, his parents sent him to boarding school in Switzerland. My heart nearly broke in half, even though he'd never spoken two words to me. My aunt eventually had enough of my mooning and went to the boy's house. She sneaked inside and stole a photograph of him. Later, she presented me with a houseplant. 'Paola, I've enchanted this peace lily with a sliver of that boy's essence,' she said. 'If you give the lily his name, tend to it, love it, and watch it flourish, when that boy returns, he will be yours.'"

I rolled my eyes and made an impolite sound in my throat. "That's a lot of superstitious hooha," I muttered. "That's not how magic works."

Paola's head snapped around, meeting my eyes with an icy gaze. "Well, pardon me. I had no idea I was in the presence of an expert on the arcane arts! If I had known your pedigree, I would have worn something more appropriate." She cast me a dark look, her eyes narrowing. "May I continue?"

I lifted my shoulders with casual indifference, but

really, I felt like a jerk. Nothing will make you feel worse than being called out on your own BS.

"So, I tended that peace lily," Paola continued. "I gave it the young man's name. I doted on it. And it grew and grew and produced the most beautiful blooms. But eventually, as girls do, I lost interest in both the plant and the boy I hadn't seen in a year. And as it happens, if you don't tend to a plant, it will not be long for this world. It was Christmas when I got the news."

The room was so quiet, I could hear the humming of the refrigerator from the kitchen. Gluttony hauled himself forward, massive shoulders bunched up to his ears as he asked through a mouthful of lemony vanilla mush, "About the young man?"

Paola nodded stiffly. "About the young man. There'd been an accident. He never returned home from Switzerland."

"And you think *he* died because the *plant* died," I said.

Again, that curt nod. "I know it. You cannot link two things in this world without one affecting the other. Call it sympathetic magic or quantum physics—it doesn't matter. The principle holds." She was silent for a little while, staring down into her hands curled in her lap. Without looking up, she said, "Worlds beyond what we can see present far more danger than Mexican cartels."

I wasn't sure I agreed with that. Every murder I'd run across came at the hands of real, live humans, not some mysterious unseen force moving us around like chess pieces. But I thought it best not to say that. "Do you think *worlds beyond* are responsible for the Star of the Sea?" I asked finally.

Now Paola smiled and pointed a gnarled finger in my direction. "That statue was my masterwork," she said. "I poured everything into her—my heart, my soul. Sometimes I forgot to eat, forgot to sleep. She became my obsession. Unfortunately for me, I gave it *too* much. And I paid the price for it."

"Paola?" Claudia appeared in the doorway, hands twisting nervously at her chest. Her eyes darted around the room. "Are you all right? I mean—is everything okay here?"

The artist smiled at her caregiver and gave a crisp nod. "I am fine. Thank you." As Claudia dipped her head and left the room, Paola turned her eyes to me. "Where were we?"

"You said you gave the statue too much."

"Of course." Paola's hands fluttered to her temples, then to the base of her throat, then finally back to her lap. She cleared her throat a few times before continuing. "When the sculpture was finished, I was elated. I'd worked hard on her, and she was beautiful. But then something unexpected happened."

Paola's gaze drifted to a window, and she sat motionless, not even blinking. I glanced at Gluttony, but he just shrugged and waited.

"I came to my warehouse one day after an excruciating argument with a former client," Paola said finally. Her voice was light but strained, like she was trying to feign nonchalance. "I needed to make preliminary arrangements for transporting the Star of the Sea to the city. But when I went to take her final measurements, I found she had changed. She was no longer wearing the expression I gave her. She was furious. Her eyes were narrowed, and her lips were pressed into a hard line. Even her body language changed. She was stiff and regal like a virago. I stared at her, hardly able to believe what I was seeing. In fact, I *didn't* believe it." She paused, shaking her head at the memory. "I figured I must be hallucinating. So I went home, retired to my boudoir, and took some sleeping pills. I assumed my exhaustion was getting the better of me. But the next day, I returned to find the statue's expression had changed again. Except now, instead of looking angry, she appeared frightened."

Paola settled back in her chair, and for the first time, she looked frail, as though recounting this story was taxing her. "From that point on, the Star of the Sea refused to keep the expression I gave her. Sometimes she looked happy, other times embarrassed. Still others, distressed. One day, I came to the warehouse to see her expression had changed again. I couldn't take it anymore. I closed my eyes, leaned my head back, and screamed. When I opened my eyes, I saw the statue was also open-mouthed, head tilted back. Screaming."

"She was screaming when she appeared on our yard," I recalled.

"Yes, well. I suppose she's had practice." Paola shifted again before continuing her story. "At that moment, I couldn't overlook the obvious. The statue was mirroring my feelings. You see, in my ardor to craft my masterwork, I gave her too much of myself. She was linked to me. My aunt buried a photograph of a boy in the soil of a houseplant, and afterward, boy and plant were linked in life and death. I gave my heart and soul to a statue." She shrugged and tossed her hands into the air. "I suppose you could say I brought her to life."

Immediately, Brittany Miller's words filled my mind. *"Either we're all being pranked, someone is moving the statue with their mind, we are all imagining this, or the statue is, for lack of a better word, alive."* I was reeling, trying to fit the pieces together. But there was still so much I didn't know.

"Hold on, though." Gluttony leaned back, clasping his hands across his mound of belly. "The statue didn't move for *decades*," he said. "Not her expression, not what she was holding—nothing about her changed. Not until recently."

"Of course not," Paola snorted, eyelids fluttering as her mouth tightened and her brow wrinkled. "You didn't think I would deliver a defective statue to a client, did you? No. I fixed the problem before I turned her over to the city."

"And how did you do that?" I asked.

Now, Paola turned a smug grin in my direction. "I gave her a name. A *proper* name. An identity of her own, so she didn't feel the need to appropriate mine. I called her Luis—I even scribbled her name in black magic marker onto her base."

Ah. That explained the name written on the pedestal. But then I remembered my encounter with Brittany Miller and frowned. "We tried to remove the writing with acetone. It didn't come off."

"I should think not," Paola said. "She always liked that name. Why should she let it go so easily?"

It was a nonsensical answer, but then, the whole scenario was nonsensical. "Okay. But…well, that's a man's name. Why give the statue a man's name?"

Paola tutted, her brow wrinkling in reprove. "Surely you don't believe a collection of *sounds* can be male or female. Neither, for that matter, can a bronze statue, no matter how delicate the features or how perky the breasts. But if you must know, the name feels good on the tongue. Try saying it. Go on. It feels tender and sensual."

Both Gluttony and I sat there a moment, neither of us willing to do as we were commanded. It was too mortifying. But finally, Gluttony gave in. "Luis. Luis. Luis." He turned to me. "She's right. It feels beautiful to say."

I dipped my chin. "I'll take your word for it."

"And anyway," our host continued, "it suited her. Once she had her own name, she found peace. Our link was broken. Her face returned to its original state, and she never again so much as blinked."

"Until recently," I reminded her. "So, what changed? What happened decades later to bring the statue back to life?"

The woman sniffed and shrugged. "I couldn't say with any certainty. But if I had to guess, some kind of new magic has moved into your town. A new magic that stirred my beautiful girl back to life. Perhaps brought to Odyssey by someone like me."

"You mean a *witch?*" Gluttony snarked. I shot him a cranky look, which he ignored.

"Do you *intend* to be rude to the woman whose hospitality you are currently enjoying, or does it merely come naturally?" she shot back.

"Paola, you said you paid the price to create your masterwork," I said, steering the conversation toward safer ground. "What did you mean by that?"

The old woman was still staring daggers at Gluttony, but eventually, she relented and returned her gaze to me. "Some say creating my greatest work drove me mad. You were here yesterday. You likely heard the din from the street. My mind is not entirely my own. But then again, I wonder—is anyone's? Why do we dream of things we cannot understand? Why do we dream at all? Is the mind really ours in its entirety, or is it just on loan from something greater—perhaps from worlds beyond?"

This conversation was getting so far outside my wheelhouse, I felt I might need a passport to get back. But just as I was trying to find a polite way to say I thought maybe she should try talking to someone, an alarm went off somewhere in the house, and Paola's demeanor instantly changed.

"I think that's all I can do for you today," she said archly, sitting up straight and flicking her eyes to the room's entrance. Claudia came in then, cleaning up our refreshments and casting furtive glances in our direction. "I wish I could help further. Now, if you please, it's time for my nap. You can show yourselves out, yes?"

I faltered, wanting to say more but having nothing more to say. I didn't know how much of Paola's tale I believed, but I had no other specific questions, and Claudia was already opening the front door for us. As we made our way out, I was suddenly struck by how little art was in Paola's home. Arjun's house was bursting at the seams with art of all kinds, but Paola's place was austere in comparison.

"Thanks for your time," I called out. Paola didn't respond, so I turned around. She sat motionless in her chair, eyes closed, her head leaning back. "I'll be in touch!" I said more loudly. She gave no response.

As we stepped into the sunlight, Claudia poked her head through the door. "Before you go." She hesitated and dropped her voice. "There's something—"

"Claudia!" Paola called out from the other room, her voice slightly shrill. "My medicine, please. Now!"

The caregiver wavered, eyes still searching our faces. Then she deflated, her gaze dropping. "Have a safe drive."

She closed the door.

thirteen

. . .

A police car was parked in front of Sinful House when we returned. Envy sat on the porch steps, chin cupped between her hands, looking glum and mildly annoyed. She was wearing cutoff jeans and an old t-shirt with a cartoon frog on it that said, "Kiss me!"

Two uniformed officers stood before her, notebooks in hand. They looked young—the guy was tall and skinny, with a long face and big ears. His female companion was small and tanned, with a round face that was probably pleasant under different circumstances. Now, however, her lips were puckered like she'd just bitten into a lemon.

We hauled ourselves from the car and walked across the lawn. As we drew closer, the officers glanced over, shielding their eyes from the sun with their hands. I asked, "Everything all right, Officers?"

"No," Envy answered. She folded her arms across her chest, hands jammed under her armpits. "Everything's not all right. I've been trying to tell the geniuses from Odyssey PD that I don't need their help, but they won't listen!"

The woman cop—her badge read MAYS—gave me a disinterested once over. Then she looked back at Envy, cocking her head in my general direction. "Who are they?"

"The other housemates," Envy said, her voice breathy and growly with exasperation. "They don't know anything. Nobody knows anything. Can't you just —can't you just leave this alone? It was probably just a stupid prank. You know, a stunt for likes and follows. It's not like anybody got hurt."

"What's going on?" Gluttony stepped forward and took charge, placing himself in front of Envy and between the two officers. "What do you mean, nobody got hurt?"

"We got a call from another housemate, a Mr. Greed…" The oafish officer, whose name tag said YANG, glanced down at his notes. "Well, it just says Greed. Mr. Greed presented video evidence of an intruder at this address. We're here to take statements and have a look around."

Gluttony and I exchanged looks. "An intruder?"

"It's nothing," Envy whined again. "Seriously, it's—"

"Why don't you tell us what happened," Gluttony said, "and we'll decide for ourselves if it's nothing. How's that sound? And don't leave anything out, Envy."

Envy glared at Gluttony before finally relenting, her shoulders sagging. "Everything is on Instagram," she said. She fished her phone from her pocket, pulled up her account, and then shoved the phone at Gluttony. "See for yourself."

I peered over Gluttony's shoulder as he played the video. The footage showed a woman's bedroom—Envy's bedroom. The person holding the camera walked over to her closet and began rifling through her clothes. Then they walked to her dresser and opened the top drawer. A man's hand came into view and pulled a pair of Envy's underwear from the drawer. He spread them on top of the dresser and then gave the camera a thumbs up. That's where the video ended.

I looked over at Envy, my mouth hanging open. She was still pouting, arms over her chest, but at least she had the decency to blush. "Envy," I drawled, "someone was in your room going through your undergarments? And you don't think this is a big deal?"

"It's from the same account that's been spying on Envy from the street," Gluttony pointed out, tapping the screen. The user who had posted the video was identified only as AppleJack44, with a cat for an avatar. He tossed Envy's phone back to her. "You have a stalker, and you didn't even call the cops yourself? Greed phoned it in?"

"I did." Greed sauntered through the open doorway, steaming teacup in hand. He looked unruffled—but then, he always looked like that. He was the most nonchalant person I'd ever laid eyes on, and I do not mean that as a compliment. "Envy may not see the danger she's in, but it's patently obvious to me. Assuming none of the other housemates took the video, someone has been in our home. Uninvited. That's a crime."

"You're absolutely right," Officer Yang confirmed, bobbing his head in agreement. "You did the right thing by calling us. If a creeper comes into your home uninvited and rifles through your personal items, it's just a hop, skip, and a jump to them doing something more invasive. Like sneaking in at night while you're sleeping. And then…" The officer shrugged. "Who knows?"

Envy rolled her eyes and flipped her hair over her shoulder. "I'm not worried about anything. It's just one lousy video. Some fans are just…overly enthusiastic, that's all. And you guys are all missing the bigger picture. This whole thing is blowing up my career! Tricia called me this morning and said my numbers are through the roof!"

"Nobody gives a hoot about your numbers, Envy!" I threw my hands in the air, exasperated. "This person has been watching you for weeks. Maybe longer! Too long to chalk it up to a random fan who let his overenthusiasm get the better of him while the rest of us were out investigating our challenges."

Leaning against the door jamb, Greed said, "I don't think this is a random fan, either."

Envy's face flushed hot. "What does that mean? You think someone I know is doing this?"

"I think someone with an *agenda* is doing this," Greed countered. "This is the work of someone who wants something from you, Envy. They've targeted you specifically. I worry this person might be trying to intimidate you. Or worse."

"Worse?" Now, Envy's face blanched, and her lips trembled. "What do you mean, worse?"

"They could try to blackmail you. Or scam you. Defraud you. Swindle you. Take you for everything you have, leaving you destitute and—"

"And I thought Sloth watched too much TV," I interrupted. "Greed, stop. You're scaring her."

"Well, if I may," Officer Mays said, "she should be scared. At the very least, cautious."

"But why should I be scared?" Envy asked. "I mean, Odyssey's finest are on the case now, right?"

The officers exchanged a dubious look. "Well, ma'am, resources are stretched thin right now, you see. You know, what with the statue causing all that chaos and that dead actress and everything?" Officer Yang ran a hand over his face. "We've never had much crime in Odyssey—"

"That's not even remotely true," I countered.

"—so, we just don't have the budget to cover cases like this," Yang went on, ignoring my interruption. "But we've taken your statement, so at least we're establishing precedent. If anything else should happen, we might dredge up enough evidence to take this more seriously."

"Well, despite what all you Scaredy McScaredy-Pantses think, I think this is all very exciting," Envy said. "I mean, it's not every day my life is the center of an investigation!"

I snorted. "Didn't you just hear what they said? There won't be any investigation. We're on our own."

Envy spread out her hands and looked from me to Gluttony to Greed and back again. "Well, you'll all investigate, though, right? I mean, your old buddy Envy might be in danger. And you wouldn't want anything to happen to me, would you?"

Greed tsked and slurped his tea. "I'm afraid I simply don't have time for that. I have a hectic schedule. My publisher has pushed up the deadline for my book. I simply can't spend more time investigating nonsense cases."

Envy's eyebrows shot up. "Nonsense cases? If it's such a nonsense case, then why'd you call the police?"

"Because I thought they'd be competent," Greed answered with a carefree lift of a shoulder. "In any case, good luck to you. I need to get back." He turned and headed back into the house, closing the door behind him.

"Well, ma'am, I think we've done all we can do here today." Officer Mays slipped her notebook away and gestured toward the house. "In the meantime, you guys might want to look into a security system, or—"

"Hang on a second," I interrupted. "Did anybody check the cameras?" I turned to Gluttony and gestured toward the house. "This entire house is basically a set, right? We've got cams and mics in every room. There's no way someone snuck in without getting caught on video."

Gluttony whistled and motioned for me to follow him as he marched into the house. "Let's go find out if our mystery intruder made an appearance on Candid Camera."

While Envy finished up with the cops, Gluttony and I found Craig playing a solo game of foosball in the recreation room and explained the situation. "So, we know we're not supposed to see the raw footage from the house and everything, but—"

"No worries," Craig said. "This is an emergency. Let's see what we can see."

After tapping in a code, Craig retrieved a laptop from a secret nook behind the wall-mounted television. "The video footage captured in the house is sent to a central server," Craig explained as he opened up the computer. "I'm pretty sure I can find the footage taken in Envy's room. What time was that Instagram video posted?"

I opened my phone to discover that I had a missed phone call and a voicemail. In all the excitement, I hadn't heard my phone ring. I made a mental note to check my messages later. I opened the Instagram app and navigated to AppleJack44's account. "Noon yester-day," I said.

"So then, the footage was probably taken yesterday morning while everyone was out working on their tasks. Let's…just…" Craig's voice trailed off as he performed his video voodoo, and a moment later, he clapped his hands and punched the air. "HA! Here it is."

Gluttony and I crammed next to Craig and watched the video now playing on the laptop. A man dressed in black jeans and a black hoodie with the hood pulled over his head walked into Envy's room. Besides the nondescript clothing, he wore dark sunglasses and a surgical facemask. All I could tell from the video was that the person was Caucasian, of medium height and build. I couldn't even be sure it was a man.

"That could be anyone," I sighed, pushing back into the cushions. "Is there any footage from other parts of the house? Maybe he took his hood or glasses off at some point."

Craig tapped around to various videos. There was footage of the man walking through the living room, up the stairs, and down the hallway. There was video of him going into and coming out of Envy's room. But in every frame, his face was entirely hidden.

"Well, at least we know it isn't one of us," Gluttony said.

"It could be Wrath," Craig said. "The height and build are pretty close. And the skin tone's not far off, either."

"That's not Wrath," I snorted. "Wrath wouldn't be caught dead posting Envy's underwear online. It would be an affront to his anti-misogynist sensibilities. Or something."

"Well, if the cops won't take this seriously," Craig said, "that leaves us no choice but to take care of this ourselves."

"Take care of what yourselves? What are you three plotting?" Envy came into the recreation room and flopped down on a beanbag chair across from us. "You're not planning a stakeout, are you?"

She'd said this with a laugh in her voice, but when I looked at Craig, I saw he wasn't joking. "That's exactly what we have to do," he said. "We have to catch this creep before his behavior escalates. And I don't want anyone at the network getting wind of this, either. More oversight from Tricia just means more problems for the rest of us."

"Ain't that the truth," I grumbled. "Okay, so a stakeout to catch the peeping Tom. What do you propose?"

Craig set the laptop aside and rubbed his hands together with glee. "Here's what I think. At first, this dude was taking video from the street. Now he's taking vids from inside the house when we're not home. He's getting braver, and he's gonna want to up the ante. So, here's my plan. What if we lure him into the house and spring on him when he least expects it?"

I nodded. "Yeah, okay. Sure. Lure him into the house how?"

"We get the word out that the house will be empty except for Envy. Then we wait for him."

"We?" I blinked, surprised. "You'd want to help?"

Craig chuckled. "Well, I can't leave it to you, can I? No offense, but you don't exactly look like the grappling type."

He was right about that, and the truth was, it warmed my cockles to think Craig cared enough to put himself in harm's way. Then again, Craig was no stranger to danger. He'd already thrown himself at a gunman to save my life.

Did Craig have a crush on me? But even thinking about that was too mortifying for words, and I flushed bright red at the thought. I waited for the cameraman to continue. But then I realized he was watching me with equally bated breath. "Hold on, Craig," I said. "That's your whole plan? We use Envy as bait, and then we wait?"

"Well, yeah." The cameraman wrinkled his brow. "Did you have a better idea?"

"No, but that's not really a plan," I said. "That's… well, that's just an idea. We need something more concrete. For example, how do we get the word out?"

But as soon as I said it, I already knew the answer. I looked over at Envy and saw that she was thinking the same thing I was. "I'm not going with you," she said before I could even dredge up the courage to ask for her company. "I can't stand that woman. And you can't make me. After all, you guys are the ones scared of little old Creepy McCreepyPants. I'm enjoying my 15 minutes of social media glory, thank you very much."

"Fine," I said. "But when I've saved us all from ruin and embarrassment, you're all gonna owe me one."

"Thank you for your service," Gluttony intoned. "Don't nobody want to see my drawers posted all over the socials. You're doing the Lord's work."

I grunted and got to my feet. "Better not put off till tomorrow what can be done today," I said. "Wish me luck."

Envy chortled and rolled off the beanbag chair. "You're gonna need it!"

fourteen

. . .

All Dogs Go to Odyssey was a pooch salon specializing in toy poodles owned by the infamous Stephanie Jones. Stephanie ran a "community newsletter" where she aired everyone's dirty laundry and frequently opined about Odyssey's steady decline into debauchery. I'd had multiple run-ins with Stephanie, and it was safe to say she and I wouldn't be buying friendship bracelets together any time soon. Still, she was the busiest body in all of Odyssey, and if anyone could get the word out to the masses, it was her.

I braced myself as I walked into the salon. Something about small, yapping purse dogs gave me the willies, and the salon was filled with them. Poodles in every color of the rainbow were getting their fur fluffed and their nails painted. The air smelled like puppy treats and cotton candy dog shampoo.

The bell over the door tinkled as I came in, but Stephanie didn't see me. She was too busy standing behind the reception counter being berated by an irate woman with a helmet of platinum blonde hair.

"Well, I just don't see how this could've happened!" The woman was saying, her hands fluttering in the air. "How do you *accidentally* dye a dog blue?"

Stephanie took a deep breath and gave the woman a world-class customer-service smile. I knew that smile. The lips said, "I'm here to help you any way I can," while the eyes said, "You're lucky murder is a criminal offense."

"I am *so* sorry, Celeste. I really don't know what happened. Whoever took your phone request wrote down sky blue instead of sunshine yellow. It was an honest mistake."

But Celeste wasn't mollified. "Tell me how that makes any sense, Stephanie. Why would I want my Sunshine to be dyed sky blue? Her coloring is *in the name!* Of course I wanted her dyed sunshine yellow. You shouldn't even need to ask!"

Stephanie nodded in faux agreement. "I understand completely. And like I said, I'm happy to give you your money back. We'll do whatever it takes to make it up to you."

Celeste gestured erratically to her freshly dyed sky-blue poodle. "I don't want my money back. I want you to fix the problem! I can't very well walk around Odyssey with a blue dog! What will people think? They'll think I've absolutely lost my mind! They'll say, 'Oh my gosh, did you hear about Celeste and that dreadful blue dog of hers? Whatever was she thinking?'

And they won't be wrong, Stephanie! They won't be wrong!"

Stephanie pinched the bridge of her nose, her indulgent smile faltering. "Celeste. What's done is done. I can't get the blue dye out. It's the hardest color to remove. It has to fade over time by itself. Even if I tried to take the blue out and add yellow on top of it, it still wouldn't work. Your dog would just end up minty green. Would that be better?"

Celeste's eyes were so big, I thought they might pop right out of her face. "Of *course* that's not better, Stephanie! How could that possibly be better?" The woman seemed on the verge of a breakdown, but before she completely lost it, she recomposed herself, her voice lowering an octave. "Well. I see now you aren't going to help me. And that's fine—it's your business, after all. But you will rue this day, Stephanie Jones. You think you have this town wrapped around your little finger because of your little gossipy newsletter. But I'll have you know, I'm at the top of the phone tree for the Odyssey Elementary PTA. I have the ears of all the mothers in this town. And once they hear what you've done to my poor Sunshine, you won't be getting any of their business any time soon. I hope your husband's law firm is doing well. Because after I'm done with you, you'll need that income."

Gingerly, Celeste plucked a whining blue Sunshine from the counter and pressed him to her chest as she stormed past me, leaving a trail of blueberry puppy perfume in her wake as she left the salon. The bell tinkled merrily at her departure.

Stephanie closed her eyes, and her lips moved as she breathed. It looked like she was counting to 10. When she opened her eyes and saw me, however, whatever fleeting calm she'd cultivated went right out the window.

"Well, if it isn't Pride," she said, her voice dripping with disdain. "I was hoping to never see you again. So, what brings you to my humble establishment?"

"I need your help with something," I said.

Stephanie huffed. "Of course you want my help. Nobody ever wants to talk to Stephanie Jones unless they need a favor. Why should you be any different?"

"Well, there's something in it for you, too," I said. "This is about your newsletter."

The goddess of gossip looked taken aback. "You want to help me with my newsletter?"

I clucked my tongue. "Let's just say I think we can help each other. Did you know that Envy has a stalker?"

Stephanie rolled her eyes and leaned her head to the side. "That kind of gossip isn't worth the paper it's printed on," she said.

"Your newsletter is digital," I pointed out.

Stephanie stared at me for a beat or two before waving a hand airily. "Whatever. The point is, no one cares about Envy. No one—"

"Someone does," I interrupted. "Someone broke into our house and posted a video of themselves going through Envy's unmentionables. We already took this story to the cops, but they're too busy with the celebrity murder and the statue to help us catch a would-be predator."

"That ridiculous statue," Stephanie muttered, her

lips curling in a snarl. "You know, my business has dropped 15% since that thing appeared at Julio's. And now it's over at the courthouse? Who needs the distraction of candy-colored pups when you can gawk at a 20-foot abomination? The whole thing is a mess."

"Right," I said quickly, not wanting to get roped into an unproductive conversation about inconvenient art. "Well, that's not why I'm here. We have an idea to catch the intruder red-handed, and we need your help. Can you post a story in your newsletter saying…I don't know, that the house will be empty for a night except for Envy? I have a hunch that if our prowler thinks he can catch Envy alone in the house, he'll jump at the opportunity. And then we'll bushwhack him."

Stephanie made a derisive sound in her throat and glanced around the salon. "I suppose I could do that. In theory."

"I'm sure I can convince everyone to stay at the Grand for a night," I continued. "All except for me, Envy, and Craig, the cameraman."

Stephanie pondered this a moment, her long, lacquered nails tapping the desk. "The trouble is, how to make this newsworthy," she said. "There must be an angle. Otherwise, why would anyone care you were gone for a night?"

"I'll leave that part to you," I said. "But will you do it? This is really important, Stephanie."

The dog groomer paused. "Can I say anything I want?"

I shrugged. "Anything within reason. As long as it's legal and not, you know—slander or libel or whatever.

The last thing we need is to get in trouble with the network. But if you think it'll bait someone into breaking and entering…"

"All right," she said finally. "I'll do it. Give me a couple days, though. I already have some juicy stories in the queue, and I'm not bumping my article on Dewey Delaney's new toupee for some fluff piece on Envy's night alone. I don't want to get scooped."

I couldn't imagine anyone scooping a story about a fake hairpiece, but it definitely wasn't worth arguing over. "Thanks, Stephanie. Will you let me know when the story's live?"

"Of course. Good luck with your home invader. And give Envy my love."

I was back out on the street when my phone buzzed. It was a text from Gluttony that read, "Can you stop by the grocery store on your way home? I got a mad hankering for Dorito's."

I was about to slip my phone away when I remembered I had a missed call. I pulled up my voicemail screen and noticed the call was from Paola Barbosa. I hit play.

"Hello, Pride. This is Claudia. I'm sorry to bother you, but there's something you should know. I don't want to speak out of turn, but it might be relevant to your case. I couldn't help overhearing your conversation with Paola today, and I'm afraid she hasn't been entirely straightforward with you. You should talk to Margot True at the True Love Adoption Agency in Odyssey. Ask her about an arrangement she brokered for Miss Catherine Pennington. I'm sorry, that's all I can tell you. Please don't mention any of this to Paola—she'd never forgive me. Good luck. Oh, one more thing. You'll need to bribe Margot to get her to talk. Your friend is a kitchen witch, right? I'll just put it this way—Margot loves veggie samosas."

The message ended there, and I slipped my phone away as a dozen thoughts ran through my mind. True Love Adoption Agency? I couldn't see how this was relevant to my case, but any lead was better than no lead. I pulled up the website for the adoption agency. The office was located not far from the house, but it didn't accept walk-in appointments. Under normal circumstances, that might be a problem. But thanks to Claudia, I had an advantage.

I navigated back to Gluttony's text and typed, "You feel up to making vegetable samosas tonight? Maybe with a little magic baked in?"

The response came seconds later. "Always. I'll send you a list of ingredients I need."

———

The following afternoon, Gluttony, Sloth, and I arrived at the True Love Adoption Agency. Sloth was chewing the end of her pigtail, fretting over our lack of appointment. "It says plain as day on the website. We need an appointment."

"We don't have time for that," I explained. "We're about to run out of time on our case. And anyway, you trust Gluttony's magic, don't you?"

Sloth turned her big, gray eyes to Gluttony and grinned. "Completely."

"Ok, then," I said. "Let's go inside. And get your hair out of your mouth. For goodness sake."

The True Love Adoption Agency was in a posh building a few blocks away from where the Star of the Sea was still holding court for the civic-minded residents of Odyssey and their out-of-town looky-loo counterparts. This part of town was peaceful. Aside from the ghost I saw floating around the parking lot—died of old age by the looks of her—it was downright pedestrian.

True Love was on the fourth floor. Their lobby was empty, and the front desk was staffed by a dark-haired young woman with a septum piercing and too much eyeliner. At the moment, she was captivated by her own fingernails.

"I'm sorry, but I can't help you if you don't have an appointment," she was saying, staring down at her nail beds. "Ms. True is with a client right now, and—"

"No, she isn't," Sloth interrupted. "No, there's no one else in the office beside us."

The receptionist looked up. "Sorry?"

"Well, I would hear their thoughts if there was anyone else in here," Sloth explained. "And there isn't. I just hear our thoughts, yours, and Ms. True's. Ms. True is thinking about grabbing lunch, and wouldn't you know it?" Sloth held up a picnic basket. "We brought some."

The receptionist leaned back in her chair, unimpressed by Sloth's mindreading routine. "Can I make an appointment for you? I think Ms. True has some time next—"

A door opened down the hall, and a woman stepped into the corridor. She was older—well past retirement age. Still, she looked sharp as a tack. Silver hair was cut into a stylish bob framing a thin, brown face with a prominent chin and high cheekbones. She was dressed in a navy pantsuit and wore delicate, tasteful gold jewelry. She looked like the head mom at a PTA meeting —if head moms were old enough to have adult grand-children. She brushed past us to stand before the recep-tion desk. "Gina, I'm just gonna run down to JB's for a sandwich before my next meeting. Do you want me to pick up anything for you?"

Gina opened her mouth to respond, but Sloth stepped between them, flashing her best smile. "Are you Ms. Margot True?"

"I am. Can I help you?"

"I was wondering if we could have a moment of your time," Sloth asked. She glanced at Gina, who was glowering at us with a disapproving frown. "Could we just step into your office for a minute?"

Margot offered Sloth an apologetic smile. "I'm sorry, but I'm just stepping out to lunch. If you'd like to make an appointment—"

Sloth lifted the picnic basket once again. "I wouldn't dream of taking up your lunch hour," Sloth breathed. "Do you like Indian? We have a basket full of veggie samosas. Homemade!"

Margot stammered, her eyes flitting from the basket back to Sloth's face. Sloth lifted the lid just enough for the toe-curling aroma of curry, fried dough, and hot potatoes to waft into the room. My belly growled at the delicious scent, and Margot's stomach rumbled in response. Eventually, she shrugged in defeat even as her face broke into a warm smile. "Well, it would be a tall task for me to resist home-made Indian food." She glanced down at her watch. "I don't have a lot of time, but I can give you about 15 minutes. Will that work?"

Sloth nodded, and we followed Margot into her office. The woman closed the door behind us and gestured for us to take our seats. While Margot moved around some paperwork, Sloth fished around in her picnic basket for a plate she'd already prepared. She gave this to Margot, who beamed as she accepted it, eyes growing wide as saucers.

"I don't know if I've ever had homemade samosas before," she purred, rubbing her hands together in expectation. "These look amazing. Did you make them yourself?"

"I did," Gluttony answered, hand raised. "They're my specialty."

I chuckled. He wasn't lying about that exactly—but it wasn't the crispy pastry or the delectable, savory filling that made these samosas stand out. (And believe me, they were absolutely, astoundingly delicious.) Gluttony had imbued every bite with what he called "The gift of gab." I waited for Margot to take a bite, and when her eyes rolled to the back of her head, I knew we had her.

"We don't want to take too much of your time," I reiterated. "We just have a few questions about an adoption you brokered for a woman named Catherine Pennington."

Margot dabbed at her mouth with a napkin before answering. "I'm sorry, but it's wildly unethical for me to discuss the details of an adoption without consent from the families involved. Not to mention, I don't even know who you are." She paused. "Who are you?"

"I'm Pride," I said, "and these are my friends, Sloth and Gluttony. We're contestants on a reality TV show —*Sinful House*. Have you heard of it?"

"I've heard of it," Margot said, nodding, "but I've never seen it myself."

"Well, we're looking into the Star of the Sea—trying to understand why she's been traveling around," Gluttony began. "And we got an anonymous tip to talk to you."

"Well, like I said, it's highly unusual to give out information about an adoption without going through the proper channels, but I suppose this one time won't hurt anyone." Margot took another huge bite of samosa. "After all, that adoption happened decades ago."

"Decades ago?" I repeated. "Do you remember much about it?"

"Yes, because it was an unusual circumstance." Margot set her lunch aside and took a breath, crossing her legs and folding her hands atop her knee. "Catherine Pennington came to me wanting to adopt a newborn baby from an unwed mother here in town. In those days, Odyssey was still a very conservative place, you see—being an unwed mother wasn't as accepted as it is today. The problem was, adoption is a highly regulated service. And while it's much more common today, placing a child with a non-traditional family was almost unheard of at the time."

Sloth raised an eyebrow. "Non-traditional family?"

Margo nodded. "That's right—Ms. Pennington, the potential adopting mother, was also unwed. However, several mitigating circumstances ultimately swayed my decision. First, Catherine and the birth mother knew each other. It has always been important to me to assist birth mothers as much as possible, and she wanted her child to go to Ms. Pennington. Second, Catherine's family was quite wealthy. I suppose you've heard of Pennington Bank?"

I shook my head. "No, but the clue is in the title. I get your point."

Margot smirked and dipped her chin in a tacit nod. "Third, Ms. Pennington was engaged, so she ultimately wouldn't be a single mother. Plus, her fiancé also came from a wealthy family. So, considering all these factors together, I was persuaded that the situation might be amenable for the child in the long run. And of course, the child's welfare was my number one concern."

"So, the adoption went through," Gluttony prodded.

"It did. As far as I know, everything worked out for the better. Ms. Pennington married her sweetheart, Nathan Burton, and together they formed the Burton Foundation. I suppose you've heard of that, right?"

"I haven't," Sloth said. "But we're new in town, so maybe—"

"Wait a minute." I leaned forward in my seat, my heart rate picking up as recognition dawned. "The adoptive mother was Cate Burton? The philanthropist civil rights attorney?"

Margot grinned, nodding jovially. "Yes! So you've heard of her, at least."

I sat back, gobsmacked. I recalled her name from the newspaper article I'd read at Aaron's house the night I perused his place for ghostly activity. "Yeah, I've heard of her. Ms. True—who was the birth mother in this case?"

Now, Margot fidgeted, clearing her throat and averting her eyes, clearly wrestling with her conscience. But in the end, Gluttony's gab magic won out, and she said, "Her name was Paola Barbosa."

fifteen

. . .

"I'm sorry, but I absolutely do not have time for this."

Cate Burton was striding through the parking lot's unruly crowd like a soldier heading off to war. Thanks to the leftover gabby snacks, Sloth's mind-reading, and the general incompetence of her staff, we'd tracked Cate Burton to the courthouse.

Of course, we should have known to find her there. A quick perusal of the top news stories in Odyssey showed that Aaron Burton's arraignment was this morning. He'd pleaded not guilty to a charge of second-degree murder. The reactions on social media were varied:

MakeOdysseyGr8Again wrote: "This is what happens when mothers give sons girly names. And she didn't even bother to spell it right! Our boys need strong role models and masculine monikers. Otherwise, young men become predators! And by the way, ERIN is Irish for IRELAND. We should be promoting AMERICA!"

Eatmycoleslaw wrote: "Let his mommy and daddy buy him a Not Guilty verdict and save us taxpayers the cost of this trial. Who even was Tabitha Antoinette, anyway?"

Hangryhangryhymnals wrote: "Our thoughts and prayers are with you, Aaron!"

DeweyDelaneyforMayor wrote: "This whole trial is a conspiracy to cover up the TRUTH about ODYSSEY! PLEASE DONATE TO MY CAMPAIGN! I am accepting donations on my BuxApp, username 2Good2B4Gotten."

I was pretty sure that last one wasn't the real Dewey Delaney. Especially since his social media account wasn't even verified. But the fact that I wasn't 100% sure goes to show what a circus the mayoral campaign was becoming.

Anyway, back to Cate. She was dressed in trial-ready attire—a dark, well-tailored suit with a pinstriped silk blouse accompanied by low-heeled shoes that clacked along the pavement. Perfectly coiffed salt and pepper hair was styled away from her face, and she wore modest makeup. She was probably an attractive woman in different circumstances. But with her mouth twisted into a snarl and the dark circles beneath her eyes, she didn't look like anyone you wanted to reckon with.

I practically had to jog to keep pace with her. Sloth and Gluttony were hopeless—they were still bogged down by the crowd, which had grown impossibly denser since last we'd visited. "Ms. Burton, I just have one question. Which of your sons did you adopt from Paola Barbosa? Aaron or Cary?"

Cate faltered, swiveling her head to really look at me for the first time. Then she grabbed my arm, dragging me out of the crowd to a somewhat secluded patch of shade beneath a tree. "Who are you?" she hissed. "What do you want?"

"I just want to talk," I said. "I'm not a reporter or anything like that. I'm just trying…I'm just trying to…"

Cate squeezed harder, eyes flashing bright with rage. "Trying to what?"

I clenched my jaw, suddenly embarrassed. I was trying to solve the mystery of a stupid traveling statue while her son was about to face a jury trial for murder. The importance of what was on her mind versus mine was so stark, even I couldn't bring myself to tell the truth. I didn't want to come off as the most cold-hearted or tone-deaf person in Odyssey, even if half the time I probably was.

So instead, I said, "I know both your sons. And I know this must be a terrible time for you, but please. I need your help. I don't think Aaron did this, but something's not right with him, either. If I could just have a moment of your time…"

Cate swore and tipped her face to the sky. She was so still and quiet that I thought maybe she was praying. But finally, she spoke. "When Aaron was little, I used to say to him, 'It doesn't matter where you came from. All that matters is that I'm your mama, and I love you.'" She choked out a sound approximating a laugh and wiped her nose with the back of her hand. It took me a moment to realize she was crying. "But that was a lie. Or maybe it wasn't a lie, exactly—I was just wrong. I didn't think what happened to Paola would affect Aaron. But now, I don't know. I just don't know."

By now, Sloth and Gluttony had finally caught up with us, but they hung back, probably so they didn't overwhelm Cate, who was wiping frantically at her face and sniveling as she tried to collect herself. I retrieved a packet of tissues from my backpack and pressed them into Cate's hand. She accepted them graciously.

"So, it's Aaron," I said. "He's Paola's son."

"He's *my* son," Cate shot back. "He's *my* baby. I would do anything for my children—anything. But I just…you can't protect a person from their own DNA. You just can't."

"Can you tell me what you mean by that?" I asked. "What happened to Paola?"

Cate gave another dark chuckle as she dabbed at her eyes. "Have you met her?"

I nodded. "Just once. She claims she's connected to worlds beyond."

Now, Cate's chuckle rang true, and she blew her

nose, a ghost of a smile flitting past her lips. "Yes, well, she claimed a lot of things, and you never know what's true and what's fancy with her. Her mind is…" Cate shrugged, and she glanced down at her feet, giving her shoulders a tiny lift. "Well, she's an artist. I suppose lots of them have madness in their blood." She laughed again, but it was dry and brittle and laced with more than a bit of sadness. "My father was Odyssey's mayor at the time that statue was commissioned. That's how I knew her. She came to our house a half dozen, dozen times to discuss the project before it began, and many times during the course of the work. My parents were wealthy, but they were kind. They liked all kinds of people."

"Maybe that's where you get it from," I said. "The philanthropy, I mean."

She shrugged. "I like to believe I am who I am because I *made* myself this way, but you're right. You can't deny genetics." She sniffled and shook herself, choosing another tissue from the pack. "Paola got ill when she was working on the Star of the Sea. Morning sickness, the midwife said. Paola didn't tell anyone she was pregnant—she even went so far as to hide it. She didn't want anyone telling her to stay off her feet and rest. She was ornery that way. However, morning sickness is the most inaptly named malady of all time. She was sick constantly—morning, noon, and night. Yet Paola didn't let it hold her back. She never took days off. She powered through her illness and weakness to deliver what she considered her masterwork."

"She must have been a very strong woman," Sloth

put in, taking a tentative step forward. "I go down for a nap if I get so much as the sniffles."

"She was," Cate hedged, "but she was also troubled. I don't know if she ever had an official diagnosis. I just know there were days where she wasn't herself—she talked to people who weren't there. She'd shout, cry, throw things..."

Cate's voice trailed, and I recalled the first time Gluttony and I had gone to Paola's. We'd stood in the sunshine outside her home while someone inside threw things, hollered, wept. It seemed little had changed. Paola was still wrestling with whatever demons plagued her.

"Anyway, to make a long story short, when the baby came, she was weeks away from completing the statue. She was utterly spent emotionally, mentally, and physically. She didn't believe she could overcome her illness to be the kind of mother she wanted for her son. So she asked me to take him, and I said yes."

"And what about the father?" Sloth asked. "Was he in the picture at all?"

Cate faltered, her cheeks and ears growing pink. "I'm afraid I can't discuss the father. Paola didn't want Aaron to know anything about his parentage. I feel guilty enough discussing Paola with you." Cate cleared her throat and gestured to the crowd behind us with a lift of her chin. "These people are only interested in the Star now that she's become a spectacle. But the Star of the Sea was always important to me because of what she represented. That's why I did that interview with the

Trident. I had to stand up for Aaron's heritage, even if he doesn't *know* it's his heritage."

I spread my hands out, imploring. "But why didn't Paola want him to know about her? She's just a twenty-minute drive away! They could have a relationship! They could—"

"It wasn't what she wanted," Cate said, her voice suddenly hard. "Look, not that it's any of your business, but my son has always struggled with his mental health. From the time he was a child, psychologists and therapists have always been part of our family repertoire. I taught the boys that mental health struggles are the result of healthy individuals living in a broken society—not the result of their DNA. Nature versus nurture."

She looked so smug and sure of herself, which I thought was funny because I was pretty sure this was a both/and situation, not an either/or. Why are people always content to see the world in black and white when almost everything is some shade of gray? Even I know that. But in any case, I wasn't interested in having a philosophical debate with Cate Burton in the parking lot, so I sidestepped the whole thing by asking, "What's that got to do with Paola?"

"I never wanted Aaron to think himself limited by her genetics. Do you understand?"

At that moment, I understood three things:

1. Paola's estrangement from her biological son didn't sound like her choice. It sounded more like Cate wanted to exert some weird control over her son's mental health narrative;

2. Cate didn't really understand that a frank conversation about one's mental health could be very healing for some people, and

3. I didn't especially like Cate Burton. I wasn't overly fond of control freaks in general, but I was especially less thrilled about people who treated mental health like something to be embarrassed about. If Aaron had known his biological mother struggled with her mind, would it have helped?

Maybe. Maybe not. But it was no use navel gazing over what could have been, so I redirected the conversation. "All right. So, back to the adoption. Your family was fine with it?" I asked.

Cate nodded and squared her shoulders. Her tears had dried, and she once again looked every bit the fierce lawyer I believed her to be. "Of course. More importantly, my husband-to-be was fine with it. Nathan and I adopted Aaron and Cary within weeks of each other—we wanted Aaron to have a sibling. And they've been thick as thieves ever since."

"And Cary is Aaron's agent now, isn't he?" Gluttony asked, stepping into our circle. "So they're not just brothers, but business partners."

Cate snickered, eyes rolling. "That whole agent thing is such a disaster. I love Cary, but...well, he's trying. Between the two of them, Aaron got far luckier in the smarts department. Nathan and I have always had to pay special attention to Cary. It's like he can't hack life on his own. The moment he runs into trouble, he comes crying to me for help."

She paused, dabbing at her eyes with her fingers. "But one thing I can say in Cary's favor—he adores his brother. He just wants Aaron to be happy, and Aaron doesn't know what he wants. Painting, acting…" She shook her head, frowning. "He's always jumped from interest to interest. This acting thing wasn't even Aaron's idea. It was cooked up by that girl from the dry cleaner, the one he recently broke up with. They were living together over at Hightide, and she was always having people over to run lines or whatever these aspiring actors do. She just kind of roped Aaron into it."

Something she just said snagged my attention. "You said Aaron and his girlfriend lived together at Hightide apartments?"

Cate nodded, eyes squinting with sudden apprehension. "That's right."

"And she worked at a dry cleaner?"

"She did. Why are you asking?"

In my mind's eye, I was back at Aaron's apartment, wandering the rooms looking for ghosts. I hadn't found any paranormal activity, but I did find a bag of art supplies in his bedroom. I recalled the lettering on the bag—Parsimonious Art Supply. In the kitchen, I'd found a half-eaten sandwich on the counter. It was still wrapped in the paper from the deli—the deli at JB's Grocery. I recalled the dry cleaning I'd found in the closet—undoubtedly from Tigh's Dry Cleaning.

In other words, all places the statue had appeared over time.

"Ms. Burton, is Aaron a server at Surfside Grille?"

The woman nodded. "Yes. We cut the boys off financially some time ago to help them build character. And Aaron's always been so proud. He likes to pretend he can take care of himself."

I didn't care about the Burtons' economic arrangements or the character-building lessons of Odyssey's embarrassingly rich. But I *was* interested in connecting all the dots of this mystery. "Does Aaron frequent Sailor's Drink and Sink?"

Again, that careful nod. "He and Cary play trivia down there every Friday. Sometimes Nathan and I join in."

A tingle ran up my spine. "And let me guess—the drive-in, Flix on the Rocks? Did you take the boys there as kids?"

Cate's mouth twitched open, and her face darkened. "What is this? You said you weren't a reporter. Why are you asking me these things? How did you—"

"It's Aaron!" I turned to my companions, hardly able to contain my excitement. "The Star of the Sea has appeared at all Aaron's favorite haunts. I'm not exactly sure what the statue was doing at Julio's, but otherwise, it fits. The art supply store, the dry cleaner, the grocery." I counted off these locations on my fingers. "Aaron had recently been to all those places. I saw the evidence in his apartment. And now that we know Paola was his birth mother…it all makes sense. Aaron and the statue are linked."

"But how?" Sloth asked, spreading her hands out before her. "Paola said she accidentally linked the statue to herself because she poured her heart and soul into it. But Aaron had nothing to do with the sculpture."

"Well, she was pregnant with him when she worked on it," Gluttony mused aloud. "So maybe there was some kind of transference…?"

I turned back to Cate. "Paola said that when she was young, her mood affected her surroundings. If she got angry, the power went out. If she was sad, it would rain. Does Aaron have any abilities like that?"

For a moment, it looked like Cate would answer. But then a cloud passed over her face, and she shook herself from her trance. "I really have to go. I have a trial to prepare for." And without another word, Cate Burton shouldered past me and, a moment later, ducked into her Range Rover and disappeared.

sixteen

. . .

On the drive home, Gluttony opened the glove compartment, pulled out a bag of licorice and ripped it open. "So we know Aaron's responsible for the statue. Any theories as to why or how?"

The radio was playing something jaunty, and I tapped my fingers on the steering wheel in time with the tune. "I don't think he even knows he's doing it. He was pretty freaked out about the idea of a ghost in his apartment. I think if he knew he was psychically linked to a statue, he'd find the prospect of a ghost a lot less concerning."

From the back seat, Sloth said, "Assuming the ghost thing was real to begin with."

"It was real," I said. "I'm sure of that. I saw things when I touched him. I felt how scared and confused he was."

"In that case, I wonder if the ghost thing and the statue thing are connected."

Gluttony shrugged, stuffing two whole lengths of

licorice in his mouth. "I still think he's sleepwalking," he said. "What the guy needs is a better doctor and maybe a girlfriend. There ain't nothing the love of a good woman can't cure. And some home cooking can't hurt. Did y'all get a look at that kitchen? I don't think that man's ever turned on a stove in his life. How you gonna get a good night's sleep when you're living on take-out your whole life?"

The song on the radio ended just as my phone buzzed with a text from Stephanie Jones. I tapped it open and read it. It said, "FYI, I just sent out the news-letter with your story in it. Please make sure the house is vacant tonight. Don't turn me into a liar!"

I sighed. So much for giving me a heads up. "Looks like we need to get everyone out of the house tonight. Stephanie published the story about the house being empty," I said.

"She sure did," Sloth confirmed. "It's right here in my inbox."

I quirked an eyebrow. "You subscribe to Stephanie's newsletter?"

"Of course I do." Sloth brought her phone close to her face, squinting down into the screen. "Whoa, Nelly. Envy is gonna be super unhappy when she reads this."

My hands gripped the steering wheel so hard, my knuckles turned white. "Why? What does the article say?"

Sloth giggled. "Want me to read it out loud?"

"Not really," I sighed. "But do it anyway."

Sloth cleared her throat dramatically and began to read.

Subject: Sinful House gets a host of unwanted new roommates

Unless you've been living under a rock, you already know that Odyssey is hosting 7 undesirables in one of our much-coveted beachfront neighborhoods. Known as the 7 Deadly Sins, these so-called witches and psychics are competitors on a cheesy reality TV show where they solve crimes and mysteries. Not that they've proven themselves especially useful. In fact, they've caused more harm than good. My astute readers will remember the havoc two cast members caused in the grocery store recently. Drama seems to follow the contestants wherever they go.

However, the tables appear to be turning. Drama has finally invaded Sinful House itself. In what can only be called a righteous twist of fate, one cast member has come down with a terrible case of head lice. Although she likes to think of herself as a social media princess above reproach, Envy has contracted a highly communicable nuisance in those long, luscious locks of hers. Bringing a parasite into the house is bad enough, but worse is Envy's attitude about the whole thing.

"I don't see what the problem is," Envy says. "People get head lice all the time. It's nothing a trip to the salon can't cure."

While Envy might think her infestation isn't that big a deal, her housemates disagree. Until Envy gets her 'visitors' sorted out, the other Sins are taking up residence in an alternate, undisclosed, bug-free location for the evening.

"They've only given me one night to get the lice removed," Envy whined to our source. "After that, they said I'll have to move out of the house! It's discrimination is what it is! Unfortunately, none of the local human salons have lice-pickers on staff. The only place that will take me is All Dogs Go to Odyssey! Can you imagine my humiliation? I have to get my lice removed at the *dog groomer!*"

As much as I hate to defend any of the house-mates, it must be said that head lice actually don't make their homes in dirty hair. They prefer nice, clean shafts to lay their eggs. So, kudos, Envy—your gorgeous locks are lice approved! We look forward to seeing you at All Dogs Go to Odyssey! The lice picking is on us!

That's it from me, friends! As always, stay shiny and don't get too close to Envy,

Stephanie

I sat in stunned silence. I don't know what I expected, but it wasn't a story about Envy's unfortunate case of head lice. Finally, I let out a low whistle and said, "I guess we'll cross the Envy bridge when we come to it. In the meantime, can one of you text everybody at the house and tell them to pack up? And then can the other one of you make the reservations at the Grand?"

"Reservations are already made," Gluttony said. "We just got a group text from Tricia. Seems she's also subscribed to Stephanie's newsletter."

"Wonderful," I grumbled. "Then can somebody text the house?"

"Done," Sloth said, still peering into her phone. "Greed is organizing everyone now. Lust says we need to make sure she gets a suite. And Wrath says he'd like to be compensated for the inconvenience of missing out on tonight's raid, whatever that means."

"Tell him I'm sure he can bring his gaming rig with him to the hotel," I said.

Sloth yawned and smacked her lips. "He says he doubts the internet will be fast enough. He's worried he'll just get one-shotted into oblivion."

I didn't know what that meant, and I didn't bother to ask because just as we pulled into the driveway of Sinful House, Envy came tumbling out the front door looking like heck on wheels. I knew right then and there I was in for it.

She was holding her phone aloft, shaking it as I got out of the car. Her face was red with fury, and snot trickled from her nose. She'd apparently been crying. "Did you see this?" she screeched. She made a beeline for me, shoving her phone in my face. "Did you see this diabolic trash garbage Stephanie Jones sent out about me?"

"I saw it," I said, taking Envy by the arm and guiding her back to the house. "Or rather, Sloth read it to me. And keep your voice down. We don't want to cause a scene."

"Well, too late for that!" Envy thundered. "Everyone is going to be talking about this if they aren't already! Pride, you said you'd take care of this! Why did you agree to let her print such vile, horrible, ridiculous lies about me?"

"I had no idea what she was going to print," I explained. "I just told her—"

"*What do you mean you didn't know?*" Envy was still shouting as I dragged her into the house and slammed the door behind us. "You didn't give her a script? You just let her say whatever she wanted? Didn't it occur to you she'd have a *field day* writing a story about why I was left alone in the house? Didn't you realize she would go to these lengths to embarrass me?"

"No, I didn't," I admitted. "I had no idea she'd write something specifically to embarrass you. How could I know that?"

"Well, you've met her!" Envy threw her hands in the air, her eyes once again welling with tears. "She's a viper, Pride! A cold-hearted, mean-spirited old wench! Oh, just wait until I get my hands on her. I'll wring her scrawny little neck!"

"You won't do anything of the sort," I said. "Look, this was low, even for Stephanie. And I understand why you're mad. But don't forget she did us a favor. If your stalker takes the bait and we catch him, this will all have a happy ending."

"For *you*," Envy whined, fresh tears falling down her cheeks. "I'm the one that'll have to live with the stigma of head lice. What will my fans think? Oh, I'll be the laughingstock of social media! My ratings will plummet! I'll never recover from this. Never!"

And with that, Envy ran up the stairs. I heard her door slam when she reached the top.

I sighed and flopped down on the couch. Greed

came into the room, knapsack in hand. "I take it Envy saw the article."

"She's going to be impossible to live with," I said.

"I'm sure she'll get over it. So. Do you think it will work? Your ruse?"

I shrugged, sighing out my frustration. "I have no idea. Who knows if her stalker even reads the newsletter?"

Greed tittered, a condescending smile twisting over his mouth. "Everyone in Odyssey reads that newsletter."

"I don't."

Greed's smirk deepened. "Very well. Everyone but you. Well, I need to finish packing. Good luck tonight." He paused, his smile falling away as he added, "You know, I hope you catch him. I really do. I know Envy thinks we're all being overprotective and harshing her vibe, but…" He grimaced, shaking his head. "He was in our *home*. He means business. This cannot stand."

"I know, I know." I leaned back into the cushions and closed my eyes. "Tell me something, Greed. If you had known at the beginning what being on this show would mean for your joy and sanity, would you still have done it?"

Greed clucked his tongue. "Of course. I've never been more satisfied in all my life. The book deals alone are worth the price of celebrity. Though I understand your concern."

I half-smiled. "Is my stress that evident? I feel like it's giving me wrinkles."

"It's giving you more than that," Greed said, his tone somber. "I've seen your future, Pride. From here on out, everything changes for you. Whatever you think you feel now is just the tip of the iceberg. This show is your Pandora's Box. And you've left it sitting wide open."

I opened my eyes, ready to ask Greed what that was supposed to mean. But he'd already gone.

———

Lying in wait for our predator would have been more fun if Envy were speaking to me.

Hours after everyone else had packed up the cars and retreated to the Odyssey Grand Hotel, Envy and I were holed up in her room with the lights out. That was Craig's idea—he said if the house looked asleep, the stalker might be emboldened.

I'd thought it was a great idea when he suggested it, but now that I was sitting in the corner with my knees pulled up to my chest listening to a podcast in the dark, I wasn't so sure. Envy was sprawled out on her bed, watching something on her tablet and steadfastly ignoring me. Craig was next door—Envy's room was too small for the burly man to be comfortable while we waited. But he'd assured Envy that all she needed to do was shout, and he'd be on the intruder in two shakes of a lamb's tail.

I assumed that meant quickly.

I glanced at the clock. It was a little past 1 a.m., and I was starting to get drowsy. I plucked an earbud from my ear and cleared my throat, hoping to invite Envy's attention. When that didn't work, I spoke into the darkness. "Hey, Envy?"

She didn't answer.

"Well, I know you haven't gone deaf in the past few hours, so I assume you can hear me," I said. "I just wanted to say—you're being a really brave sport about this. And about the lice—"

"Don't."

"I was just going to say I'll find a way to make it up to you."

Envy only grunted in response.

I was about to put my earbud back in when I heard a creak.

It sounded suspiciously like a footstep.

I froze, ears cocked toward the door. Envy must have heard it, too, because she slid her tablet soundlessly beneath her blanket and rolled to her side, pretending to be asleep. I held my breath, still and silent as a shadow as we waited.

A moment later, Envy's bedroom door creaked open.

A man stepped inside. He was dressed in black sweatpants with a matching hoodie just as he was in his underwear video. He paused in the center of the room and removed something from his pocket. Carefully, he stepped toward Envy's bed. He paused again at the edge, then lifted the object he'd retrieved. It was his phone. He pushed a button and framed his shot so Envy was centered in the middle. He leaned down to get a close-up.

I waited about three seconds and then made my move. I shouted, and Envy bolted upright, kicking the phone from the intruder's hands. He screeched as the device flew across the room. I leaped from my corner, grabbing the intruder around the ankles. He stumbled backward and crashed hard to the floor. At the same time, Envy's door burst open, and bright light streamed through the doorway as Craig flung himself inside. He grabbed the interloper by the collar and hauled him to his feet, knocking off the dark sunglasses in the process.

Wordlessly, Craig snatched the surgical mask from the man's face and threw back his hoodie. When we saw the man's face, we gasped.

"Cary?" I croaked.

Cary Burton blinked rapidly, his eyes adjusting to the light. He wasn't a big man under the best circumstances, but being gripped at the throat by over 6 feet of pure muscle, he looked like a chihuahua. His jaw trembled, and his lips quivered as he tried to make words. His voice broke when he spoke. "Please," he said. "Please, I can explain."

From her perch on the bed, Envy's eyes grew wide as she looked from Cary to me and Craig. "You know this creeper?"

"We know him," Craig said. None too gently, he released the gibbering Cary, who coughed and grabbed his throat like he'd just been strangled to within an inch of his life. "He's the brother of the guy the cops arrested for Tabitha Antoinette's murder."

Now it was Envy's turn to gasp. "You're brothers with a *murderer?*"

"Alleged," I cut in. "And for what it's worth, I don't think he did it."

"Alleged, schmalleged," Envy retorted. She turned her ire back to Cary. "You should be ashamed of yourself! What do you think you're doing, creeping around my bedroom while your brother…your own *brother…!*"

"I can explain," Cary said again. He stumbled backward into Envy's desk chair, holding his head in his hands at the temples, elbows on his knees. "I've actually been trying to help my brother this whole time."

"You better explain that," Craig grumbled. "Because if you think me grabbing you was uncomfortable, wait till you feel my fist cracking into your nose."

I watched this exchange with no small amount of delight. I'm generally not a violent person, but you can't just break into someone's house and not expect to get clocked in the face.

Cary glanced up, still shaking. "The whole thing…it was a setup. I was never going to hurt Envy or anyone else. This was all just a ploy."

Craig cocked an eyebrow, and I saw him clench a fist at his side. "Keep talking. And speed it up."

"My brother's acting career has gone nowhere," Cary jabbered. "I'm his agent, as you know. I'm not great at it, but I'm not terrible. It's Aaron who's the problem. I send him on auditions, but he doesn't get cast. But then *Sinful House* came to Odyssey, and I saw my shot. If I could scare Envy into leaving the show, my brother could replace her. He's *perfect* for the part. He's handsome, charismatic, jealous…"

"And in jail!" I shouted, incredulous. "He's been arrested for murder, and you're still trying to get him a part on a show? How does that make any sense?"

Cary licked his lips, eyes darting around the room.

"Mom will get him off eventually. I know she will. And he'll still need work, so…"

"That's about the most tone-deaf thing I've ever heard," Envy said. "Who would cast someone accused of murder on a show like ours? Even if they got off—the damage to their reputation is done. Nobody would ever vote for him!"

"Convicted serial killers get *fan mail* in prison. Geez, some of them even get *married!*" Cary pinched the bridge of his nose. "Anyway, you might not think it was a good idea, but that's what this has all been about. The pictures, the videos…I've been trying to scare you. Hoping to get you to leave the show."

Envy stared at him open-mouthed. Slowly, her expression changed, and color flooded her cheeks, her nostrils flaring. "Do you know what I've had to sacrifice because of you?" she asked. "Do you know what that ridiculous article in the newsletter cost me? All because you wanted your brother to take my part?"

"Does Aaron know you've been doing this?" I asked, incredulous. "Did he put you up to it?"

"Of course not." Cary snorted in amusement. "He has no idea. He would never let me go through with it if he did. Aside from being kind of a goody-good, he'd be too worried that I'd get caught. Which is crazy because he's my little brother, you know." He looked up and offered a thin smile—all rubbery lips, no teeth. "But it's usually him looking out for me. This time, I got to look out for him."

"That's all super honorable and everything, but boy, did you ever pick the creepiest Creepy McCreepyPants way of getting a role possible. Did you really think it would work?" Envy was on her feet now, hands planted on her hips as she towered over the seated Cary. "Do I really seem like the kind of girl who would just walk away from all this? People know my name. People know who I am. People follow me on social media!" Envy threw her hands up in exasperation. "I mean, goodness gracious, I'm not *Sloth!* This is all I've ever wanted! Maybe *she* was ready to walk away from fame and glory over some spiritual awakening but not me, buddy! I plan to become America's Favorite Sin! You have no idea who you were messing with!"

Envy stalked over to where the phone lay broken on the floor. She picked it up and shoved it in Cary's face. The facial recognition unlocked the phone and Envy began tapping.

"What are you doing?" Cary's eyes were locked on his phone. "That's private!"

"Oh really?" Envy snickered and cocked her head as she scrolled. "So are all the photos and videos you took of me. So you'll have to forgive me if I want to delete them all." Her fingers flew over the interface, presumably deleting videos Cary had taken without her permission. Almost a minute into it, though, she stopped, her finger hovering over the phone. Her mouth worked, and her eyes widened. I couldn't see whatever she was watching—I only saw the glow of the screen lighting up her features.

Her eyes lifted slowly. She turned to Craig and said, "Hold him. Hold him down, and don't let go."

Craig hesitated. "Hold him? What—"

"Just do it!" Envy snapped.

Craig lifted Cary by the collar, hauled him from the chair, and threw him down, pressing his back to the floor. Then the big man straddled him. Cary yelped, ineffectually slapping Craig until the cameraman pinned his arms by his side. "Don't make me knock you out," Craig said.

Cary stilled.

"Pride, call the police," Envy continued, her voice conspicuously calm. "Tell them a violent criminal broke into our house, that he's currently immobilized, but we need immediate backup. I'm sending a video to the Odyssey police department."

Confused but willing to trust Envy, I did exactly what I was told. When the call was finished, I crossed my arms over my chest. "Envy, you wanna tell us what's going on?"

Instead of answering, Envy got down on her haunches until she hovered over Cary, still prone and motionless on the carpet. She cocked her head to the side and folded her lower lip beneath her teeth as she cracked each of her knuckles one by one. Then, without blinking, she asked, "Why did you do it, Cary? Why did you kill Tabitha Antoinette?"

seventeen

. . .

Cary was a blubbering mess, snot dripping from his nose. "You don't understand," he said. "It was an accident. You can see that in the footage! It was an accident!"

"Footage?" I repeated. "What footage?"

"You better start talking," Envy said, hands on her hips. "Or I'll have Craig here crush your skull."

I didn't actually think Craig was the skull-crushing type, but Cary didn't know that. "I went to see Tabitha about Sloth," he explained. "I knew she planned to leave the show to start a foundation or something with Tabitha. And—well, I couldn't have that. I've been working all angles to get my brother cast as Envy. But Sloth leaving…that would put the show in danger. The network might just cancel it. I mean, there can't be that many lazy psychics out there running around. She's irreplaceable."

"No one's irreplaceable," I said. "Cary, why didn't

you just pitch your brother as Sloth? If she was leaving the show, anyway—"

"Aaron can't play Sloth," Cary snorted. "Are you kidding me? She's lazy and sloppy and that's the whole point. You've seen his apartment. He's the anti-Sloth."

"Forget Sloth," Envy said. "How did Tabitha end up dead?"

Cary looked at me and licked his lips. "When you were looking for ghosts in my brother's apartment, you mentioned he had a shotgun in the closet. A fake one," he amended. "But if it fooled you, I figured it might fool others, too. So I got an idea. I thought…I thought I could go over to Tabitha's and just scare her a little. Just scare her into backing off of Sloth. So I went to Aaron's, got the gun, and went over to Tabitha's."

He paused, sniffling. Craig was still pinning his arms down, so he couldn't wipe away the snot that dribbled down his face. "It was early. I parked a few blocks down and entered the house through the sliding glass door in the back, which opened right into the kitchen. Tabitha was standing there making coffee. I never pointed the gun at her or anything, I swear. I didn't even say a word. But I guess if someone breaks into your house with a gun in tow, you assume the worst."

"You think?" Envy snapped. "A woman alone in a strange city? You must have scared her half to death! I'd put you in jail for the rest of your life just for that."

"I know," Cary moaned. "In retrospect, it was so stupid. But I wasn't thinking clearly. I just—I was desperate to save the show. For Aaron. I swear I never meant to hurt her. But when she saw me with the gun, she immediately started scrambling away from me. And that was the problem because she'd left the dishwasher door open. She tripped over it and fell backward. She hit her head on the counter. Then she hit the floor and…"

He was crying openly now, and if a woman wasn't lying cold in the ground, I might have felt sorry for him. "I was paralyzed. I had no idea what to do. I didn't even want to touch her, you know? Fingerprints and everything. So I did the only thing I could think of."

I finally understood what Envy saw on Cary's phone. "You started filming," I said.

"I tried calling my mom first, but she didn't pick up. So I made the video. I didn't know what to do! I needed her to tell me how to fix it! But then Aaron showed up. I don't know what he was doing there—he must have followed me. I guess I woke him up when I went to get the gun."

I held out my hand to Envy. "Let me see the video."

She hesitated, but eventually handed me the phone.

By the time the police arrived, I'd already watched the incriminating video about a hundred times. Well, maybe not a hundred, but it was a lot of times, anyway. The video went something like this:

A blurry kitchen comes into view. It's well-appointed but not expensive. Formica counters, not granite. Vinyl tile, not ceramic or hardwood. Typical made-for-vacation-rental type stuff. The camera is shaky, and the operator—Cary—is breathing hard, on the verge of hyperventilating. Then the camera pans down to a woman sprawled on the floor, motionless. Before her is an open dishwasher door.

Cary's voice from behind the camera whispers, "Oh no oh no oh no. I don't know what to do! Mom, please, help me—I don't know what to do!"

His voice is almost unrecognizable, pitched an octave higher than usual. The camera pans away from the woman and lingers on the open dishwasher. "I didn't see that—I just…Mom, I don't know what to do!"

The camera pans away again, but for a split second, something long, dark, and skinny is lying on the vinyl in the corner of the video. It took me a few watches to realize it was Aaron's fake shotgun.

Then, off-camera, the sound of a sliding door opening. The cameraman swings around and, standing in the entryway, is Aaron. He looks dazed and confused, his hands buried in the roots of his hair as he says, "Cary, what's going on here? What did you do?"

The camera shakes violently, like Cary is flailing about. "Aaron? What are you doing here? What are you —you can't be here! You didn't see anything, do you hear me? Get out! Get out!"

The camera is still not focusing on anything in particular when a man's voice starts shouting frantically. It's Aaron's voice, but he's speaking a language I don't recognize. It sounds like Spanish and Russian had a baby.

The next few seconds are hard to make out. The video gets dark and fuzzy; everything goes out of focus. Then the camera hits the ground and everything goes still until Aaron's face appears in the frame. He reaches down, and that's where he must have turned off the recording because that's the end of the video.

I looked over at Cary, my brows drawn together in confusion. "What language is that?"

Cary shook his head. "I have no idea."

"Does Aaron speak anything beside English?"

Again, a vehement head shake. "Straight Cs in high school Spanish. I have no idea what language that is. At the time, I had better things to worry about."

I supposed that was true, but the language wasn't the only thing bothering me. "Did you see the look on his face?"

Cary looked annoyed. "His face?"

"Yes," I nodded. "He looked…not like himself."

"Well, he was probably in shock," Envy said. "It's not every day you catch your brother murdering a woman in her kitchen."

"It's not that," I said, rewinding the video to watch again. "It's his eyes. It just doesn't look like him."

I recalled the video of Aaron being interrogated at the police station. He'd insisted he had no idea why he was at the crime scene. That he had no memory of going there. That he couldn't fathom how he ended up lugging Tabitha's body through the front yard. He'd even gone so far as to say it could have been a twin brother.

They'd practically laughed him out of the station for that. Even I had thought it ridiculous, and I'd seen some crazy stuff. But now that I'd seen the video for myself, I wasn't so sure.

I was still thinking about Aaron's evil twin theory

when the cops arrived. I figured they'd send over a pair of patrol officers in response to our distress call. But it must have been a slow crime night in Odyssey because before I knew it, a half-dozen uniformed officers plus the frizzy-haired detective from Aaron's interrogation video were handcuffing Cary, taking statements, and walking around with their chests puffed out like self-important peacocks. By the way they strutted and squawked, you'd think they outsmarted Cary themselves instead of Envy stumbling onto the smoking gun via our amateur sting operation.

It was the sound of Cary's screech over the officer Mirandizing him that snapped me back into the present. "Call my mother! She can explain everything!"

I thought that was a strange thing to say until I remembered Cary's voice in the video. *"Mom, I don't know what to do!"*

I blinked. "Cary, does your mother know about this video? Did you send it to her? Does your mother know you were at Tabitha's that day?"

The detective was already hauling Cary away, but he turned to look over his shoulder. "She's my mother, Pride. She'd do anything to protect me."

I stood in stunned silence, still staring after Cary long after they'd carted him away. Another officer, someone I didn't recognize, returned to the room. "Whichever one of you sent that video to the department—good job."

"That was me," Envy said. "The officers who took my statement about the intruder gave me a number in case anything else happened."

"Well, that was good thinking to call it in *and* send supporting evidence," she said. "We'll likely have a confession out of him by morning. But I am gonna need that phone. Evidence."

I nodded absently, her words not registering. Then I glanced down at the phone still clutched in my hand. "Oh. Right." I handed the device to the officer, who slipped it into a plastic baggie. "Be careful with that," I said.

She tipped her head and strode purposefully from the room.

The house didn't grow silent until well after 3 a.m. My body was exhausted when I climbed into bed, but I couldn't sleep. I couldn't stop thinking about what Cary said as the cops dragged him off. *"She's my mother, Pride. She'd do anything to protect me."*

I understood a mother protecting her child. What I didn't understand was—if she'd seen the video, why hadn't she protected *Aaron?* Why hadn't she turned the video over to the police to get her other son out of jail?

"Because it wouldn't have made any difference. Not to her."

I didn't have to open my eyes to know the voice came from the ghost girl who was now sitting at the foot of my bed. I scooted closer to the wall to make room for her, which was silly. Ghosts don't actually take up space. But I couldn't help it—the ghost girl always felt material to me. Like a living, breathing person instead of mere ectoplasm and memories.

"What do you mean by that?" I asked her. I didn't

bother asking how she'd known what I was thinking. She wouldn't have answered me, anyway.

"Did you know that mama cuckoo birds lay their eggs in the nests of weaker, smaller birds? And then when the cuckoo baby hatches, the adoptive mama bird just acts like it's no big deal and takes care of the baby as her own, feeding it and everything?"

"I'm not in the mood to talk about cuckoo birds," I said.

"Good thing I'm not talking about cuckoo birds," the ghost girl replied, her voice strangely forlorn. She was quiet a minute, fidgeting with the edge of my blanket. Then she said, "Cary and Aaron are both Cate's sons, you know. She couldn't just turn the video over to the police and trade one son for the other. She's probably thinking she can figure out a way to get Aaron off the hook without hanging Cary out to dry. After all, Aaron really is innocent. And she's smart. She's probably counting on finding some loophole to get both of her sons out of trouble."

Part of me suspected the ghost girl was right. It made sense when you thought about it from a mother's perspective. But it also sat wrong with me. Lawyers were supposed to be committed to justice, weren't they? And didn't Tabitha Antoinette deserve justice for what happened to her? Didn't Cate Burton have a moral obligation to turn Cary in and lay that poor woman's soul to rest?

I was trying to think of how to succinctly verbalize these thoughts when the ghost girl said, "People are complicated, Pride. Much more complicated than birds.

For people, many things can be true at once. But being a lawyer doesn't trump being a mama. Maybe nothing can."

"I guess I wouldn't know," I said into the darkness. I hadn't realized how bitter I was about this whole mother-protecting-her-children thing until the words were out of my mouth. A good amount of time had gone by since I'd read that letter from my mother, and nothing made more sense now than the first time I'd read it. Cary and Aaron's mother was fighting to get one son out of jail without turning in the other. And what had my mother done? She'd written me—an infant—a Dear John letter and then walked off the face of the Earth. She left me in that commune alone, vulnerable, and completely unable to fend for myself. She hadn't fought at all. She basically just said, "Sorry about all this trouble. Hope to see you on the other side."

I sighed loudly and rolled onto my side, pulling the blankets up to my chin. "I wish I knew how to feel about this. On one hand, I feel glad Tabitha's killer is in custody. On the other hand…is it wrong for me to feel bad that Cary was just trying to help his brother? He went about it in an idiotic, irresponsible way, and of course he should pay for that, but…Is it terrible that I don't want him to hang?"

The ghost girl chuckled and wiggled her way under my blanket. "People are complicated, Pride. They can feel many things at once."

I watched her get cozy beneath my comforter. She made a cute little mound of glowing ghost skin and soft, dark hair. Her eyelids fluttered closed, long lashes dark against her chubby cheeks. Her breathing became slow and even, so I guess she must have fallen asleep. My eyelids, too, grew heavy as I watched her drift off. Then, right as the day finally caught up to me and I nearly succumbed to sleep, the little mound of blanket at my feet collapsed as the ghost girl vanished, leaving me alone and cold with nothing but my thoughts for company.

eighteen

. . .

Days later, Portia came to see me.

She was dressed more casually than I'd ever seen her in a pair of white linen pants and a pale pink silk blouse. Her hair was pulled into a carefully-styled messy bun. But she was still wearing her signature red lipstick.

We were sitting out on the back porch drinking sparkling lemonades and eating cucumber finger sandwiches. Craig was filming in the corner and slurping a beer as he watched our little exchange. Portia was smiling and radiant like she hadn't a care in the world. She took a sip of her lemonade and sighed, refreshed. "It's such a beautiful day. I really outdid myself when I chose this location for the show. Speaking of which." She leaned her head to the side. "I hear you lost your challenge."

"Big time," I said, taking a huge bite of sandwich. "We got so close. We figured out the connection between the artist and Aaron but not Aaron and the statue. That's the missing link. So the statue is still out there, free to travel the world. Or Odyssey, at least."

"Well, even Sherlock Holmes failed to solve a case every once in a while, didn't he?"

I shrugged. I'd never read a Sherlock Holmes book in my life, but I wasn't going to humiliate myself in front of Portia Cameron by admitting it. "Speaking of Aaron—has he been released yet?"

Portia nodded. "For the time being. Given his history of mental illness and his family's statements, the DA may choose not to charge him with anything. He still claims he was never at Tabitha's. If he's not nuts, he's got more guts than a sausage factory."

I frowned. "Why do you say that?"

"He's on the videos—both videos. The one his brother took, and the footage from the doorbell camera. To say you weren't there at all when your face is in plain view takes some pretty huge—"

"Right, got it." I wrapped my hand around my lemonade, tapping my fingers against the cool glass. Condensation dripped down the side, forming a puddle on the table. "Seems like this should be easy enough to solve, though. Just put him in a room with Sloth. She can figure out if he's lying lickety-split."

Portia grinned, and I got the feeling she was trying not to laugh at me. My cheeks flushed hot under her smirking gaze. "The legal system doesn't put a lot of stock in *mind-reading*, but you've got the right idea. The police administered a lie detector." She shrugged. "It came up clean."

The hairs on my arms stood up. "So, he's telling the truth?"

"I wouldn't go that far," Portia said. "Some people are just talented liars. Psychopaths, for example."

I glowered at the would-be mayor across the table. "So now you think Aaron is a psychopath?"

She shrugged again. "I'm not a doctor."

I tapped my forefinger in the water that pooled around my lemonade. "What will happen to Cary Burton?"

"He confessed to Tabitha's death and swore Aaron had nothing to do with it. After extensively reviewing the video, the DA has decided to charge Cary with manslaughter. It might have been an accident but still unforgivably negligent. And all for what? To save a preposterous TV show? No offense," she added with a smile that indicated she meant full offense.

I didn't take the bait, mainly because I agreed with her assessment. "And what about the mother? Cate Burton?"

"Accessory after the fact and obstruction of justice," Portia said. "Although a jury will probably go soft on her. She was a mother in an impossible predicament. It will be hard to find twelve people that can't sympathize with her."

I had nothing to say about that, but it tracked with what the ghost girl said. It seemed everyone had a soft spot for moms but me.

Or maybe my spot was even softer than most, and that was the problem.

"Well, thank you for the snacks. I don't want to keep

you." Portia stood and brushed at the wrinkles in her crisp linen pants. "I just thought it appropriate to come by and express my gratitude. Your service to the city does not go unnoticed."

She flashed me her best politician's smile, but I knew Portia well enough to know she was only performing for the cameras. She was probably tallying up the votes she'd won just by coming here. I'd noticed a flurry of new "Portia for Mayor" fliers all over town. She was really milking this whole thing.

She was halfway to the door when she stopped, snapping her fingers in mid-air. "Oh, I almost forgot." She dug in her purse and retrieved a newspaper, which she placed in front of me. "Some people like to keep the articles they're mentioned in. I wasn't sure you had your own copy. So, I brought this for you." She smiled and wiggled her fingers. "Toodaloo!"

I wasn't the kind of person who got sentimental about my name in print, but I was admittedly curious about what *The Odyssey Trident* had to say about Cary's arrest. The headline was typical click-bait-type stuff. "Beloved Actress Tabitha Antoinette's True Killer Unmasked!" But when I read the first paragraph, my heart stopped.

I looked up and did something I knew better than to do. I caught Craig's eyes, cracked a huge smile, and said into the camera, "Too little, too late, but I just solved our case."

nineteen

. . .

Thirty minutes later, my teammates and I were in Aaron's apartment with Craig filming the encounter. The place looked much the same as the last time we'd been there. It was still spic and span, and the unfinished painting still sat in the corner propped on its easel. Aaron, however, looked worse for the wear. For someone recently not charged with murder, he looked remarkably terrible. His hair stuck out like wires all over his head, and the half-circle bruises still adorned the hollows beneath his eyes. His usual five o'clock shadow was threatening to become a full-fledged beard.

"It's really good of you to come check in on me," Aaron was saying with a rubbery smile that didn't quite reach his eyes. "This whole ordeal has been rough, you know? It's one thing to be accused of a crime you know you didn't commit. It's another thing to hear your brother admit it was him all along."

"I can imagine it's been really hard on you," I said. "How is everybody holding up?"

Aaron snorted. "We're all hanging by a thread. Mom will be disbarred for this, and the DA is charging her with anything he thinks will stick. Dad is trying to salve his wounds by working 80-hour weeks. I'm not allowed to visit Cary—no one is. I can't even leave my apartment because the media is swarming the parking lot waiting for me to appear. So, I'm just sort of stuck here. I'm pretty miserable if you want to know the truth."

"I'm so sorry about everything you've been through," Sloth said. "And I hope you don't mind me asking, but...Your intruder. The presence? Has it returned?"

Aaron's eyes were unfocused as he nodded. "Almost every night now. It's gotten worse since the incident. I still don't know how I ended up at Tabitha's. I have no memory of that, I swear. None. I'm at my wit's end. I have no idea what to do or who to go to."

"You don't need to go to anyone," I said. "We've been talking about this. If you're open to it, we'd like to continue with your case."

Now, Aaron looked up, his eyes wide. "Really? You would do that for me?"

Sloth smiled. "It's the least we can do."

A faint smile tugged at the corner of Aaron's mouth. "So, does that mean you've decided not to leave the show?"

Sloth reached for a pigtail and shoved the end in her mouth, chewing thoughtfully. "I wanted to go work with Tabitha because I wanted to make my life meaningful. I want to help people. But then I thought about it and realized…I have a gift. I mean, sometimes it's a curse," she said with a nervous chuckle, "but mostly, it's a gift. And I can use it to help people here in Odyssey, too. Besides." She threw me a side-eye. "I can't leave Pride to have all the fun without me. Someone's got to hold this show together."

Everyone laughed at that, so I guess it was a joke, but I didn't really get it. "So, Aaron, what do you think?"

He bobbed his head and rubbed his hands together. "Yeah, of course. That would be great. Any help you can lend me, really. Thank you."

Gluttony leaned forward, resting his elbows on his knees. He tapped his fingertips together and cleared his throat. "Now, we need you to answer a question for us."

Aaron looked unfazed. "Of course. Anything. What is it?"

My teammate turned to me for the unveiling. This was our shining moment as contestants on the show, and I saw the excitement in their faces. From the corner of my eye, I saw Craig making a get-on-with-it motion with a roll of his hand. With the encouragement of the camera guy, I turned back to Aaron. "Aaron, what kind of psychic are you?"

For a fraction of a second, a cloud passed over his face, and my enthusiasm took a nosedive. If he got recalcitrant now, it would ruin our big reveal, and viewers hated that. But my worries proved unfounded. He recomposed himself quickly, turning on the phoniest Gee Willikers smile I'd ever seen west of the Mississippi. Not that I'd been east of the Mississippi, but he was really dialing up the fake innocence, is what I'm saying. "Gosh, Pride, I'm not sure what you mean."

"Yes, you do. You couldn't take over Sloth's role because she's sloppy and lazy, and you clearly aren't." I gestured around at the impeccable apartment. "So, Cary had you pegged for Envy, which, if you want my opinion—eh." I wobbled my hand to show I wasn't sure he (or anyone, really) was as petty and jealous as Envy. "I guess you could work Envy's angle. But there's one big thing everybody in the house has. It's kind of the premise of the show. In addition to the flaws indicated by our namesakes, we all have powers."

Aaron must have seen where I was going with this because color rose in his cheeks, and he had to bite down a sheepish grin. "So, logically—if Cary thought I was a shoo-in for a role on the show, I must also have powers."

I winked and jabbed the air with a finger. "That's right. So tell us—what's your power, Aaron?" I leaned in, closing the distance between us, and lowered my voice. "This is all for show, by the way. I already figured it out before we came over here." I cocked my head toward Craig. "But the viewers don't know, so make it good, huh?"

Aaron looked around the room at the expectant faces staring back at him. Then he flashed a camera-ready grin with just the right amount of chagrin around the edges. I could see why Cary thought he'd be great for our show. When he wanted to, he could really turn on the charm. "Telekinesis," he said. "I can move things with my mind."

Sloth made a succession of amazed noises, and even Gluttony let out a whistle. "Really? Dang, son, you must've been the *business* at high school sports! Just put that ball in the net with your mind? Captain of the basketball team over here!" Gluttony faux-shouted while pointing jovially at Aaron.

But Aaron only shook his head, the color in his cheeks deepening. "No, it wasn't like that. Not even close. For the most part, I can't control it. It's something that happens when I get emotional. Pictures fall off the wall. Items on a table will fall over. Every once in a while, I'll think about something—like the TV remote or a blanket—and it will appear next to me. But that's rare. Mostly, it's just chaos."

That part I didn't know, but it made sense. It explained why, the last time I had been at Aaron's apartment, I'd seen the container of paintbrushes spill over and a tumbler of water fall onto its side unprovoked. "Is that why you don't have much artwork on your walls? Why your place is so…bare? So stuff doesn't just fall randomly?"

Aaron looked around as though noticing the lack of decoration for the first time. "I guess unconsciously. It just didn't seem worth the hassle."

"You know, your biological mother doesn't have much artwork in her house, either. That's one thing you both have in common."

I had been looking for a segue into this conversation from the minute we stepped into Aaron's apartment. And although I wasn't sure I'd switched gears elegantly, at least I'd gotten us there. Aaron looked up, a frown scribbled over his face. "My biological mother? You met her? In person?"

I nodded. "We did." I paused to consider how to address what could likely be a very sensitive issue. "Is it okay if I share information about her with you? I won't if you're not okay with it, but—"

"I don't mind," Aaron interrupted. "I mean, I've never felt the need to connect with her, but I'm not opposed to learning more."

I let my breath out in a relieved whoosh. Nothing I was about to say would make much sense if he'd declined to discuss his ancestry.

And boy did I have a lot to say.

"Your bio mom," I began, "is the artist behind the Star of the Sea."

Aaron sat in rapt silence as I told him everything. I told him how Paola was pregnant with him when she worked on the monument. I recounted her story about growing up with a magical aunt in Portugal, her tale about the plant and her adolescent love interest, and her discovery that the statue was mirroring her emotions.

And then I got to the part where she figured out how to fix it.

"She discovered the only way to get the statue to leave her alone was to unlink herself from it," I said, my heart pounding in my ears as I finally got around to the big payoff. "She did that by giving the statue its own name. At least, that's what she told us. But I'm pretty sure it was partially a lie."

I pulled the newspaper Portia had left me from my backpack and handed it to Aaron. "My last clue was right in front of me this whole time if I'd only thought to ask." I shrugged, donning an oafish grin. "Well, what can I say? Even Sherlock Holmes overlooks a clue or two from time to time, right?"

Aaron glanced from me to my teammates and back again. "I'm sorry, but you lost me," he said. "What clue?"

"The statue has a name scribbled on its base. I didn't think it significant until I read the paper today." I pointed to the first paragraph of the newspaper article and read it aloud. "'Previously arrested for the egregious crime was Luis Aaron Burton, brother of Cary Burton.'" I cocked my head to the side. "Your first name is Luis."

Aaron pressed his lips together in a thin line. "I don't use it except for legal purposes," he explained. "It was the name my birth mother wanted me to have, so Mom agreed. But I've never liked it." He paused, looking confused. But then a light bulb must have gone off because when he looked up, wonder was written all over his face. "Is the name written on the statue…Luis?"

I nodded. "It is. Paola told us she gave the statue that name because she liked how it felt in her mouth, and I didn't press her on it because, to be honest, your mother is kind of weird."

Aaron barked out a dry laugh. "Yeah, so I've heard."

"But now I think she had a plan." I paused and glanced down at the bracelet on my wrist. It was glowing with a soft lavender glow, which meant Lust was feeling content. And for some reason, it did my heart good to know it. "She didn't give the statue its own name. She gave it *your* name, so you and the statue would be linked."

"But why?" Aaron asked, his hands spread before him, supplicant. "Why would I want a statue linked to me? It doesn't make any sense."

"It does if you think about it from a mother's perspective," Sloth answered. "She didn't do it for you. She did it for herself. By the time she wrote the name on the statue, the Burtons had already adopted you. I think she did it so she could look at that statue and get a glimpse into your life. How you were feeling, what you were thinking..." She shrugged, an awkward smile on her lips. "The statue was like a baby monitor, but one she could look on for the rest of her life."

Aaron's frown deepened. "She knew my parents. She could have just reached out if that's what she wanted."

Sloth dithered, bobbing her head side to side. "She had her reasons. She wasn't well. This was her way of keeping you close without influencing you. The irony is that she moved away before the statue ever began manifesting your emotions. So it never actually functioned the way she expected."

Aaron was quiet for a long time, and while he mulled this over, Gluttony retrieved a glass of water from the kitchen and pressed it into Aaron's hands. He accepted it gratefully, took a long drink, and then wiped his mouth with the back of his hand. "So, what's up with the statue flitting about town? Is that related to me, too?"

"I think so," I said with a nod. "Every place the

statue appeared was somewhere you frequented often or had strong emotions about. Like the Hightide apartments, where you lived with your girlfriend, and the drive-in theater you visited as a kid."

"JB is a good friend," Aaron mused aloud, speaking of the proprietor of the grocery store. "I get lunch at his deli several times a week. He recently got a gig playing a Russian gangster on a new show."

I smiled. That explained why the statue had once appeared at the grocer's carrying an AK-47 and a bag of cash.

"JB is an actor?" Gluttony asked, surprised.

"Everybody's an actor in Odyssey," Aaron said without a trace of a smile.

"But what about Julio's?" Sloth asked. "That's how we got put on the case. The statue was messing up the boutique's opening, and Julio was plenty hot about it. It's new, though, so you can't have had strong feelings about it. So…?"

Aaron set the water glass on the table and dropped his eyes to the floor. "I can't say for sure, but that was probably because of Cary. He's the one who found that property for the boutique—he's Julio's virtual assistant."

"I thought he was your agent," Gluttony said.

"He is, but he has lots of jobs. He's…trying to find his passion or something. Trying to find something he's good at. He doesn't just want to be a brain-dead socialite." He chuckled wryly. "Not much room to be a socialite in prison, is there?"

"Don't go there," Sloth said, her voice soft. "Stay with us. What happened with Julio?"

"Nothing," Aaron said with a shrug. "I was just stoked he was working an honest job. Because up until then…"

Something about that felt ominous, and after all my time in Odyssey, I was getting good at recognizing ominous when I heard it. "Until then, what?"

Aaron cleared his throat several times before closing his eyes and dropping his head into his hands. "I knew Cary was taking pictures of Envy without her consent."

A gasp went around the room, and Aaron waved his hands as though shooing away any personal responsibility for not saying anything before now. "I told him it was uncool—"

"Uh, it was actually *illegal*," Sloth cut in.

"—and he swore he wouldn't do it again, which was obviously a lie. I had no idea what he was taking the pictures for. I figured he was selling them to magazines to make ends meet. So, when I heard he got a job with Julio…"

"You were relieved," I said. "And that's why the statue paid Julio a visit. And it also explains her expression."

"Huh," Gluttony grunted. "I thought she just looked hungry."

"How does one look hungry?" Sloth asked.

"Like this." Gluttony sat still, offering no expression at all.

"You just look like you always look," I said.

"Exactly." Gluttony scowled. "What's the matter? Y'all don't get jokes?"

"Anyway," I said, returning my attention to Aaron,

"I guess relief can be as powerful an emotion as anything else."

"This also explains why the statue appeared screaming at our house," Gluttony said, deciding to add value to the conversation once again. "You were upset about your brother snapping the pics there."

"This is all still a lot to process." Aaron stood and walked over to the painting on the easel, arms wrapped protectively over his torso. "I guess I believe you about Paola and the statue and everything, but it's a lot. Like… a *lot*."

"It's how I knew your power was telekinesis," I explained. "Your mother made the statue change expressions. But she never caused the statue to travel. That's your specialty alone."

Aaron chewed over this a while before asking the big question. "So, I guess the million-dollar question is… why did it start moving recently?

I took a breath. "I suspect the bottles in your bathroom might explain it. I think she started moving around the time you stopped taking your meds."

The apartment fell silent. Here's the thing about talking to people about their mental health medication: that conversation is almost always filled with land mines. I know this because Dr. Xena told me. As part of our check-ins, she'd ask me if I was still on my meds, and I'd get huffy and impatient with her, even though as my doctor, it was her literal job to ask. But she said my reaction wasn't unique. Lots of her patients got defensive when asked about their meds.

So I was prepared for Aaron to get upset, but he

didn't. Instead, he offered a sad smile and folded his hands in his lap. "Well, I guess that makes sense. That's around the time I started to feel things."

Aaron looked like he might cry, so Sloth walked over to him and put a hand on his shoulder, giving a gentle squeeze. He laid a hand atop hers and squeezed back. "The meds are great at evening me out. There are no real lows, but no real highs, either. Every day is the same flavor of gray. Is it wrong I wanted to find out what the world was like in Technicolor?"

I shrugged. "That's a decision only you and your doctor can make. It's got nothing to do with anyone else."

Aaron nodded, and the relief on his face was evident. "Yeah, that's my thought, too. I've been on mental health medication since I was a kid. ADHD meds, anxiety meds, depression meds—you name it. And I never questioned it until recently. I'm not saying I shouldn't be on medication. But I am saying adult-me should decide that—not child-me's parents. You know?"

There didn't seem to be anything else to say about that, and I have to admit I was proud of my companions for not saying anything stupid about Aaron just needing more sunshine or exercise or whatever. As that chef woman on TV says, if you can't make your own serotonin, store-bought is fine.

"Well, now that we know why the statue has been traveling, it's time to make her stop." Everyone looked to me, expectant. I smiled and said, "Anyone have a Sharpie?"

———

We waited until after dark, when the throngs of people camped out around the statue had gone home. When we arrived at the courthouse, a few stragglers were left, but Gluttony scared them away with his booming threats to call the cops on them for loitering. I guess they weren't local and didn't know Odyssey had no loitering laws because they scurried off without putting up a fight.

Alone with the statue under the moonlight, she was even more impressive than ever. She gleamed in the starlight. She was still standing with her arms raised, carrying a sign proclaiming Aaron's innocence. Aaron walked up to her and placed a hand on the curved tail of her mermaid body. He never tore his eyes away from her when he said, "I never had any idea my bio mom made this statue. All this time…I never knew. This is the first real contact I've ever had with her. It's making me unexpectedly emotional. Is that weird?"

I didn't know if it was weird or not. I wasn't exactly an expert on normal. But I could at least relate to what he was experiencing. When I first read that letter from my mother, I'd felt an array of emotions I'd never had before, almost none of which I could name.

"How does it feel?" I asked, hoping Aaron might have a better emotional vocabulary than I did.

He chuckled, pulling away and jamming his hands into the back pocket of his jeans. "Good. It feels good."

I sighed. So much for borrowing his emotional thesaurus.

At my side, Gluttony removed a black Sharpie from his pocket and uncapped it. "You ready to do the honors?"

Aaron glanced over his shoulder, checking to see if we had an audience. "I don't want anybody to think I'm defacing the statue," he explained as a blush crept up his neck. "The last thing my family needs is more trouble with the law."

"I've already taken care of that," I said. "I called Portia and told her the plan. She's very okay with it. Anything that will get the statue out of her hair and back in front of City Hall is good with her."

Aaron nodded, a thoughtful expression on his face. "Well then, I guess this is the moment of truth. Does anybody have any idea what we should name her?"

We were all silent as we waited for someone else to speak. Finally, Sloth said, "You should ask her."

Aaron's brow wrinkled. "Who? The statue?"

Sloth nodded. "I know it sounds crazy, but hear me out. When she first appeared on our lawn, I had a feeling she wanted something. I tried talking to her, asking her what she needed from us. I didn't get an answer, of course. But then again, that's not my name scribbled on her base. She's not linked to me."

Aaron chuckled and thumbed his nose, sniffing with newfound confidence as he squared his shoulders. "You're right," he said. "Let's see what she has to say."

He stepped forward and placed both palms on the statue again, eyelids fluttering closed as he caressed the cool, smooth metal. Then he let his hands fall to his sides, and he stepped back and opened his eyes, head tilted back as he gazed up into the mermaid's face.

"You know, I've heard guys say that women can be hard to understand," he said. "I've never found that to be the case myself. But this lady?" He chuckled warmly. "Even easier to comprehend than most."

He held his hand out to Gluttony, who slapped the Sharpie down in his open palm. He dropped down onto his haunches, placed the nib of the Sharpie to the metal, and added a single letter to the word already scribbled there.

He stood up and gestured to his handiwork with a satisfied nod. "There. I think that's it. That's all I needed to do, right?"

We all peered down at what Aaron had written. "Luisa, huh?" Gluttony glanced from the name up to the statue's face. "That's what she wants to be called? She kinda looks more like a Monique or a Shaniqua."

"I guess you never can tell with mermaids." Aaron slipped the pen into a pocket and folded his arms over his chest, looking up at the sculpture in admiration. "I guess now we wait. If she's still here tomorrow…"

"She won't be," Sloth said. She yawned and stretched as she dug a knuckle into an eye and rubbed. "This is it. This is what the statue wanted all along. Her own identity." She nudged Aaron in the side with an elbow. "Though I guess she didn't want to *completely* abandon you, huh? I mean—you're Luis. She wants to be Luisa. That's kinda sweet, right?"

"I guess so," he agreed. "If Paola was pregnant with

me while she was creating the statue…I guess she and I are twins. In a manner of speaking," he added with a self-conscious chuckle. "You know, it's funny. I don't know what I expected but…well, I don't feel any different."

"Give it time," Gluttony advised. "Sometimes it takes a minute to come to terms with a new reality."

We admired the statue together for a little while longer before it was time to head home for the night. By the time I woke up the next morning, the news was already all over town: the Star of the Sea was back at City Hall where she belonged holding a mirror and a lantern.

I showered, brushed my teeth, and was about to go down to breakfast when my phone pinged, letting me know I had a new email. It was from an unknown sender, which was unusual. I clicked the message and froze, staring at my screen for a long time. There was no subject, no greeting, and no closing sentiments. All the email said was, "Thanks."

I'll probably wonder for the rest of my life if mermaid statues can send emails.

twenty

. . .

"Okay, everybody. Settle down, please. I have something super important to talk with you about."

It was the much-dreaded day of Tricia Woodward's visit. We had all just finished watching the most recent episode of our adventures—which, if you've never had to watch yourself on TV, let me tell you, it's the most mortifying experience in the world. There you are on a 70-inch screen in high definition with all your pores, pimples, and wrinkles shining in the light for God and everyone to see. And if that weren't bad enough, life doesn't give you a script, so you get to watch yourself fumble your dignity by saying the cringiest, most awkward things ever.

Watching myself on TV is seriously the worst part of my life.

Anyway, I was sitting on the floor with my back propped against the couch, eating handfuls of Chex Mix and counting down the minutes until this forced camaraderie was over and I could go back to reading the new thriller novel I'd just picked up. It had been almost a week since we solved our case, and I was enjoying the slow, quiet days where the only mysteries on my mind were the fake ones invented by authors. It was cathartic to experience tension with no skin in the game.

"As you know, this is the part where I would usually go over everyone's scores for the week." Tricia was standing in her usual spot in front of our enormous TV. Today, she was wearing a lavender polo shirt with matching pedal pushers that looked like the rejects of a Vineyard Vines Easter collection. "But this week, there's been a problem."

"Hold on." The minute I heard Wrath's voice, I groaned inwardly and prepared to be regaled with stories about the unfairness of a fascist television organization for the next 10 minutes. Even Tricia looked annoyed, though she did a pretty good job hiding it. "Why aren't we getting our scores today? What's the problem?"

Tricia's mouth twisted. "Well, I was just getting to that if you would give me the chance to speak." She heaved a sigh and planted her hands on her hips. "Look, there's no elegant way to put this, so I'll just come out with it. Some vital information that wasn't supposed to air for a few weeks has been leaked to the public. And as a result, the network is concerned that this week's votes may have been unfairly swayed."

Sounds of surprise went around the room. One of the rules for living at Sinful House was that we weren't supposed to watch the news. (Though, of course, we sometimes did.) We weren't supposed to know what was happening in the world, and the world wasn't supposed to know what was happening with us. At least, not in real time. One drawback of having lag between when the show was recorded and when the show aired was that everyone had to keep mum about the situation at the house. Ours was a carefully regulated existence.

So, hearing that somehow information got leaked was actually a big deal.

"What kind of information?" Greed asked. "I think we have the right to know."

Tricia fidgeted and cleared her throat, nodding while she thought of what to say. "Yes, of course you do. Well, it's like this. Some of you may know that Pride went to Santa Barbara to see a piece of art created by an artist from the Sam Lovelace commune. Your housemate then stumbled upon a letter written from a mother to her child, and we all agree that Pride is the child in question. Now, I don't know how many of you have read it, but we didn't plan to release the contents of that missive for a few weeks still. Unfortunately, somehow, the contents of that letter have leaked out to the public. All the gossip sites are talking about it."

All eyes turned to me, some faces friendlier than others. But I held my hands up in defense, shaking my head vehemently. "Don't look at me," I said. "I've never wanted anything to do with this."

"We have no evidence suggesting Pride was behind the leak. In fact, for all we know, the letter's original owner may have been the source. All we know for sure is that viewers were supposed to vote for their favorite Sin based on the footage they saw this week. But Pride got so many votes this round, we just don't think that's what happened."

At the risk of drawing the ire of my fellow housemates, I raised a hand, my brows drawn together in confusion. "Uh, not to be that person, but isn't it possible I got all those votes because people just really liked me last week?"

Tricia smiled icily. "Anything is possible, Pride. But based on what the viewers saw and the social media sentiment up until the letter was leaked, our statisticians believe Lust should have gotten the most votes. She was the most likable, and she got the most airtime. By comparison, you came off a little stiff. So, no, we are all adequately convinced that the contents of the letter biased the viewers in your favor. And as that goes against the spirit of the show, we're canceling all of this week's votes."

"So, what's the plan, then?" Envy asked. "We just don't have a winner this week?"

"I know this is very disappointing to all of you," Tricia said in a voice that indicated she really didn't care one way or the other. "The network is working hard to ensure this doesn't happen again. But as for now, I'm sorry to say, Envy, but there will be no winner this week. I wish you all better luck next time."

Before the groans of protest could rise to the level of mutiny, Tricia moved on to the next topic on her list. "As you all know, local celebrities make the best endorsements for local politicians. So, as a thank you for all the hard work Portia Cameron has already put into our show by finding you a place to live, the network has agreed to allow each of the Seven Deadly Sins to appear on a commercial endorsing Portia Cameron for mayor."

Tricia was smiling like she had just bestowed the greatest gift humanity had ever received. But I found her wording suspect. *Allowing* us? That made it sound like we were all champing at the bit to say what a great person Portia was and how excited we were to be under her thumb. But the truth was, I could hardly think of a person I wanted to endorse less than Portia Cameron. At least, no one still alive.

"When you say we are *allowed* to endorse her," I began, "you mean we have the *choice*, right?"

Tricia sighed and stood akimbo, all her weight on one foot as she gave me an admonishing glare. "Why does everything have to be so difficult with you, Pride?"

I threw my hands up in defense. "I don't think that's fair. I'm asking a straightforward question, and I can't be the only person in this room who wants to know, right?" I looked around at my companions, but nobody seemed that fussed about the situation. "I mean, politics is supposed to be about the freedom to use your voice for causes you believe in."

"That's right," Wrath added, rising to his feet. "We should each choose for ourselves who we want to endorse for mayor. Because if you ask me, that dude running against her with the goofy glasses and the crazy toupee? He's *hilarious*. And since politics is nothing but theater anyway, I'd rather vote for the clown that's gonna grant me the greatest amusement."

I threw my loudmouth housemate a dubious look.

"Wrath, do me a favor and stay off my side." I returned my attention to Tricia. "No, but seriously. I don't have to endorse her, do I?"

"Our endorsements can't possibly mean much, anyway," Sloth added as she stretched out on the sofa, her feet propped in Lust's lap. "We're not even citizens. We can't even vote."

Tricia tutted and winked as she pulled her phone from her pocket. "Oh, that's not true. We checked. As long as you have mail delivered to this address—which you all do—you are legally allowed to vote in local elections. And anyway, you think the people of Odyssey care one fig about the letter of the law? They'll see your smiling celebrity faces and flock down to the voting booth to do what you say. So, according to the email I just got from corporate, the camera crew will be here tomorrow bright and early. I expect you all to be ready for your closeups."

"Tomorrow?" I blurted. "Tricia, you didn't give us any warning. We won't have time to—"

"To pack your bags and get out of town for a nice, long weekend? Yes, I know. We thought it over carefully. Now, I don't want to hear any more about this. The matter is decided. We will give you the scripts in the morning. So! Are you all ready for your new assignments?"

Tricia didn't wait for our responses as she began reading from her phone. "Team one this week will be Gluttony and Wrath. Team two is Envy and Sloth, and Team Three is Pride, Lust, and Greed."

While Sloth and Envy were screaming something

about girl power and giving each other high fives, my stomach fell through the floor. I knew I couldn't avoid being partnered with Greed forever. But I did not expect to be put on the same team with both him *and* Lust.

But when I saw Tricia's devilish smile, I realized this was intentional. The stupid network was setting me up for a final showdown. *"Who will walk away with Lust on their arm? Freak Show—or the Creep? Stay tuned to find out!"*

"Well, well, well," Greed ambled over to where I sat motionless on the floor, staring down at the mood bracelet on my arm. It was glowing red. I didn't even want to know what red meant. "Looks like we're finally partnered up. And with Lust as our delightful third, too! The network is just full of surprises, aren't they? I wonder, though—who will be the third wheel in this intimate little trio? Will it be the ravishingly desirable charmer? Or—"

"Or will it be you?" Lust asked with a throaty chuckle.

Greed wagged a finger in her face, stepping so close she could probably smell his aftershave. "Very funny, Lust. I do so enjoy your coquettish sense of humor."

I hadn't even begun to formulate a response to any of this when Lust said, "If you want to know the truth, though, I'm betting the odd man out will be me. My money's on you and Freak Show falling hopelessly in love and running off together into the sunset." She paused, giggling like a teenager. "What do you think? Possible?"

"It's more likely I'll sprout wings and soar into the sun," I said with more disgust than I meant to leak out. I knew Greed got off on pushing my buttons, and I didn't want him to know he was getting under my skin. But it wasn't like I was hard to read. I was practically vibrating with discomfort. "Anyway, let's just get this part over with. Who wants to read our assignment?"

Greed cocked an eyebrow at Lust, who sighed beautifully and pulled her phone from her hip pocket. "All right, I'll do the honors. Here goes." She cleared her throat and began to read. "Lust and her two suitors: Assignment #5."

"Two suitors?" I repeated, my whole face numb from embarrassment. "Is that really what it says?"

She winked at me and tossed a long lock of hair over her shoulder. "It might as well. Shall I continue?"

I nodded mutely, feeling more miserable than I ever thought possible.

"An unexplained illness is sweeping the halls of a local performing arts boarding school. Half a dozen teenage girls have been hospitalized after freak incidents that ended in convulsions, foaming at the mouth, and finally, coma. To date, doctors have found no cause to explain their symptoms. Their illness remains a medical mystery. Your task is to uncover the source of their ailment and return the girls home to their loving families."

She paused and looked at Greed and me, her lips trembling. "This is nuts, right?" she asked. "I mean, this is a medical problem. We shouldn't be getting involved in this."

Greed, however, wore an expression I couldn't read. "Is there more?"

Lust swallowed and nodded. "Yeah. Each girl shares a single characteristic. Upon falling ill, an image of a butterfly appeared on the underside of the girls' forearms, just above the wrist. Despite best efforts, the butterflies won't come off."

Lust dropped her arm to the side, a frown etched deep into the lines of her face. "I don't like this. This is serious. We should let doctors handle this, not three amateur psychics with **IMDB** profiles as our sole qualifications. *I'm not a doctor!*" she said in a mocking voice. *"I just play one on TV!"*

But now, Greed's fingertips brushed Lust's skin as he cocked his head and offered a low-wattage smile. "Oh, but you forget. I'm a board-certified psychiatrist. An actual, degree-holding MD. The doctor, as they say, is in."

Lust giggled and tittered with relief and batted her long lashes at Greed, and my insides shriveled. If there was any doubt about who would be the third wheel in this cursed trio, Greed had eliminated it in a single bound.

I sighed and hung my head between my knees. This next challenge was shaping up to be a doozy in all the worst possible ways. And then, if my new partnership wasn't bad enough, I thought of Greed's earlier ominous message. *"I've seen your future, Pride. From here on out, everything changes for you. Whatever you think you feel now is just the tip of the iceberg. This show is your Pandora's Box. And you've left it sitting wide open."*

A shiver ran down my spine as I wondered what that meant. Pandora's Box? What had Greed seen in my future? Should I be worried? Thankfully, I didn't have time to ponder for long. A few minutes later, Gluttony shouted that a fresh batch of cannoli was ready. So, I followed my housemates into the kitchen to gobble down delicious pastry and ignore my looming problems for what I hoped would be a long, blissful calm before the storm.

Sinful House Mysteries continues with

KEEP YOUR SIN UP

"I've learned several important things from watching that TV show *House MD* over the years: 1) It's never lupus, 2) Love sucks, and 3) Everybody lies.

I just never thought I'd have an opportunity to put all three to the test in a single case."

thanks for reading!

Sinful House Mysteries was so much fun to write, and I'm thrilled to share these adventures with you.

I'd love it if we kept in touch.

If you'd like that too, please sign up for my newsletter on my website. Use the QR code to go directly to the site:

If a newsletter isn't your jam but you'd still like to support me, please consider leaving a review. This is the easiest and best way to help other readers connect with the weird and wonderful cast at *Sinful House*.

See you soon!

about the author

Amber Fisher is the author of urban fantasy and paranormal mysteries. She lives in Austin, Texas, where she enjoys watching sci-fi shows, making things by hand, baking, and playing tabletop games with her husband.

Connect with me at: amberfishermedia.com

Facebook at: facebook.com/amberfisherauthor

Twitter: @amberla

Sign up for the newsletter: bit.ly/332eurl